The
Woman Lit
by Fireflies

Books by Jim Harrison

The
Woman Lit
by Fireflies

Jim Harrison

Houghton Mifflin / Seymour Lawrence

Boston 1990

For information about permission to reproduce selections from
this book, write to Permissions, Houghton Mifflin Company,
2 Park Street, Boston, Massachusetts 02108.

Library of Congress Cataloging-in-Publication Data

Harrison, Jim, date.
The woman lit by fireflies / Jim Harrison.
p.   cm.
Contents: Brown dog — Sunset limited — The woman lit by
fireflies.
ISBN 0-395-48884-2
ISBN 0-395-55107-2 (Limited Edition)
I. Title.
PS3558.A67W6   1990   90-4161
813'.54 — dc20   CIP

Printed in the United States of America

FFG 10 9 8 7 6 5 4 3 2 1

Portions of "Sunset Limited" appeared in the
January/February 1990 issue of *Smart* magazine.

"The Woman Lit by Fireflies" first appeared in
The New Yorker in slightly different form.

The lines of poetry on page 213 are from *Roots and Branches*
by Robert Duncan. Copyright © 1984 by Robert Duncan.
Reprinted by permission of New Directions Publishing Corporation.

To Anna

Contents

Brown Dog

JUST BEFORE DARK at the bottom of the sea I found the Indian. It was the inland sea called Lake Superior. The Indian, and he was a big one, was sitting there on a ledge of rock in about seventy feet of water. There was a frayed rope attached to his leg and I had to think the current had carried him in from far deeper water. What few people know is that Lake Superior stays so cold near the bottom that drowned bodies never make it to the surface. Bodies don't rot and bloat like in other fresh water, which means they don't make the gas to carry them up to the top. This fact upsets working sailors on all sorts of ships. If the craft goes down in a storm their loved ones will never see them again. To me this is a stupid worry. If you're dead, who cares? The point here is the Indian, not death. I wish to God I had never found him. He could have drowned the day before if it hadn't been for his eyes, which were missing.

These aren't my exact words. A fine young woman named Shelley, who is also acting as my legal guardian and semi-probation officer, is helping me get this all down on paper. I wouldn't say I'm stupid. I don't amount to much, and you can't get more ordinary, but no one ever called me stupid. Shelley and me go back about two years and our love is based on a fib, a lie. The main reason she is helping me write this is so I can stop lying to myself and others, which from my way of thinking will cut the interesting heart right out of my life. Terms are terms. We'll see. Shelley believes in "oneness" and if we're going to try to be "one" I'll try to play by her rules.

I'm a diver, or was a diver, for Grand Marais Salvage Corporation, which is a fancy name for a scavenging operation. You'd be surprised what people will pay for a porthole, even though they got no use for it. An old binnacle is worth a fortune. We sold one last July for a thousand dollars, though Bob takes three quarters because he owns the equipment. Bob is a young fellow who was a Navy SEAL, the same outfit that lost the hero, Stethem, who was beat to death by the towelheads. Bob is still damned angry and hopes to get revenge someday.

"Vengeance is mine; I will repay, saith the Lord," I quoted.

"Do you believe that, B.D.?" he asked.

"Nope. Can't say I'm sure. But if you believed it, it would save you from going way over there and having the Arabs shoot your ass off."

Bob is a hothead. A salvage bunch up in Duluth owed him a compressor so we drove over. The three of them were sleeping off a drunk so we took two compressors, and three portholes for interest. Two of the guys woke up punching but Bob put them away again. I'm not saying Bob is a bully, just a bit quick to take offense.

I've been reminded to get the basis of my salvation out of the way, to start at the beginning, as she says. Shelley is twenty-four and I'm forty-two. That means when I'm one hundred she'll be eighty-two. Age is quite the leveler. She is a fair-size girl by modern standards, but not in the Upper Peninsula where you would call her normal-size, perhaps a tad shy of normal. In a cold climate a larger woman is favored by all except transplants from down below (the southern peninsula of Michigan where all the people are) who bring girlfriends up here who look like they jumped right off the pages of a magazine. Nobody pays them much attention unless the situation is desperate. Why take a little girl if you can get a big one? It's as simple as that.

Anyway, on a rainy June evening two years ago Shelley came into the Dunes Saloon with two fellows who wore beards and hundred-dollar tennis shoes. They were all graduate students in anthropology at University of Michigan and were looking for an old Chippewa herbalist I was talking to at the bar. They came over and introduced themselves and Claude announced it was his birthday.

"How wonderful," said Shelley. "How old are you? We've driven three hundred and fifty miles to talk to you."

Claude gazed at the three of them for a full minute, then sped out of the bar.

When the screen door slammed Shelley looked at me. "What did we do wrong?" she asked.

"Goddammit, we blew it," said the redheaded fellow with a big Adam's apple.

"You missed your cue. When Claude says it's his birthday you're supposed to ask if you can buy him a drink. If someone else is buying he drinks a double martini," I said.

"Is there a chance we can make up for this?" said the third, a blond-haired little fellow in a Sierra Club T-shirt. "We were counting on talking to him."

Shelley pushed herself closer, unconsciously using her breasts to lead. "Are you related? I mean are you an Indian?"

"I don't talk about my people to strangers." Now I'm no

more Indian than a keg of nails. At least I don't think there's any back there. I grew up near the reservation over in Escanaba and a lot of Indians aren't even Indian so far as I can tell. What I was doing was being a little difficult. If you want a girl to take notice it's better to start out being a little difficult.

"We're really getting off on the wrong foot here. I didn't mean to intrude." She was nervous and upset.

"How the hell could we know he wanted a double martini," whined the redhead. "'You don't push drinks on an old Indian. I've been around a lot of them."

"What do you know about my people, you shit-sucking dickhead?" I yelled. The three of them jumped back as if hit by a cattle prod.

I moved down to the end of the bar and pretended to watch the Tigers-Milwaukee ball game. Since we are much farther from Detroit than Milwaukee there are a lot of Brewers fans up here. Frank, the bartender, came over shaking his head.

"B.D., why'd you yell at those folks when the lady's got beautiful tits?"

"Strategy," I said. "She'll be down here with a peace offering pretty soon."

The three of them were huddled by the window table, no doubt figuring their next move. I began to question my yell. In fact, I'm not known to raise my voice unless you set off a firecracker right behind me. Finally she got up and walked down the bar toward me with a certain determination.

"I'm Shelley Newkirk. Let's start all over again. The three of us have a great deal of admiration for Native Americans. We love and respect them. That's why we study them. We want to offer you an apology."

I stared deeply into my glass of Stroh's while Frank darted into the kitchen. When she spoke I thought he was going to laugh, but he's too good of a friend to blow my cover.

"The name's B.D.," I said. "It stands for Brown Dog, my Anishinabe name." At this point I wasn't bullshitting. Brown Dog, or B.D., has been my nickname since I was in the seventh grade and had a crush on a Chippewa girl down the road. I played ball with her brothers but she didn't seem to care for me. Their mother called me Brown Dog because I was hanging around their yard all the time. Once when she was slopping their pigs this girl, Rose by name, threw a whole pail of garbage on me. I actually broke into tears on the spot though I was fourteen. Love will do that. Her brothers helped clean me off and said they guessed their sister didn't like me. I didn't give up and that's why the name stuck with me. I was sort of following her around before a school assembly to see where she was going to sit when she hit me on the head with a schoolbook and knocked me to the floor. "Brown Dog, you asshole, stop following me," she screamed. I got to my feet with everyone in the gymnasium laughing at me. The principal tapped the microphone. "Rose, watch your language. Mr. Brown Dog, I think it's evident to all assembled here that Rose wishes you would stop following her."

So that's how I got my name and how, much later, I met Shelley. Right now it's October outside and already snowing though we're sure to have a bit of Indian summer. I don't care because I like cold weather. The farthest south I've ever been is Chicago and it was too goddamned hot down there for me. It was okay when I got there in March but by June I was uncomfortable as hell with the bad air and heat. That was when I was nineteen and was sent off on scholarship to the Moody Bible Institute, but then I got involved with the student radicals who were rioting and my religion went out the window. It was actually a fire-breathing Jewish girl from New York City who led me astray. She wore a beaded headband and flowers in her hair and kept telling me I was "one of the

7

people," and I had to agree with her. At her urging, when we were camped in the city park, I led a charge against the cops and got the shit kicked out of me and got stuck in jail. She bailed me out and we went off to a commune near Buffalo, New York, where they didn't eat chicken or any other kind of meat. They supposedly ate fish though I didn't see much of it around, but that's another story. At honest Shelley's insistence I will add here that I was kicked out of the commune because I snuck off to a bar, got drunk and ate about five hamburgers. They didn't drink either.

Just four months ago in late June was when I found the Indian. You'll have to understand how the cold at the bottom of Lake Superior preserves things. It was hard on my partner Bob. On one of our first dives together off Grand Island near Munising he came across a Holstein cow as big as day and looking damn near alive. He said the cow scared him as much as any shark he'd seen in the tropics. Then, as if to cap it off, a week later we found a new wreck off Baraga and the cook was still in the galley of the freighter. The cook didn't look all that unhappy in death except for his eyes, which like the Holstein's plain weren't there. The cook seemed to be smiling but it was the effect of the icy water tightening his lips. After the Holstein and the cook Bob was ready for anything, which didn't prove true when he saw the Indian.

Shelley just came in from the cold and sat down next to me. Before I get on to our drowned Native American friend, she wants me to lay down a few more background effects, partly so I won't appear to be worse than I am when we get to what I did. I keep wanting to get to the Chief, he was dressed in the old-time clothes of a tribal leader, but she says my actions will not be understood without an honest "confrontation" with the past.

8

To me the past is not as interesting as finding a three-hundred-pound ancient Indian chief sitting bolt upright on the bottom of Lake Superior. Your average man on the street doesn't know that the hair continues to grow after death and the Chief's long black hair wavered in the current. Besides, you can't walk right up to your past, tap it on the chest and tell it to "fess up." It has reason to be evasive and not want to talk about the whole thing, which for most of us has been a shitstorm.

Luckily there are methods for digging up the past and confronting it, and Shelley knows these methods like the back of her hand. This knowledge didn't come from her university training but from her troubled youth. Her dad was and is a big deal gynecologist in the Detroit area and his overfamiliarity with women on the job made him act remote and impersonal to Shelley. Or so she tells it. "Too much of a good thing?" I offered, which she didn't think was funny. The upshot was that Shelley went to psychiatrists, therapists and psychologists, and learned their methods. How you tell the difference is the first can give medicine (not cheap), the second goes deep into your past, and the third offers cut-rate tips on how to get through the day. That's my rundown on it anyway.

So we set aside an hour or two each day and she asks me questions in a professional manner. She calls this "probing," just as she was probed because of her haywire times with her dad. They're in fine shape now. He even gave her a new 4WD made in England when she got her master's degree. I'd call that a top drawer relationship for a father and daughter on a certain level. Anyway, Shelley was probed from eight to eighteen at who knows what cost because she says there's no way to add it up. It seems the real problem was that her mother's younger brother, Uncle Nick by name, used to make Shelley play with his weenie on camping trips. Between this and her

9

father's occupation father and daughter kept their distance until it all came out in the wash. I suggested we go find Uncle Nick and kick his ass but she said that was missing the point. What's the point then, I wondered. She's pals with her dad and fearless about weenies? That was part of it but mostly it's that she's not upset for mysterious reasons. That made a lot of sense to me because you can't even shoot a grouse or a deer properly if you're upset about something vague.

And now that she's at one with herself and the world she can work my brain over with high horsepower energy. For instance, she nailed me to the wall on the story of how the student radicals in Chicago had ruined my future in Christian work. She got me all soothed on the sofa by talking about things I love like all the different kinds of trees and fish in the U.P. Sometimes her voice gives me a boner but I'm out of luck because this business does not allow a quick time out, sad to say, for fucking.

We went back to the ordinary sadness of those hot days in Chicago and what really happened, not all of it my fault. The church treasurer in Escanaba had made a mistake and sent the scholarship check directly to me instead of to the Bible Institute. I didn't even open the envelope right away because I thought it was just another letter saying that everyone in the congregation back home was praying for me. I just sat on my bed in the Christian rooming house (no smoking or drinking) and had a sip of after-school peppermint schnapps. I remember I was thinking about Beatrice who was a bubble-butted waitress at a diner near the school. She was a dusky beauty but when I asked her what nationality she was she said, "What do you care, you snot-nosed little Bible thumper?" We had to carry our Bibles (King James Version) at all times. I guess I looked so downcast that she came over when I finished my oatmeal and said she was part black and part Italian. I told her that to me she was the most beautiful woman in the world. I'd have my oatmeal and breakfast coffee and spring a hard-on just watching Beatrice wipe off a table.

So I was sitting there in my room thinking of Beatrice, and not wanting to exhaust myself on unclean thoughts, I opened the letter from the church. It was a check made out for three hundred and ninety dollars. The possibilities hit like lightning so I dropped to my knees and prayed for strength which did not arrive.

I hit the bank as if shot from a rocket, then trembled my way over to the diner for an early supper. Mind you, I didn't order thirty-cent oatmeal for breakfast out of choice but because it was all the budget would allow. It was irksome to sit at the counter and watch a neighbor eat ham, eggs and potatoes. I have always had a weakness for catsup, but it didn't go too well with oatmeal. I tried it once and it wasn't a popular move at the diner. For days afterwards other customers would look at me and shake their heads. So when I got to the diner I took a full-size table in Beatrice's section and ordered a T-bone steak with all the trimmings. She doubted I had the money, so I flashed my roll and she smiled. I had become handsome between breakfast and dinner. The owner even nodded to me when he saw me eating a steak. I admit I was feeling like an instant big shot when I asked Beatrice to go out.

"You looking for a chance to talk about yourself or are you after free pussy? In either case, the answer is no."

"I'd be a fool to think anything was free in Chicago except hot weather and bad air," I said, catching the drift. I'd always flunked the courtship routine so I might as well try to sin boldly and quick.

Well, she wrote down her address and told me to come over at nine, but not unless I had a fifty-dollar bill in my pocket. I said I'd be there, though fifty bucks about equaled the largest amount I'd ever made in a week. This fact and a lot more caused the next three hours to be pretty uncomfortable. There was a sense in my small room that I was wrestling with Satan and I somehow knew I was going to lose to His power. I felt the overwhelming heat of His presence in the room though I realized it was mostly the weather. I prayed and almost wept and even gnashed my teeth. The guy in the next room, Fred, a poor kid from Indiana who was also a Moody Bible Institute student, heard the noise and came over to pray with me. Of course I didn't tell him the nature of the problem. The trouble with Fred's prayers was that he sounded like the popular comedian from Indiana, Herb Shriner. At one point the devil made me laugh out loud. I gave Fred ten bucks and he ran out with plans to eat a whole fried chicken. My food budget was two dollars a day and his was only one. The week before his mom had sent him cookies and he ate them all at once and puked.

I worked on my term paper on Nicodemus but the bubble-butt of Beatrice seemed to arise from the page and smack my nose. How could I think of spending fifty bucks straight off the collection plate of the poor folks back home? Few unbelievers and upper-class-type Protestants understand this kind of test and the fact that deep faith is a sure-fire goad to lust. Forbidden bubble-butt fruit is what I was dealing with. Years later when President Carter spoke of the lust in his heart I sure as hell knew what he was talking about.

To be frank, as some of you might have guessed already, I failed the test. I still feel a trace of shame over my five days in Beatrice's school of love. That's what we jokingly called it.

We started slow but soon enough we were on the fast track, me to perdition, and for her, business as usual.

When I got to her small apartment the first evening she was still in her waitress uniform making late dinner for a little boy about four years old. While she took a shower I read the kid a book called *Yertle the Turtle* about ten times, which was not much of a warm-up for sex. She came out of the bathroom in a blue satin robe and white furry slippers and took the kid down the hall to a babysitter. While she was gone a mean-looking black guy peeked in the door and tried to give me a bad look which didn't work. I was known around my home-town as a first-rate fistfighter and I had dug enough eight-foot-deep well pits by hand not to take any bullying.

So she came back, we went into the bedroom and it was over in less than three minutes. What I bought was what she called a "half-and-half," which is half "French" and full entry. She took off her robe and had nothing on but a teeny pair of red undies. I was dizzy from holding my breath without knowing it. She undid my trousers and let them drop to my ankles, went down on me for a few seconds, and when I groaned she jumped up, pulled down the undies and bent over. I had barely plugged her when I shot and fell over backwards to the floor, where I thought for a moment of my young love for Rose. I looked up in despair at Beatrice's fanny, then she turned and started laughing. She put her robe back on and went out to the other room still laughing. Was it for this that I had betrayed all my principles?

We sat on the couch and had a beer and I became cagey. I pointed out that at her current rate for work done she was making a thousand bucks an hour which was more than the President of the United States. "Fuck the President," she said, still laughing. I tried to slide a hand in on her breast and she

slapped it away. I developed a lump in my throat and got up
to leave with shame sweating out of my pores. She stopped
me and said for another twenty bucks we could transfer the
deal to an hourly rate. She let a breast slip out of her robe and
I agreed. I also had to do the dishes because she was sicker
than shit of dishes and food.

It was while washing the dishes that I realized I was in the
hands of forces far larger than myself. There was a temptation
to cut and run, reduce my losses to the T-bone dinner and
seventy bucks (I had immediately turned over the twenty for
the hourly rate). I could tell the Institute that the money had
been stolen from my room while I was at prayer service. Tears
formed at the image of me on my knees while some craven
thief stole the church's money, stealing money from God Himself. Only that isn't what happened, I corrected myself.

I turned then to see Beatrice on the sofa, now with her robe
off and only the red panties to cover herself. She was reading
Life magazine which seemed to me a coincidence.

"What I was wondering is this. Is the dish-washing time
using up my hourly rate?"

"It depends. It all depends. I'll take another beer."

I brought her a bottle of beer and she set the cold bottom
of it first on one nipple, then on the other. The nipples perked
up and she shivered.

"It concerns me that you don't know fuck-all about what
you're doing. You're an amateur at this, aren't you?" She slid
off her undies and took another drink.

"You're crazy if you think it's my first time. I'd say you were
about number eleven. Maybe twelve."

She was actually number three. The first, by the name of
Florence, was thin as a chicken carcass and we did it standing
up against a pine tree in a cloud of mosquitoes. The second,

Lily, was enormously fat and drunk, and I can't even guarantee I was on target, though I suppose it's fair to count it.

"Let me tell you, B.D., I don't like men who don't know what they're doing. It's simple as that. You're one of them. I have feelings. We all need pleasure, you understand."

She tugged my arm and I knelt down by the couch. She rubbed a hand through my hair and laughed. "You got the ugliest head of hair in the world." True, my hair is bristly and will stand straight up without a good soaking of Vitalis. She tugged my ears, then pressed a hand on the back of my neck, pushing it downward. And thus I faced the beautiful mouth of hell.

Five days of this and I had run out of money. I went over on the sixth evening and she was friendly enough but it was no dice. Her "professional standards" made what she called "freebies" out of the question. Her heart of gold was actual gold and not very warm at that. She was cooking spaghetti for her boyfriend and served me a single meatball before showing me the door. I tried to get a little sentimental and she just shook her head like she did the day I tried catsup on my oatmeal. It is hard for me to admit that I didn't turn her head one little bit. But still, a wise man would do well to go looking for a woman who's half black and half Italian. There's no point in searching the U.P. because the population is too scant for such a combination.

Within a week I was locked out of my room for nonpayment of rent and was bumming around the park. When I think of that room now I wonder what they did with the new robin's-egg blue suit Grandpa gave me, my schoolbooks and Scholfield Reference Bible (KJV), the single dirty picture of Beatrice, a present, stuck under the mattress. The last must have been an eye opener for the kindly old landlady, at least she was kindly until I ran out of money. I was lower than a snake dick until I cast my lot with the student radicals in the park who assured me I was one of the people. I couldn't wait to disrupt a political convention, though we never got inside to see the big deals. At least there was plenty to eat. I didn't realize at the time that college students were expert thieves.

I'm running on at the mouth a bit here at Shelley's insistence. What happened to me was in her terms a "key experience." This doesn't mean what I thought it would. According to Shelley, what I did with the church money and Beatrice wasn't necessarily wrong, only that it established a pattern of failure as a self-fulfilling prophecy that I never got over. I was involved in failure as a habit, according to her. This is curious as I never felt I did all that badly at life, at least for up here. I'd say half the men I know are worse off one way or another, either from drink or jail or because a tree fell on them while cutting pulp. I never owned a house but my van is free and clear, though it's a '78 Dodge and could use some work. I rent deer cabins real cheap to keep a roof over my head. You just have to be out during the season from November 15 to December 1. Sometimes I live rent free if I do some improvements.

Also I relish parts of what Shelley calls my professional guilt trip. The battle between good and evil is entertaining and is supposed to be instructive. Just about everything seems to be in the gray area these days, at least according to the newspapers. I only read the newspaper on Sunday like Grandpa did. I was just remembering that right after the brief trial Shelley's father called me a scoundrel. Ten minutes later he asked me not to tell his daughter that he called me a scoundrel, to keep it between us. I agreed which lightened up his mood. After all, he paid my legal expenses, otherwise I'd be in jail like my partner Bob, or any other poor guy without a first-rate lawyer.

To be frank, my life in crime started right after Rose hit me over the head with the schoolbook. About a week later when I still wasn't feeling all that well a sheriff's deputy shot my dog Sam for killing chickens, domestic ducks and geese, ripping the mailman's trousers, chasing a stray cow into a fence and tearing the tire off a kid's bike, that sort of thing. I'll have to admit he wasn't much of a companion, but I loved him, and he stood for something to me, something like Old Glory to a veteran. He even bit me once when I tried to take a fresh deer bone from him to destroy the evidence that he had been running deer.

Grandpa had found Sam two years before while he was skidding logs in Dickinson County. The dog had no doubt been lost by bear hunters as he was part terrier with some Plott hound on the other side which made him large. Sam's muzzle was full of porcupine quills, also his sides, as if he had bowled it over after biting it. Sam wanted help in a real unfriendly way and Grandpa said the only reason he tried is another logger bet him a quart of beer he wasn't man enough for the job. It wasn't that hard, he said. He took a tarp from the truck, threw it over the dog, wrestled him down and rolled him up in the canvas with the dog's head poking out. Then he wedged a stick sideways in Sam's mouth, tying it behind the head, and pulled the quills out with a pliers. When he unrolled the canvas the dog stood still for the side quills and Grandpa had the notion this had happened before. Certain dogs are so ornery they can't learn from their first porcupine experience. He washed Sam's mouth out with whiskey and water, then the dog jumped in the truck and went to sleep, so we had a dog.

Unfortunately, as we were to see, a dog that is bred, raised and trained to chase bear was not the best choice for our small farms, one near Bark River and the other outside Escanaba, where we lived depending on where Grandpa was working. To call them farms is a bit of a joke as both of them were Depression brick shacks sitting on forty untilled acres of swamp, woods and meadow. I liked the one in Bark River better as there was a small creek and a beaver pond where you could catch brook trout. Living in two places allowed two school systems to share the load of my behavior without totally outwearing my welcome.

In her search for problem spots and "glitches," as she calls them, Shelley sometimes gets a bit loony in my book. For instance, she made a big deal about the fact that though Escanaba and Bark River are only twenty miles apart they are in different time zones which must have confused me. I said no, though I generally preferred the central time zone in Bark River, but I couldn't say why. Grandpa said all the world cares is that you get to work on time. I never owned a timepiece but I could see the need for one if you had to catch airplanes, or were having business-type dealings. Of course Bob had an underwater watch for me when I was diving. When you're down deep you have to come up slow, otherwise you'll get the bends and die. If you don't time your air and leave enough for a slow climb you may as well cut your throat and stay down there. The late afternoon I found the Chief I had to spend a full half hour moving slowly up the line, looking down at his black hair wavering below. It made me want to draw up my feet closer to my body.

But what I said about time isn't what Shelley means. If you don't have a sense of time you tend to drift along without any plans. You'll just be another working stiff waiting for his next day off. That's what she means by calling it a glitch in my brain, not thinking ahead pure and simple. For instance, if I had kept closer track of Sam the deputy wouldn't have had to shoot him, she said. Just try keeping up with a bear hound, I replied. Then keep him tied up, she said. He would just be a piece of meat tied to a dog house if he didn't get a daily run. Mind you, the dog has been dead nearly thirty years.

What happened was that I was walking home looking for Sam when he appeared with a white chicken in his mouth. I tried to get it away with no luck. I heard a car and turned to see the deputy coming at me at top speed, then I tried to get Sam to run but he stood his ground. In the winter he'd stand in the road and the county snow plow would stop and lay on the horn. The dog would piss on the snow blade and walk off. The deputy jumped out with this woman from down the road screaming "My chicken!" The deputy drew his gun and when I tried to get in the way he pushed me in the ditch. Maybe he tried to shoot Sam in the head, I don't know, but I do know he caught him in the gut which was sad indeed. Sam started howling, still with the chicken in his mouth, and ran into our yard with me right after him. When I reached him the chicken was turning red from the blood coming out of Sam's mouth. He was hanging his head but unwilling in death to let go of the chicken. The deputy came up to finish the dog off but Sam tried to attack him and the deputy ran backwards while I hauled on Sam's collar. Then Grandpa drove into the yard, home from work and beered up. He read the situation right and grabbed the pistol from the deputy, then walked up to Sam, gave him a goodbye pat and a bullet in the head. He threw the deputy's pistol across the road into the weeds and told him if he came on our property again he'd stomp him until he had to be hauled off in a gunny sack. We buried Sam with the chicken still in his mouth. Even now, across all these years in between, my eyes get wet thinking of my beloved dog.

Shelley and I had a terrible shitstorm of an argument. She hates animal cruelty and the story about Sam. I said that I was only writing what had happened. The argument went on to my other shortcomings and my lack of sympathy for her work. She wants to dig up this old burial mound I found way back in the forest exactly thirteen miles from the nearest people. She said it dates from the time of Columbus. I showed the burial site to Shelley the day after we met so she'd make love to me which she did on the spot, so she fulfilled her side of the bargain. The trouble is that when I had showed the spot to Claude he asked me never to disturb it and I promised. My word is not too reliable in most matters but this one was important. I took the precaution of using a roundabout way and Shelley could never find her way back. Now she nags at me like a sore tooth over this matter. The Chippewa are tough folks and won't stand still for the digging up of their relatives like they do out west.

After the big argument I ran off to the bar, which violates my probation. I came home just before dawn smelling of perfume. Who wore the perfume I can't say except she was not local. I finally made peace with Shelley when I got up in the afternoon. She is to continue probing me an hour a day but will not interfere in or read this story until I'm done. In turn I had to promise to drive her down to Escanaba and Bark River to see where I grew up, something I don't want to do. When Grandpa died about ten years ago I sold both places for a total of thirteen thousand dollars, bought my vehicle and took off for Alaska to seek my fortune. I never made it past Townsend, Montana, where I got beat up by some fellows in a misunderstanding about a girl. The money went for repairs at the hospital in Bozeman, but that is another story.

I was just thinking that my mind became a tad criminal after my dog was shot. Shelley told me that suffering, as opposed to what they say in the newspapers, does not necessarily make you a better person. I'd have to agree with that notion. I waited for two months before I burned down the deputy's chicken coop, though at the last moment I took mercy and opened the coop door so the chickens could escape. My friend David Four Feet, who was Rose's brother, stood watch. He got his name Four Feet because when he was a little kid his spine was haywire so he scampered around on his hands and toes like an ape. Then the government took him away for a year and when they delivered him back he could walk, only the name stuck.

The deputy had a pretty good idea who burned his chicken coop but he couldn't prove it. I hoped it would make me feel better but it didn't. You can't compare a chicken coop to a dog.

For Christmas that year Grandpa bought me a big heavy punching bag. He knew I had set the fire though he didn't say anything, and I think he wanted to get me interested in something, which was the sport of boxing. But boxing turned matters worse. I worked so hard on it for two years I became a bit of a bully, winning all my bare-knuckle fights in the area. I wasn't any good at anger so I had to rely on technique, most of it taught to me by an Italian railroad worker from the east side of Escanaba. My fighting career ended when I was seventeen one night over in a field near Iron Mountain. My Italian railroad worker organized the thing to win some betting money. I only weighed about 170 at the time and my opponent was a big pulp cutter in his thirties, real strong but too slow. There were two rows of cars lined up to cast light. It was supposed to be a boxing match but right away the guy choke-holded me in a clinch and I got the feeling he was trying to kill me. I got free by stomping on his instep and then, since he smelled real beery, I worked on his lower stomach and then his throat. The feeling of nausea and choking will weaken a man faster than anything else. Finally the guy was down on his knees puking and holding his throat. What ended it all for me was when a little kid about five ran to the guy and hugged him, then came at me and hit me in the legs with a stick over and over. I never knew my own father but if I had I sure wouldn't want to see him get beat up. The whole thing was awful. I never fought again except on the rare occasion when I was attacked by surprise in a bar.

It just now occurred to me that Bob was right when he yelled at me during a recess in the trial. He said that if I had acted like a real partner we wouldn't be in this mess. The afternoon I found the Chief I was off by myself in the rubber tender dinghy near the Harbor of Refuge at Little Lake. Bob was farther down west in the main skiff with a metal detector where the *Phineas Marsh* went down in 1896. Mind you, everything we do is against the law as all sunken ship artifacts are the sole ownership of the state of Michigan. When I made it up to the surface and to the dinghy I rigged the smallest buoy I had so it wouldn't be noticed, then thought better of it. Any diver will check out a stray buoy and I didn't want the straight arrows over at the Shipwreck Museum at Whitefish Point to find my prize redskin. I sat in the dinghy for a long time making triangulation points on the shore about a mile distant.

When I joined up with Bob an hour later at the Little Lake

dock I had good reasons, or so I thought, for not telling him about my find. I was still sore over my arrest in the Soo (Sault Sainte Marie) a few weeks before. Bob had sent me over to sell a brass ship's whistle to a nautical antiques dealer. Most of the time we work through a dealer in Chicago to escape detection, but we needed some quick cash as the lower unit of our Evinrude was in bad shape. I dropped off the ship's whistle and got the cash in a sealed envelope which was an insult in itself. I said, How's a man to count the money? The dealer said he was just told to give a sealed envelope to a messenger.

The downfall in this situation was that I only had gas money to get back to Grand Marais and I was hungry and thirsty. I went into the bathroom of a bar down the street, opened the envelope and took out a well-deserved twenty. I had a few shots and beers and went over to a cathouse for a quick poke with a black girl I knew there. This girl has three years of college yet works in a whorehouse, which shows that blacks don't get a fair shake. Maybe I just liked her because she reminded me of long-lost Beatrice, though like Beatrice she wasn't especially fond of me. Anyway, it was slow time in the afternoon and I worked up an appetite doing "around the world" instead of the usual half-and-half. It cost me an extra twenty bucks but I was still within my share of the take on the brass ship's whistle. Then I figured Bob wouldn't want me to drive home hungry so I went out to the Antlers and had the Deluxe Surf 'n' Turf for the Heavy Eater, which was a porterhouse and a lobster tail, and a few more beers to fight the heat of the evening. I had every intention of leaving town, but was struck by the notion I could get some money back by going to the Chippewa casino and playing a little blackjack. Wrong again. I was out another hundred bucks when I walked over to the bar at the Ojibwa Hotel for a nightcap to help on the lonely ride home. This turned out to be the key mistake of the many I made that cursed day.

The seafood had given me a tingle of horniness which it is famous for and I asked a real fancy woman to dance. She and her girlfriends were all dressed up from their bowling league banquet, and her pink dress was open-necked like a peck basket. She said, "Get out of here, you nasty man." I went back to the bar feeling my face was hot and red. I admit I wasn't looking too good in my jeans and Deep Diver T-shirt. I hardly ever get turned down when I'm in fresh, clean clothes. Sad to say, the weight of failure of the day was pissing me off so I went back over to the table and asked her to dance again. She said the same thing and all the women at the table laughed, so I poured a full mug of cold beer down that big open neck of her pink dress, then I said something impolite and stupid like "That should cool off your tits, you stupid bitch." I was not prepared for what happened next. All five of these women jumped me as if they were one giant lady. They held me down with the help of the bartender until the cops came and hauled me off.

The upshot was that the next morning in jail when I called my partner Bob to come bail me out he wouldn't do it. He said, "Use the money from the ship's whistle and bail yourself out." I had to explain over half of it was gone which left me fifteen bucks short of bail. He yelled "Then fuck you, sit there" into the phone and let me cool my heels for three full days. A lesser man might have sat there and moped, and I could have called Shelley down in Ann Arbor, but I decided to guts it out. Grandpa used to say "Don't Doggett," meaning don't act like his second cousin with the truly awful name of Lester Doggett from Peshtigo, Wisconsin. Lester used to stop by for a visit and piss and moan about the likelihood of a forest fire. That's about all he talked about, and true, his grandparents had died in the great Peshtigo fire which killed thousands, but that was over seventy years before. "Don't Doggett" was what Grandpa said to me when I whined, complained or expressed any self-pity. It still means to stand up and take your medicine, though it doesn't mean you can't get even, and that's what I was doing two weeks later when I didn't tell Bob about finding the Chief.

One afternoon it was wet and windy and we were almost done with our probing when Shelley's cousin Tarah and her boyfriend Brad showed up at Shelley's cabin. I had heard about this Tarah and was curious to meet her. Tarah is not her real name but was given to her during a ceremony of "empowerment" in a place called Taos in New Mexico. That's what Shelley told me anyway. I could believe it as this Tarah had green eyes that could almost hypnotize you. She was a bit thin for my taste but her satin gym shorts pulled up her butt in a pretty way. She was brown as tobacco and had a clear musical voice. The minute they arrived this fellow Brad unloaded a thick-tired bicycle from his van and dressed up a bit goofy in black, shiny stretch shorts, a helmet, goggles and special shoes. He was a real ox and I asked him what the bike set him back and he said a thousand dollars. I was not inclined to believe the figure and I said for that amount they should throw in a motor. He said "Ha-ha," asked directions and rode off at top speed on the dirt road, farting like a bucking horse.

Back inside Tarah made us some tea out of secret Indian herbs and we sat before the fire. I can't say I felt anything different from the tea but I had high hopes, sobriety being a tough row to hoe. Then Tarah spread out a velvet cloth and put this rock which she said was crystal in the middle of the cloth. She stared at Shelley and me and said in a soft, whispery voice, "You are more than you think you are." I didn't exactly take this as good news because what I already was had gotten my ass in enough of a sling. Then Tarah said a whole bunch of what sounded like nonsense symbols as if she were trying to make a rabbit jump out of a top hat, though maybe it was another language. I wasn't concentrating too well as Tarah was sitting cross-legged like an Oriental and you could see up her crotch past her shorts to where we all come from. I already said she was a bit thin but she was also smooth and healthy. She had Shelley and me put our hands on the crystal. "We all go back many, many eons. We started when time started and we end when time ends. We have been many things. We have been stones, moons, flowers, creatures and many other people. The source of all beingness is available to us every day."

I admit I was a bit swept away, at least for the time being, by this mystical stuff. We had to sit there in complete silence for a half hour just like you do for long periods when you deer hunt. It sounded good because since I was a kid I wanted to be a bear or a sharp-shinned hawk or even a skunk. If someone gives you a hard time you just piss in their direction and they run for it. At one point Shelley frowned at me, thinking I was looking up under Tarah's shorts when I was supposed to keep my eyes squinted almost shut. "Seeing but not seeing," Tarah called it. I was wishing my old buddy David Four Feet were here. We used to spend money we earned hoeing at a raspberry farm to send away for books we saw advertised in *Argosy* or *Stag* or *True* magazine that would give us what they called secret powers. If you're hoeing raspberries for thirty cents an hour in the hot sun what you want is secret powers.

We never got back anything we could understand but neither of us was good at school. The toughest book was about the Rosy Cross put out by the Rosicrucians. It mostly reminded me of David's sister Rose, the one who knocked me down and also threw pig slop on me.

Tarah rang a little chime to end the period of silence. I remembered when the bell rang that what I was supposed to be doing was getting in touch with a past life. Shelley went off to start supper because Tarah wanted a private time with me. Tarah moved closer to me and held my wrists. She was sitting in what she called a "full locust" and you couldn't help but wonder what was possible with a woman with that much stretch in her limbs. She fixed her green eyes on me.

"What did you become? I could see your trance state was very deep."

"I became a big condor from olden times. I was feeding on a dead buffalo I scared off a cliff." I fibbed, remembering a trip to the Field Museum when I was on the bum in Chicago. If you're in Chicago you should go see these ancient stuffed animals.

"That's truly wonderful, B.D. It means your spirit wishes to soar far above your current problems. Your spirit wishes to use your condor being and blood to help you. In order to do this you must not deny the proud heritage of your people. You must let us help you rediscover your heritage."

I dropped my head as if lost in thought. Despite how many times I've told Shelley I don't have a drop of Chippewa blood in me she refuses to believe it. She feels I am ashamed of my roots and how do I know anyway since I'm not all that sure who my parents were? I've said I'm just as likely to be an Arab or a Polack, but she won't hear of it. All of her anthropology friends think I'm at least half Chippewa but she's told them I won't talk about it. I've been tempted a few times but then was worried about being caught out. After all, these people know more about Indians than any Indian I ever met, except what it is like to be one. I never saw David Four Feet's family having all that much fun.

"It would be nice if you'd give me a hand during these troubled times," I said. "Sometimes this probing I do with Shelley just wears me out."

"There are many ways rather than a single Way. Shelley is dealing with your past and I'm trying to reach into the past before your past. Do you understand?"

I nodded as she stood up stretching a few inches from my nose. I breathed deeply so as to catch a general whiff. It was somewhere between watercress and a rock you pick out of a river, way up near the top along with wild violets and muskmelon.

"I sense that you are responding to my womanness," she said, twisting at the waist to loosen up. "But you are not responding to me, Tarah, but to the female porpoise that has been my other mode for the last month or so. Porpoises are deeply sexual."

Then Brad came in from his bike ride. It turned out he had ridden all the way to the Hurricane River and back on a dirt road in less than two hours. That happens to be about thirty miles which I found amazing. I got out my topo maps and he was thrilled to see that there were hundreds and hundreds of miles of small dirt roads in Alger County. I was brought up short when I asked him if he had seen the moose that had been hanging around the Hurricane. "I see nothing but the road," he said. Then he grabbed a towel to go swim in the bay even though the temperature was only in the mid-forties and the foghorn was going full blast. I watched him through

binoculars and he swam all the way out to Lonesome Point
and back which was three miles. I didn't bother asking him if
he had seen any fish.

It was during my after-dinner nap that I got a real eye opener.
Tarah and Shelley had fixed the food of far-off India which
didn't sit real well in my stomach, mostly because there was
no meat, chicken or fish, just rice and vegetables. Old Brad
really tied on the feedbag. It was the most quantity I had seen
anyone eat since I watched a friend of mine eat twenty-three
whitefish fillets. It was all-you-can-eat for a fixed price and he
wanted to get a deal. Tarah said Brad needed ten thousand
calories a day while he was in training. Brad didn't talk while
he ate or after he ate. Anyway, while I was napping and trying
to digest the food I heard my name mentioned through the
thin wall by Shelley and Tarah who were in the kitchen cleaning up. I pretended I was snoring to urge them on. I just
heard bits and snatches but it was a plot for me to take Tarah
out to my secret burial mound and for her to try to remember
the route. Shelley knew I'd never take her back there and
here she was trying to rig it for her cousin to do the job. My
feelings were so hurt I eased out the window and walked down
to the Dunes Saloon.

Morning dawned bright and clear for me, if a little late. Shelley couldn't very well say anything about my getting drunk
when she was busy hatching a plot. She sat at her desk surrounded by a pile of books, writing a semester paper on how
Indians preserved their medicine herbs for use in winter (they
hung them out to dry after they picked them). Tarah was in
the kitchen packing a knapsack of food for Brad's all-day ride.
While I poured my coffee I saw her stick in twelve apples, a

sack of carrots, a head of cabbage and a jar of honey. She wondered if I could catch some fresh fish for dinner and I said yes. She was all dressed up in the Patagonia clothes that Shelley wears, including green shorts that did a good job on her rump. She had on great big hiking boots that looked funny at the end of her brown legs. Meanwhile, out the window I could see Brad stretching with a leg so far up a tree you'd think he'd split himself. Two old Finns I knew were standing out on the road on their way for the morning opening of the bar. They were watching Brad with polite interest.

Finnish people don't judge other folks too harshly. My partner Bob says no one knows where their language comes from and that they migrated to the U.P. because they liked pine trees and cold weather just like me. Grandpa said I liked cold weather because of the sunstroke I had once when hoeing. Also, when I was a baby I had been left in this closed-up cabin for two days and when he found me I was about dying of thirst. Ever since those two experiences I can't handle hot weather. I like to dive to the bottom of Lake Superior and be cold, and in the winter I keep my cabin about fifty degrees which also means you don't have to cut so much wood. Sometimes in winter I'll stand outside in shirtsleeves just for the fun of getting cold.

I turned from the window where Tarah was giving Brad his ten-pound bag of lunch. I was wondering what he was going to do with that whole cabbage when Shelley came into the kitchen. She asked me to take Tarah out to the burial mound, not to try to fuck her if you please, and perhaps she could go along though she already knew the answer was a "negativo" as Bob says. He had picked up a lot of Spanish in the tropics and owns a bunch of treasure coins from diving on the *Atocha* wreck off Key West. I tried to act stunned at the idea that I'd make a pass at Tarah, but Shelley just crossed her eyes which is what she does when she knows I'm bullshitting.

"Take my car. It's more comfortable," she said.

"Nope. You got a compass on the dashboard. I'm wise to your tricks."

"Do you think Tarah is sexier than me?"

"Of course not. She needs some more meat on the bones. You might catch a splinter with that girl."

That seemed to satisfy Shelley. Then Tarah came in and when they were standing next to each other the idea came to me how nice they'd look naked in bed with me in the middle. I mean for the contrast, like autumn leaves, brown grass and white melting snow. Something like that. I did it with two big ole girls over in Munising once but I didn't write home about it. One of them fell down in the motel shower and we had a deuce of a time getting her out until I turned on the cold water to sober her up. I had met them at the Corktown Bar with Frank my bartender friend, but he backed out. "B.D., you better go it alone," he said. I went ahead so they wouldn't feel bad, also I was curious. On the way out of the house with Tarah I saw her slip one of those flat compasses out of her knapsack and into her pocket, so driving out of town I asked her for it. I slowed down and tossed it out by a hemlock where I could find it on the way back.

"I'm getting the vibes you don't trust me," she said.

"I don't want anyone digging up my grandparents," I said, remembering that's what Claude said when he saw the mounds.

"How can they be your grandparents when Shelley said the burial site was from the Hopewell Period? That's why it's so important to her. It would be the northernmost Hopewell site. She'd be famous."

"Fuck famous. Everyone who came before is my grandparents." I was getting on thin ice here and wanted to change the subject. Once when she went for groceries I tried to read one of Shelley's books on the Chippewa but it was slow going. I either needed some pointers or had to keep my mouth shut. "I don't want to dig up graves. I just want to communicate with the Ancient Ones." She twisted in the van seat and put a hand on my leg. I was already noticing how sharply she looked at the landscape. I was sure I could confuse her, though, because she was used to out west and in the U.P. you don't have the elevation for landmarks. It's just woods beat up by logging, or bare gullied areas where the soil is too weak to grow a tree, or just plain bogs and swamps. She put her feet up on the dashboard and squinted her eyes. I could see pretty far down the underside of her shorts but wasn't going to let myself lose caution. I was willing to bet that within her "seeing but not seeing," Tarah was trying to remember all my turns.

I could tell this girl was playing hardball when I parked near the river and said from then on we had to go by foot. I could have damn near reached the site by two-track in the van but thought I'd make her pay some dues. It had become a fair day for mid-October, what we call Indian summer, but I knew the river water would be cold from the frosty nights. I waded right in, then turned to watch her take off her boots and socks, shorts and panties, so she was only wearing her shirt. She plunged right in and crossed the river's waist-deep water and scrambled up the far bank ahead of me, a pretty sight for the eyes. I just stood there waiting for a few minutes while she air dried and got dressed. My plan was not to be a pushover for any tricks but my heart was like a deer's that's been chased by dogs, so I just stared off in the distance, taking only the shortest peeks at the lady.

I hauled ass off on a zigzag route for the burial ground, but

I sure was wrong thinking I was going to tire her out. When I paused after two miles to catch my wind she wasn't even breathing deeply, and this raised a certain resentment in me that came from a lot of directions. For instance, how could Shelley really care for me, then try to trick me out of my secret place using her cousin? There's no way I'm going to try to jump this girl, I decided, just to spite Shelley who thinks I'm going to try. Maybe they even talked about it.

"I just can't do this," I said, and sat down on a stump, facing away from her.

She walked around the stump and faced me with tears coming into her eyes. "I can tell what you're thinking by the way we walked here. You don't trust me. I want to commune with these people, not dig them up."

I reached out and caught a tear that had made it to her chin and was about to fall off. Tears have a powerful effect on me because I doubt if I ever cried myself since I was a baby.

"I'll tell you what. We'll go there but if you try to bring Shelley back I'll put a Chippewa curse on you that will short-circuit your entire life. You'll damn well wish you really was a porpoise. In fact, within a year you'll be praying to die, *wagutz*." *Wagutz* is a real dirty Chippewa name for a woman but it was the only thing I could think of.

She nodded and put her arms around me. This had to be the best-smelling woman in the world, despite the hike. I thought she was going to kiss me but I slid off the stump, not wanting to lose control of the situation. I never have been in control which means someone else is, and at this moment I didn't want it to be her.

So we came to a natural clearing in the woods and I pointed out to her the seven large mounds and four smaller ones about thirty yards away, then I sat down under this small tree that had been blasted and burned by lightning. I don't have an ounce of superstition in me but you have to draw the line and I wasn't going near the mounds this time.

When I thought about it later it seemed that the light was too clear, the clearest I had ever seen, and the area was full of ravens whirling and croaking. She walked right out there and sat in the middle of those graves and began chanting in another language. After a while she lay face down on one of the larger graves which I wouldn't have done at gunpoint.

As luck would have it, from way off there came a howling and bawling sound. Now I knew very well it was just a baby bear trying to locate its mother but there was a split second of doubt and I jumped up before relaxing again. Tarah out there on the mounds heard it and started flopping around and crying out. I thought, Jesus Christ, she's gone goofy on me, and I shouted out it was just a bear at least a mile away. Now she was rolling around shrieking and I had half a mind to leave her there. Of course I didn't. I ran out and grabbed her, dragging her away. She was flat-out hysterical for the first ten minutes I led her back toward the van. She didn't hear anything I said about the noises bear cubs make when they've lost track of their mothers.

It didn't take us long to get back to the river because I could see I was safe not retracing the crooked route. In fact, I was worried because she was acting like some of the crazy folks in the County Home I saw when I visited Grandpa before he died. She just lay down on the bank of the river and cried, then started to take her boots off but I had to help her. She lay back in the sand and I pulled off her shorts and undies. It was at this point I got an idea, and not the one you might think, as my notion of fun isn't fucking a crazy woman. First I bit her on the leg to get her attention, then picked her up and threw her head first into the river. By the time she came up sputtering I was right beside her, shaking the living shit out of her. "In the name of the sacred coyote, get the fuck out of here, demons," I shouted. I used coyote because I couldn't think of anything else at the moment but raccoons and wood-chucks and they didn't seem right. Then she calmed way down though she was still crying. I went back to the bank, picked up her stuff and helped her across the river and up to the van.

Everything was going fine up to this point, all considered, until I looked at her tiny white panties in my hand. Without question I deserved something for my efforts. I got an old blanket out of the van and used it to towel her off. Then she grabbed hold of me so legally speaking it was more her fault than mine, not that I was exactly a victim though this girl was as strong as any. It was quite a chore getting me out of my wet trousers and shoes and my body was real cold so that it made her seem hot as fire. To be frank we wore off some skin right there on the ground which at least served to make her stop crying.

We returned home to a tragedy of sorts though Shelley had the situation well in hand. It seemed that Brad had been rid-ing full tilt on a deer path off the Adams Trail and rounded a bend and ran smack-dab into the Golden Age Dirt Trackers, which is a fine club of senior citizens who ride three- and four-wheel ATVs. I hate the racket these machines make which is worse than a chainsaw or snowmobile but it's the only way real old folks can get around in the woods. The collision was of such force that Brad got a spiral leg fracture when he flew through the air and about crushed an old man. The local res-cue squad took Brad to the Munising Hospital, then on to Marquette because a spiral fracture was too much for Munis-ing to handle.

The upshot was that Shelley and Tarah took off right away

for Marquette and I got a few days of solitude. I was about peopled out anyway though my solitude didn't start too well. It was a fine afternoon and Frank stopped by and we went out bird hunting with his springer spaniel. We shot three grouse and five woodcock, and picked up two T-bones down in McMillan at Rashid's, also making the mistake of buying a half gallon of wine and a bottle of whiskey because it was Frank's day off. We grilled the birds and steaks over a wood fire and finished off the beverages to the last drop.

I woke up early not feeling too well and drove out to the deer cabin. I brought along some groceries, my tablet and three pencils (Dixon Ticonderoga number 3's) so as to get on with my "memoirs" as Shelley calls them which is another word for your memories. I partly wanted to get out of Shelley's place because of the phone. Not just Shelley calling, because if I wasn't there she could check with Frank, but all the phone calls she gets from her friends in the anthropological business, and her parents who she talks to nearly every day, and whoever else. When the phone rings it's not for me is the rule of thumb. I've lived pretty well at times on what she pays out in phone bills. When the people I know have to talk long distance they keep it under three minutes. With Shelley it's like talking across a kitchen table.

By mid-morning a northwester had come up and the temperature dropped thirty degrees so I let the deer cabin get real cold before I stoked a fire. I don't take aspirin for a hangover because Grandpa said if you do you'll never learn anything. I drank about a gallon of water from the spring and just sat there hurting and collecting my thoughts. About midafternoon I had a glass of peppermint schnapps to settle my stomach.

Now hangover thoughts are real long thoughts and I was

feeling damned near like an orphan because I was standing outside listening to the wind and waves come up on Lake Superior some two miles distant through the woods. The stormy season was beginning. About ninety percent of all the shipwrecks that Bob and me dove on took place in late October and November. You'd think someone would learn from this fact. I was out near Whitefish Point when the *Fitzgerald* went down with all hands that November afternoon. The wind came up to ninety knots and the waves were cresting near forty feet. That day a friend of mine was on the ore freighter *Arthur Anderson* which was trying to stand by for help. When he reached the Soo he got off the boat and never got on another. The Coast Guard didn't agree but my buddy said he knew the *Fitzgerald* sprung her hull on Caribou Shoals and despite having four seven-thousand-gallon-a-minute bilge pumps she went down in six hundred feet. Not a single body was found, for reasons I already said. Those thirty-four men will still be down there when the world ends as it surely must. Our preacher used to say nothing manmade lasts except real big stuff like the pyramids and even they show signs of wearing out.

Anyway, I was standing outside the cabin in the cold wind thinking these thoughts when I saw a big snowshoe rabbit. At the same time it occurred to me that Shelley might have been helping me out this long in hopes of finding my ancient burial mounds and becoming a famous anthropologist. A friend of hers had become famous for finding a prehistoric stone prayer wheel on Beaver Island even though a Chippewa lady had found it in a dream three years before. Maybe I was just glum from the liquor burning off and I knew Shelley really cared for me but I couldn't figure in her long-range plans. It had to be the mounds that made her hang in there and pay the legal expenses and all that. The thought was too obvious for me to be struck dumb. I stared into the evening woods behind the snowshoe rabbit which was taking bites of grass in between keeping an eye on me. I was feeling right at home all by myself. The woods can be a bit strange. It takes a long time to feel you belong there and then you never again really belong in town. It's a choice made for you by your brain at a moment you don't notice.

When I had this notion of Shelley helping me out for mixed motives I can't say I was real upset. Grandpa used to say to me, Don't just listen to what people say to you but why they say it. Shelley and me have a fine time together but my future is more of the same which I don't mind, and she's bent on making her mark. Be thankful when a woman's not kicking you in the ass one way or another, I said to myself. Also, there's the point that I'm forty-two and Shelley is the best I've ever been under the sheets with. She's like Beatrice, with four more gears plus overdrive. If I start acting betrayed I'll screw the whole thing up.

There was no point in standing there in the wind getting a hard-on thinking about my girlfriend so I went in the cabin, opened the window quietly, took my .22 rifle (Remington) and shot the rabbit for dinner. I skinned and gutted it, cut it in pieces and browned the pieces with a little bacon. The rabbit was a big male and I knew it would be tough so I stewed it with a few turnips, potatoes, onions, and a head of garlic. Shelley started me on garlic for my high blood pressure and I got to liking it even better than her. Sometimes I boil up a head and spread it on toast because I don't like butter. I put my dutch oven on the stove and sat down to think recent events over step by step.

Your thoughts jump around when you are real hung over and hungry. For instance, I laughed out loud at the idea that

Tarah mistook the bawling bear cub for the voice of an Indian dead for seven hundred years. An owl hitting a rabbit makes the rabbit scream like a woman which will startle you when you're in the woods at night. The yelping a bunch of coyotes make chasing a deer or rabbit will tend to make you light-hearted while a wolf's howl makes your mind lose its balance. The worst, the most horrifying noise I ever heard, was when the Chief asked me to bury him. How could this be, you might wonder, if he was found in seventy feet of water and his eyes were missing? When I walked to the stove to check the stew my feet dragged and the hairs rose on the back of my neck. It's like I murdered someone and I'm pretending it was in a dream and I can't admit it to myself let alone confess it in public. The judge said I was "delusional" and that's why I got off so light while poor Bob was thought to have a "sound mind" and a bad lawyer so he's doing two years.

What happened after I found the Chief was that I made a plan. Probably lots of folks make the same mistake. Your number one step on your plan might be wrong, therefore all the other steps will be even more wrong. The morning after finding the Chief I had full intentions of getting the advice of Frank who is the only man I can trust, but when I got there Frank was babysitting his kids and they were all on the couch watching the exercise girls on television while his wife was at work. Frank likes these exercise programs on television as you don't get to see all that many girls in bathing suits in the U.P., what with summer being known locally as three months of bad sledding. Well, Frank didn't have time for any advice but sat there with a kid on his lap eating eggs with its hands, and he was yelling stuff like, "I want the one in blue on my nose."

The first thing I did after Frank was to call Shelley in Ann

Arbor and ask her for two eyes. She had friends over at the medical school and I was sure they'd have some spare glass eyes lying around. I'm proud to say I've treated my girlfriends good enough so that they trust me and will help out when I'm in a pinch. I've lived with a half-dozen ladies over the years and none of them left me over any unkindness but because there was no future in staying. Grandpa always said I'd be a late bloomer so something might happen yet. I have my own theories about what people think of as the future. Imagine yourself lying in bed sleeping and dreaming of things people dream of, say fish, death, being attacked, diving to the bottom of the ocean, the world exploding, the undersides of trees, screwing women or men without faces, that sort of thing. It makes the world seem blurred and huge. Then you wake up and you're just B.D. in a ten-dollar war surplus sleeping bag in a cold cabin. The first step is to pee and make coffee, which I can deal with, and after that what happens is not in firm hands.

Part of the problem of handling the future of the Chief was the article I had read in the *Reader's Digest* in a barbershop in Munising, where like Beatrice of yore the lead scalper thinks I have the worst head of hair in the Christian world. According to him, every single hair goes a different direction. This article said it is given to every man to have a few main chances in life, opportunities that will turn the whole thing around. While getting clipped it came to me my first chance had been when I sold Grandpa's land cut-rate because I was in a rush to get to Alaska. This opportunity ended in the hospital in Bozeman. It was clear as day to me when I found the Chief that he was my second chance.

My first problem was to get a hold of one of those small trucks that deliver bags and blocks of ice to gas stations and grocery stores. I would also need a piece of gill net for towing the Chief into Little Lake. The man looked pretty big but I was sure I could boost him up onto the dock and then into the back of the ice truck, the one I didn't have.

My ace in the hole was Avakian, the nautical artifacts dealer in Chicago. I always felt that he paid us fair prices though Bob wasn't so sure and he was dealing from our side. When Avakian came to the U.P. on buying trips it was a top secret operation because, as I've said, everything we do is a tad illegal. We'd meet way out in the boonies, or in an odd place, and every time Avakian would be driving a different fancy car. Well, once this man got me aside alone and said if I came up with anything weird he'd be interested. When I asked him what he meant by weird he just said, "Think it over, think it over," twice in a row in the slick way Chicago men talk which I could remember from so many years back. Being an honest fellow I later asked Bob what Avakian meant. Bob said Avakian had pretended he wanted an old-time body for science to study the qualities of preservation in cold water, but Bob had said to him, That's bullshit. Then Avakian had said he'd pay twenty thousand for a shipwrecked body because a private customer wanted one to freeze in a big block of ice. When Bob had asked why, Avakian had just said, Who knows?

The problem for Bob was that before he signed up for the SEALs he was in a different part of the Navy working for some dentists and doctors identifying dead men by their dental records and body parts. Bob signed up for this duty because he was tired of San Diego and wanted to travel. What happened was the Navy would have an accident somewhere in the world like a plane would crash or a part of a ship would blow up. Bob and another assistant would fly to the place with a doctor and dentist and figure out which victim was which. After a half year of this Bob got sick and tired of sorting body parts and loose teeth and signed up with the SEALs. I say this because when I cut Bob in on the action with the Chief he wasn't much help because he had developed a phobia about dead bodies and he only looked at the Chief straight in his empty eyes once.

The upshot was that the first of July I stole an ice truck in Newberry by hot-wiring the ignition. I drove the truck full of sacked ice cubes directly to the deer cabin where I repainted it with seven aerosol cans of camo green spray at five bucks apiece. The next day Frank drove me to Newberry to pick up my van. I told him it had broken down, not wanting him to be involved in my criminal activity. He was my only character witness at the trial and the judge wasn't too impressed because Frank made it clear he wasn't one bit impressed by the judge.

Anyway, I switched license plates with my van and drove the ice truck to Little Lake at about three A.M. with the deflated rubber dinghy and the gill net squeezed inside with the cubes. I had told Bob I had an earache and couldn't dive so he busied himself trying to fix the Evinrude. You shouldn't dive on wrecks alone as there is too much that can go wrong. You develop an excess of nitrogen in your blood and you get what they call rapture of the deep which is about the same as smoking too much dope. I have nothing against smoking hemp except it puts me dead asleep and it's not what you'd do right before diving.

I found the Chief just after daylight as soon as I could pick out my triangulation points. I dove with a single tank and the gill net and a light to help me find the body. The Chief had tipped over on his side as if he were sleeping. There was a school of lake trout that looked like they were standing guard.

I was all business and wrapped the big body in the gill net and towed it upward with a rope. I can't tell you why things weigh less under water. I tied off the body at about fifteen feet to ensure clearance when I towed it through the channel to Little Lake.

So far so good, you might say. I thought I was making smart moves while I was doing it, all cool as a cucumber. I pulled the body up to the dock where the ice truck was parked. How was I to know there was this old Audubon-type woman down the beach trying to find a kind of plover that is nearly extinct? She was watching me all the time through binoculars and she said in court that when she saw me load the Chief into the ice truck it struck her as "peculiar." And there was another thing I was missing out on that would have given me cold feet. I always listen to country music on the Ishpeming station and never the Top Forty out of Newberry. Little did I know that the town of Newberry was treating the missing ice truck as the crime of the century. Not much has happened there since the state closed down the nut house. I bought a whole roomful of their furniture once for twenty bucks to fill an empty deer shack. I don't know why but it was comforting to have furniture that was all worn out by crazy people. So there I was driving down a two-track in a dark green ice truck not knowing that an old woman was on her way to the Rainbow Lodge at the mouth of the Two-Hearted River to call the cops.

When I reached the cabin I hid the truck in the woods and drove my van into town to the hardware store to see if the eyes had arrived by UPS. This wasn't suspicious as Bob sends out artifacts through UPS all the time. The eyes had come and I opened them in the van and rolled them in my hand. They were sort of disappointing as they were blue and not too realistic. There was a note from Shelley that read: "Dearest

B.D., Here are your eyes. My tits and pussy ache for you. Behave yourself. Your Love Pumpkin. P.S. See you this weekend."

Shelley is quite the potty mouth for such a high-class girl. I never ran into this before in a woman and it threw me off balance. After I met her in the bar that night two years ago we agreed to meet the next day. That was a downfall of sorts as I took her out to the burial mounds to impress her in order to screw her. In a way I was like Adam in the Garden I guess. We started necking out there in the clearing in the woods and she shrieked, "Stick your dick in me, you asshole," and it stopped me cold for fifteen minutes or so. I never even heard the lowest-class lady talk like this when making love. This talk took some getting used to during a sacred act (or so I am told) but I've learned to like it a bit over the past two years.

Anyway, I put the two eyes in my pocket and went in the Dunes Saloon to calm my nerves. The weather had turned hot which put me on edge and meant I'd have to keep the truck's refrigeration unit running nearly full time. My nerves forced me into a double whiskey when I realized I hadn't yet looked the Chief full in the face from close up, then I had to order a beer chaser because the whiskey was catching in my throat. Bob came in with grease to his elbows from working on the Evinrude. He asked about my earache and I said both of them were ringing. He was pretty upset because the diving season was just beginning and he didn't have the money to replace the lower unit.

"How about I offer you five thousand dollars for a day's work?" I found myself saying. I sketched out the story in a whisper leaving out the fact that the truck was stolen. At first he was angry over my breaking the bonds of our partnership so I edged up his share to seventy-five hundred. All we had

to do was drive the Chief to Chicago. He said he'd call Avakian and meet me at the cabin. Meanwhile, I should install the
eyes as he didn't want to fool with the body.

I drove out to the cabin all warm with the feeling I was no
longer in the scheme alone. It was easy enough to burn down
a chicken coop years ago but now I was in the big time and I
had to act strong like Robert Mitchum does in the movies.
Just by the way Mitchum talks or lights a cigarette you know
he's not fooling around. When I got to the cabin I stood there
in the gathering heat and watched the last of the south wind
stop in the trees. I could hear the soft *putt-putt* of the ice
truck's refrigeration unit in its hiding place out in the woods.
I strode right toward it rattling the eyes in my palm as if they
were dice. I paused at the back of the truck in full sweat because of the heat, then opened the door.

The Chief was still wrapped in the gill net and the sunlight
struck across his chest, his head still in the shadows. It occurred to me I shouldn't have painted the truck camo green
from its original white because it was absorbing too much sun
and heat. I got halfway in and unwrapped part of the gill net
around the Chief's head and slid him down so I could see
better what I was doing. He owned the biggest head I've ever
seen on a man so there would be plenty of room for the eyes.
I looked down and saw there was some water on the floor
which told me I was dealing with meltage. This didn't bother
me too much as we would be driving mostly at night which
would cool it off. I figured after I got the eyes in I would throw
some boughs and bed sheets on the truck top for the time
being. Just then, as I was looking up the Chief let out a moan
and some air which flubbered his lips. Suffice it to say I threw
myself backwards out the door, knocking my wind out when
I hit the ground. I felt like I was full of hot jelly I was so

scared. I hadn't even moved a minute later when Bob drove up and came down the trail into the woods.

He looked down at me, then in the truck door at the Chief, quickly slamming the door. "Jesus," he said, "that's fucking Frankenstein." He helped me up and I told him what happened. "Just gas," he said, having seen it before in dead bodies. Bob suggested we start right away instead of waiting for dark so the wind could help cool off my paint job. Avakian wanted us there before dawn and the trip was over five hundred miles. I'd wait and see if Avakian would pay extra for the eyes. Little did Bob and I know that bodies aren't a case of finders, keepers.

Right now I am back in present time with my rabbit stew bubbling on the stove. Old Claude just walked in without a knock. He said he smelled something to eat a half mile away, then asked for a drink. There is something in the air up here that makes us lie a lot. For instance, if you catch three brook trout you say you caught fifteen, and if you caught fifteen you say you caught three. If things are terrible you pretend you're okay, but if things are going too smoothly you tend to piss in the whiskey and create a problem. I'm not sure why this is true. I told Claude I didn't have any booze in the cabin and he started sniffling loudly and said he smelled schnapps, McGillicuddy's Peppermint Schnapps, in fact. I got the bottle out of the cupboard and took a big swig first in case he had it in mind to hog the rest. When I handed him the bottle he sat by the stove and just looked at it for a long while before drinking. He always acts like this when he has something important to say.

Claude is in his mid-seventies and he just walked seven miles out here to tell me something but he was in no rush.

He carries a big garbage bag folded up in his pocket to crawl into in case it rains or the snow is wet, or he just wants to take a nap. Claude's the one who told me that every tree is different from every other tree. I thought about this for a week, then told Bob who didn't think it was such a big deal. Claude has a weak spot for Shelley even though he thinks she's up to no good. He tells her a lot about the old ways of the Chippewa though I know he makes most of it up on the spot.

It wasn't until I set out two bowls for supper that Claude told me the news. First of all Shelley wanted me to come over to Marquette tomorrow because she and Tarah were feeling blue. Claude said they were at the Ramona Inn but I was pretty sure it was the Ramada. Then came the shocker. Just this afternoon while Claude was wandering around in the boondocks for reasons of his own, he came upon two fellows setting up camp despite the bad weather. It just so happened that the two guys were Shelley's friends and classmates, the asshole with the red hair I'd met several times and the small blond fellow who walks around being sincere about everything. The blond guy had given me a book of poetry by a fruitcake Arab by the name of Gibran that I couldn't understand, so I gave it to a tourist girl and it made her horny as a toad.

When I heard about the camp certain things were clear. Claude said when they drove off he came out of hiding and snooped in their tent, finding a whole tube of marked-up topographical maps. It dawned on me Shelley wanted me over in Marquette so I wouldn't run into the two guys looking for my burial mounds out in the woods. I got so angry that I couldn't eat my rabbit stew, then I calmed down in a few minutes and it was so good we finished the whole pot. Sad to say we didn't have a single beer to go with it, and the schnapps was gone.

I drove Claude back to town and we decided on the spur of the moment to have a nightcap at the Dunes. Sure enough Shelley's friends were there. To protect their identities I'll call them Jerk and Jerkoff. They were all smiles and pretended surprise that Shelley was in Marquette. After buying us a drink they said they were headed back to the Superior Hotel for a night's rest. When they left Frank came over and warned me that the two of them were talking about me to Shelley on the pay phone. I felt my muscles tighten as if they were steel. "I'm going to deal hard with those shitsuckers," I said. Frank offered to loan me an axe but I thought that was going a little far. You never know when Frank is kidding.

The next day dawned bright and clear. I wasn't feeling great but a lot better than the day before. I made a thick bacon and raw onion sandwich which always gives me energy. It was about seven and I knew I should wait until ten before I checked out their camp as they would likely be out on their burial search at that time. If Shelley was blue I was a whole lot bluer. I'm not talking about feeling betrayed, because I saw that coming, but the idea that far too much had been happening in the past four months for me to get my balance.

When Shelley probes me she can't get over what she calls my "preferences" and "life choices." For instance, my favorite thing is just plain walking in the woods. I can do it days on end without getting tired of it. I mix this up a bit with fishing and hunting. Of course I like to make love and drink. That goes without saying. Before I started diving for Bob I sometimes had to cut pulp which is hard work. When I cut pulp my favorite moments were drinking cold water, making my din-

ner, then falling asleep because I was bone tired. I think I've
seen every bird up here but I don't know their official names
which irritates Shelley. Perhaps no one is who they seem to
be. Shelley also thinks that what with my being pretty much
an orphan, and with an old man as a parent, I was raised as if
I myself were an old man with no expectations, no drive and
ambition. When I agreed she didn't want me to, so I said I've
been around a bit and there's a lot worse things than that. To
be sure, it is strange to be an orphan and have to invent yourself because you don't know the facts. Having parents would
give you an anchor on earth, but when you're an orphan you're
always dreaming about how you came to be, and you could
well pass your life dreaming. Or walking around in the woods.

This reminds me of the finest thing I ever saw, and which
upset Shelley so much we skipped the next day's probing. I
was about ten at the time and we were living over west of
Escanaba. It was the day before school let out before Christmas vacation and a storm had begun in the morning so we
were let out of school early. The problem was that the wind
had been coming from the south up across Lake Michigan
bringing in rain because the lake hadn't completely cooled
down. But then the wind, as it always does, came around to
the west, then the northwest, increasing to about fifty knots
and we had a full-blown gale and blizzard sweeping down all
the way from Manitoba. First it was the rain turning to ice,
then a foot or so of wet snow freezing up as it turned cold,
then another foot or two of dry snow casting in drifts so it
came halfway up the kitchen window. It was a hellish storm
and by late afternoon the electricity went off. That didn't matter to us as our heat was wood anyhow and we had twenty
cords stacked against the back of the house, with another two
cords of dry maple in the pump shed. We just lit the oil lamps

and continued to play cribbage which we always did during storms.

Somewhere in the middle of the night the wind stopped and moonlight came in my frosted-up window. I blew my breath on the window to make a peephole in the frost. I remember staring at the field outside and the woods beyond and feeling quite satisfied that I wasn't an animal freezing my ass off. Then I saw a movement way out in the field near the edge of the woods, a black shape wobbling around and coming slowly toward the house. My skin pricked up with fright before I realized it had to be our neighbors. I also remember Grandpa was worried about David Four Feet's mother because she was due to have a baby and her husband was in jail for getting drunk and slugging the deputy. The upshot was that I woke up Grandpa and he got dressed in a hurry and went plunging through the deep snow to help out. It was David, his two brothers and sister Rose dragging a toboggan with their mother aboard. She was in labor and the kids, none of them over ten, were upset and their legs were bleeding from the crusted snow. Grandpa put the mother in his bed and the kids in the parlor where he attended to their wounds with me helping out and fetching hot water, bandages and iodine.

He made the kids stay in the parlor, then put another pot of water on the stove, and we went in to help the mother. I mostly stood there and let her squeeze my arms and hands and within a half hour out came a baby girl with the help of Grandpa giving a tug or two. When he held the baby up and cleaned the gunk off and it started crying he said to me that this would be the finest thing I'd ever seen and this was how every person came into the world. I believed it though my arm hurt and was all bruised up from her squeezing. They all stayed with us for four days and we had a grand time playing

games and cards and tobogganing though it didn't make Rose
and her mother like me later on. I must have been an unlikable kid.

That afternoon in July before Bob and I took off for Chicago
with the Chief we had more than a few cold beers to fight the
heat, and me with a plumb empty stomach. The beer filled
me with courage and I took an easy chair out to the truck and
tied the Chief down on it so he wouldn't be sliding around in
an undignified way. A thing worth doing is worth doing well,
they say. I also stuck in the blue eyes. It was then I made an
important discovery I have divulged to no one. It was possible
the Chief had been murdered because of the piece of frayed
rope around his ankle. On a whim I ran my hand through his
ice-cold hair until my fingers touched a hole that could have
been made by a bullet. It was then I checked his trousers and
came up with a thin wallet which never occurred to me before. Everything in the wallet had turned to mush except a
plastic-coated driver's license that read Ted Sleeping Bear and
a Marinette, Wisconsin, address. The license had an expira-
tion date of November in 1965 so the body wasn't nearly so
old as I thought, right around twenty-five years in Lake Superior. I pitched the wallet in the brush and hid the license
in the outhouse where it still is today.

I drove first and only made it halfway between Grand Marais and Seney before the hot air and the truck's bad exhaust
system made me sick. I rinsed my face in some ditch water
but it was warm and green. I was dizzy and my clothes stuck
to me and Bob was anxious to get going. I said I'd ride in the
back with the Chief and cool off and he said, "B.D., you got
a real set of balls." By this time, though, I wasn't afraid of the
Chief, and to be truthful, while riding back there in the cold

dark I got to thinking he might be my dad. Of course I was half drunk and sick, also afraid of being caught, so my mind was a bit crazy. This is what the court called "delusional." There was nothing to say the Chief wasn't my dad. Marinette is across the river from Menominee which is less than fifty miles from Bark River. Of course Shelley has pointed out just about any man near sixty years old or older could be my dad. Be that as it may, the idea set itself in concrete in my mind, which shows again I had no talent for crime. All Grandpa would ever say was that his wife was a bad woman and so was their daughter, so he finally kicked them both out when I was a baby and raised me himself. Just before he died in the old folks' home I tried to badger him out of more information but he just said, "B.D., cut that shit out," and told the story he had told so many times about how he started to cut a big hemlock to get it out of the way for the skidder and it tipped over uprooting itself. Out popped a big bear that had been hibernating under the tree roots but the bear was still too sleepy to be pissed off. The bear just looked at him and walked away. Then when Grandpa was near death he was mumbling about Beaver Island. Sometimes in the summers we'd catch a ride with a fish tug out to Beaver Island and that was where I first learned how to dive. There's nothing to equal being down there on the bottom looking around except walking in the woods on a cold morning. Shelley couldn't quite believe how I'd take a stroll on a cold blustery night in just a T-shirt. Anyone who's not a fool should try walking in the woods on a cold night when the moon is full. That's when I learned most of life's secrets that I know.

Sitting back there with the Chief I could tell when we hit Seney because Bob stopped and turned right, heading west on 28 on a part of the road called the Seney stretch. This country strikes some as a thirty-mile swamp but it is beautiful when you get inside it. We were about five minutes or so down the stretch and I was having a chat with my presumed dad when I heard the siren and knew the jig was up. As the truck slowed I scrambled around behind the Chief's easy chair to hide which was pointless but I did it anyway. The truck stopped and in a minute or so I heard two voices besides Bob's, then the door opened and flashlights shown in because it was evening. Partway as a dumb joke I let out a howl and the police yelled. I peeked out quickly and saw one cop throw his hands back, dropping the flashlight, and accidentally hit Bob square in the face. I'll tell you that to hit Bob is to light a stick of dynamite because you better run for it. I jumped out and watched the three of them fight and it was quite a struggle. Just then I had the bright idea of jumping in the truck and taking off which is exactly what I did.

It is now nine-thirty A.M. and time to take my vengeance on Jerk and Jerkoff. I made sure I had what I needed in the van and took off for the woods. After I settled their hash I would take a powder and head over to Marquette to see Shelley and Tarah to try to lighten their hearts. I stopped short of the campsite, put on my camouflage suit, loaded my Colt .22 pistol and grabbed a gallon of gasoline I keep for the dinghy's old three-horse Scott-Atwater. The can was red so I sprayed it green with the last of the aerosol paint I used on the ice truck four months before. Waste not, want not, they say. I moved silent as a shadow through the woods, then came down a dry, brushy creekbed that only carries water during spring run-off. Just as I thought, there was no one at the campsite. Their Toyota was parked far enough from the tent and for a moment I thought of burning that too, but settled for letting the air out of all the tires. I doused the tent full of expensive camping gear with the gasoline, threw on a match and leapt back, and she burned with a fine roar. With a forefinger I traced a skull on the dusty side of their Toyota though it looked a bit more like a schmoo. For no reason at all I fired three shots in the air and hightailed it for my van. From my reckoning they'd have a thirteen-mile walk on their hands, by which time I'd be in Marquette.

Somewhat to my surprise I didn't get much pleasure out of the tent and equipment burning. On my way down toward Seney and over to Marquette I thought long and hard about protecting those ancient burial mounds. You better not hold your hand over your ass until you come up with thinking that makes a difference, that's all I can say. Mine was the original sin of taking Shelley out there in the first place in my pussy trance. I knew Tarah had been confused enough afterwards, but maybe on the way in she'd been smarter than I thought. Country people are always underestimating just how smart outsiders can be. I've seen men come way up here from Flint, Grand Rapids and Detroit with a bunch of high-price bird dogs and shoot more partridge than any fifty locals. Sometimes these same folks catch more trout on flies that you can hardly see than anyone who fishes with worms. Maybe Tarah had one of those brains like a camera you read about. The fire might slow down the effort for a while but in the long run you couldn't stop these people if they kept up their gumption. Sad to say, in my thinking there was no way to get myself off the hook.

I had to laugh when I crossed the Driggs River Bridge because this was where Bob had had his duke-out with the cops that got him two years along with illegally transporting a body. I wish I could have stayed to watch the fight. The one cop who was supposed to be the toughest around ended up in the Munising Hospital but so did Bob for a few days. While they were fighting I had turned off 28 and headed down the first of many log roads at top speed. I went so far into the brush I doubted the sunlight would ever reach me, deep into bug hell where you could grab a handful of mosquitoes out the truck window if you had a mind to. What's more, I knew that at daylight the blackflies, horseflies and deerflies would join the cops and mosquitoes in the search for the truck. I had no insect repellent and nothing to drink but two beers that were getting warmer by the minute. There was nothing to eat and though I knew I was close to creeks, the Stoner and the Creighton, I had no fishing tackle. The fifty-one dollars in my wallet couldn't buy a thing out in that black hell. If I needed to lose weight it would have been a fine time to diet.

Rather than tire myself out with fear I curled up and slept for a few hours until so many mosquitoes managed to get in the truck cab I awoke to a swollen face and hands. I got out and checked on the Chief and found it was warming up in there. Above the whine of the mosquitoes I could hear the ice melt. I started the truck and the refrigeration unit to cool it off which wasn't taking much of a chance as the search for me probably wouldn't start until daylight. I was disappointed to see that I had less than a half tank of gas which would limit the time I could hide out. I was pretty sure Bob wouldn't say anything as in the Navy SEALs he had been taught how to resist confessing under torture. And what could he say besides that he was driving a dead Indian to Chicago in a stolen truck? Of course he could name my name but everyone in Alger County knew we were partners and it wouldn't take Dick Tracy to figure out I was involved.

I turned off the ignition and the refrigeration unit and got in back with the Chief to avoid the warm night and the mosquitoes. I thought of moving him off the easy chair and taking a snooze but it didn't seem right, so I sat on the arm and leaned back just touching his left side. It remains to be seen if I was asleep or awake, and maybe I'll never know, but the Chief spoke to me there in the ice-cold dark. It didn't seem to be in English, though that's the only language I know by heart. Some of it was in a jumble but I remember it pretty well. *"B.D., my son, you haven't exactly panned out but then you didn't start with much. To whom the Lord gives much, much is expected so you are not on the hot seat in regard to gifts. Someday branches and leaves will grow out of you and you'll understand how fish, birds and animals talk and I don't mean in chirps and growls. You'll be a green man is what I mean, with leaves coming out of your ears. Don't cross the Mackinac Bridge and don't go south of Green Bay toward tropical places. Your greed got you into this. Beware of women with forked tongues. Buy yourself a hat because your hair is thinning on top. Don't rely on alcohol so much for good times. Sneak up on animals and just say hello. Don't try to take vengeance on those who killed me or they'll kill you too. It wouldn't hurt you to read a book about nature cover to cover. Remember when you were so good at square dancing in the seventh grade?"* How did he know this? *"Well, don't come tromping into the Halls of Death, but live your life with light feet. Before I forget, bury me in the forest where I belong, not with the fish."*

That's pretty much what he said. I started to relax when he stopped talking and he sang me a few songs like nursery rhymes which were beautiful. I imagine this is what fathers do for sons who are hurt and grieving.

I awoke bone-chilled on the Chief's lap to the sound of water trickling on the inside and bird songs on the outside. I opened the door to let the light in and heard the first of the spotter planes above the bird sounds. The treetops above formed a pretty good canopy and I added to it with brush. It was about six A.M. and already warm and the breeze was from the south so I knew it would be a hot one. This made my heart ache for both myself and the Chief. I cranked up the truck and sat on a stump trying to make a plan, mindful that the original one had been short on good sense. I quickly drank the two warm beers out of thirst and for courage. Why hadn't I put the beers inside with the Chief to cool off? It showed that in desperate straits you can't think clearly. By and large, though, I felt pretty strong from my talk with the Chief. There was no way I was going to get away scot-free, and the best plan had to take this into account. We should have been leaving Chicago now with a paper sack full of twenty thousand dollars. I was going to buy a newish used van and check out some locations in Canada as the U.S. seemed to be filling up. Shelley was due in the evening and would get her ears full of my fuck-up. In short, the whole damn situation didn't look good.

I opened the door and it was cooling down nicely. About all I could manage by way of a plan was to bury the Chief properly and turn myself in. I decided to remove the blue eyes but they were stuck so it meant the Chief was swelling up. I took off on foot out of the woods and across the marsh and the Stoner Spreads toward Worchester Lake where I hoped to break into a cabin and find something to eat. It was a tough walk as the marsh was spongy and two of the creeks were neck deep. I watched an otter family fooling around so long I about forgot what I was doing, but was brought awake by the DNR (Department of Natural Resources) spotter plane. I wriggled under a clump of elder until the plane got tired of crisscrossing the area. At the Stoner Spreads I drank my fill at a cold spring I knew about from brook trout fishing and smeared some silt mud on my face and arms to try to slow down the blackflies.

The cabin I had in mind hadn't been used yet this year so the pickings were slim. I ate at a can of baked beans and a can of green beans until I was all beaned out. I took a bottle of water and half ran back the Creighton truck trail because the Chief would need cooling off. Twice I had to jump off into the brush, the first time for a State Police cruiser with a big German shepherd tracking dog in the back, and the second time for a County Sheriff's car. It made me feel important for about ten minutes, then I saw the back end of the deal. I'd hate to miss the big storms of winter in a jail cell.

There's not a lot more to this part of the story. As soon as it got dark I drove over to the Bear Trap Inn near Melstrand. I knew the bartender and he sold me a six-pack and fifteen bags of ice through the side door, and let me use the phone in the back room. He said I was getting real popular with the police as they had stopped by three times that day to check on my whereabouts. I called Frank and asked him to drop off a shovel and a bottle of whiskey at a certain part of the woods. Frank said, "B.D., you got your ass in a sling." I asked if there was a reward for my capture because I wanted him to have it, but he hadn't heard of any reward. Shelley was in the Dunes Saloon waiting for me to show up and Frank put her on. "B.D., I beg you to give yourself up, my darling." I told her where she could meet me at dawn with the cops and hung up. I instantly regretted this as I had a hard night of work ahead of me and would need a nap before I turned myself in. Then I tried to call David Four Feet to see how you went about burying an Indian Chief. There was only one number under their American name and I got an older woman. I said this is B.D.

and she said "I know it." This was the same woman who I had helped have a baby over thirty years ago. Sad to say, she told me my buddy David had got himself killed in Jackson Prison ten years before. She said Rose was living in the house with her two kids and I asked to talk to her. There was a pause and voices, then she said Rose was watching *L.A. Law* and wouldn't come to the phone. Maybe if I stopped by someday with a present she'd be likable. I hung up the phone with a bad feeling in my stomach from Rose just like in the old days. The power of love to make you feel awful is something to see.

I took log trails all the way to Grand Marais and past it, picking up the shovel on the way. There was a note from Frank taped to the shovel handle: "Do not shoot it out as if you get your ass shot off we will not get to hunt and fish anymore. There is no cold beer in hell. Yr. friend, Frank." This note scared me a bit as it had not occurred to me that the cops would shoot me.

I reached the location a half mile past the burial mounds and spent the next four hours digging a hole the size of a well pit for the Chief. I hauled him out and set him down, then sat next to him and had a cigarette and a cold beer. I put my arm around him and looked up at the moon, listening to some whippoorwills from along the river, and way in the distance a gang of coyotes yipping after a rabbit. I said "Goodbye, Dad" and almost cried, and gave him a shove so he toppled into the hole. By the time I filled in the hole there were the first traces of daylight in the eastern sky and I knew I had to give myself up to the law.

Now it's October and I am a free man driving to Marquette to see the woman who saved me, Shelley, and her dingbat cousin, Tarah. I imagined Brad might be having problems getting his ten pounds of vegetables per day at the hospital. I stopped at the Corktown in Munising for a pick-me-up and felt lust in my heart for the barmaid who had a large, solid fanny. I was nervous as the thought came to me that burning up the tent and expensive equipment might be a violation of my probation. No doubt it was, but someone has to stand up for what's right. For some reason I couldn't remember why Jesus came into Jerusalem on a donkey and why they threw palm branches in front of him. There was the idea that back then they maybe didn't have riding horses. Grandpa bought me a horse once for twenty bucks and you could hardly ever catch him, but you could see him at dawn and in the evening from the kitchen window, way out at the end of the field hanging out with the deer.

I checked at the desk at the Ramada Inn but the clerk didn't want me to go up to Shelley's room until he called ahead. I should have dressed better, I suppose, and when I felt my head my hair was sticking up. I went on up and found they had two rooms, what is called a "suite" with a living room and a bedroom. If you ask me, neither of them looked too good. They were both edgy and pale around the gills and I figured they must be sitting up day and night with Brad, but I discovered later it was something else. Tarah gave me a bleak hug and went off into the bedroom to take a nap.

Shelley closed the door on her and immediately became crosser with me than ever before. She accused me of playing a trick on Tarah so that she heard a voice when she lay face down on the burial mound. This had given her a nervous breakdown as she had never got an out-loud response from the spirit world before. Shelley said she thought of herself as a scientist type and didn't believe in this bullshit but I had to have done something to freak out her cousin who was also her best girlfriend. I said I couldn't throw my voice like Edgar Bergen did to Charlie McCarthy and Mortimer Snerd, but she had never heard of these people, which shows the difference in generations. I explained like I did to Tarah that the noise was just a bear cub crying for its mother. Then Shelley accused me of fucking Tarah when she was practically passed out from fright. Shelley was standing right in front of me so I had to stonewall it by saying that Tarah was "delusional" just like they'd said about me at the trial. It seemed to work as Shelley gave me a beer from a tiny refrigerator like a boat refrigerator over in the corner. She took a vial from her purse and snorted white powder that I knew was coke with a miniature spoon. This was out of character, I thought, as she is usually down on drugs. She said she and Tarah had been tired and sad from their problems so they bought a bunch. She offered it to me and I said no. A few years before, Bob and me met some tourist girls in the bar and went to their motel room and did some coke and whiskey. I got real excitable but my weenie wouldn't stand up so I got drunk. The idea of paying a hundred bucks for a half-master is beyond me. My head hurt so bad the next morning I rolled around in the weeds next to the cabin and yelled.

Shelley perked up fast and took a sport coat she bought me out of the closet. I hadn't worn a coat like that, except a borrowed one to a wedding or a funeral, since I lost my graduation suit back in the Moody Bible Institute days. Things were looking up again, I thought, staring at myself in the bathroom mirror and wetting down my hair. Shelley came in and took off her clothes and we tore off a quick one watching ourselves in the mirror, and me with my new sport coat on. Shelley made a loud hooting noise and Tarah woke up and came out of the bedroom to see if Shelley was okay. We could see her behind us in the mirror and we all started laughing. It looked like it was going to be quite an evening.

I had the rare treat of watching cable television while the

girls spent an hour getting dressed. The cabins I live in never have electricity and Frank doesn't turn TV on in the bar unless someone wants to see a sporting contest. Strange to say, there were twenty-seven channels and nothing interesting to watch. Shelley only let me have one more beer because we were going out to dinner at someone's home and she wanted to guarantee my good behavior. I busied myself catching glimpses of them dressing through the bedroom door while I pretended to read the catalogue that lists every single Ramada Inn in the entire world. I caught Tarah bending over in a rear shot that made me wish I could work a camera so I could save the view for future generations, or at least for my cabin wall. She finished dressing first and came out and sat on the couch next to me with a dab of white powder under her nose and glittery eyes.

"Shelley said that noise I heard was a baby bear."

"I told you that about five times." I was nervous when she put her hand on my thigh because I was still a bit swollen from seeing her butt in underpants.

"No you didn't. It doesn't matter anyhow. The voice spoke right into my stomach with a weeping sound."

"That was a bear cub," I repeated. She traced a finger along the shape of my pecker and I glanced at the bedroom to make sure Shelley wasn't coming out.

"I think it's the way the dolphins used to tell me to get involved with Native Americans," she said, giving my weenie a pinch.

"Might be," I said. Then Shelley came out dressed for church and we went off to dinner.

After I thought it over later I can't say I didn't enjoy myself though I never got my balance back after Tarah's pinch. The house was big and old but inside it was brand new which was peculiar. It was owned by a doctor younger than me who was taking care of Brad. He had a beeper on his belt and didn't get to drink or do any drugs. Everybody else kept glugging drinks and disappearing into the bathroom for reasons I guessed President Bush wouldn't approve of. I'd like to take him fishing as according to the newspapers, he never catches much in the ocean. According to Bob, the Japs are raping the oceans of fish for their yellow hordes.

Meanwhile, at dinner there was also an attorney who kept saying "Super" and a newspaper guy who had been at my trial for a short period and who ignored me. The women were more pleasant than the men, also they were pretty and smelled better at close range than any bunch of women I had ever met. One of them could see I was uncomfortable at such a high-class deal and talked to me about her kids. Her husband had left for a while and came back with a fresh sack of coke. He was a nice fellow and we talked about fishing, exchanging our least-best locations as fishermen do. His wife said she was glad to see we were "bonding," and went into the kitchen to help out. I said to the guy that I always thought bonding was when you repaired your waders or an inner tube and he agreed, though he was staring across the room at Tarah as if he wanted to jump her like a flying squirrel. All the men were paying the most attention to Shelley and Tarah because they were new in town, which pissed off the other women, who pretended they weren't pissed off as they helped set out dinner.

The main part of dinner looked like a huge cornish pasty but it was baked dough covering rare meat with a liver-tasting sauce. To be frank, it was the best thing I ever ate. The doctor's wife was real happy because no one else was eating much, so she kept serving me more, and with it I drank two whole bottles of delicious foreign red wine. There was also a dish of the tiniest carrots and onions and I said the onion was one of the most perfect things God made, and everyone was eager to agree. This made me feel more comfortable though the wine might have had something to do with it. In fact, the wine was creeping up on me like a dread assassin, and when everyone got up to go to the bar where they were playing music, I went to the bathroom and washed my face with cold water. When I got out they were all gone except the doctor's wife who was cleaning up. I felt sort of forgotten but she said she'd told them she would give me a ride. I think she was fibbing but I let it go and pitched in with the dishes. There was some gravy left and I asked if she minded that I drink it to settle my stomach and that pleased her. She was the plumpest of the ladies and I couldn't help but flirt a little. Her face got red and her eyes all teary.

"I know Fred is chasing that slut friend of yours, Tarah." She threw a glass against the refrigerator and it broke all over. By Fred she meant Dr. Fred, her husband.

"Don't worry, she won't be caught. She's engaged to this fellow in the hospital." I swept up the broken glass so I wouldn't have to face her. I knew if Tarah was primed up she'd probably fuck a rock pile if she thought there was a snake in it. I could see Mrs. Fred didn't believe me either, so I gave her a simple enough hug, and when we kissed she stuck her tongue in my mouth which sets me off, but then she pushed me away though not too far.

"I'm not going to screw you. I'm pregnant and it wouldn't be right." She put her hand on my pecker under my trousers and I put one down her blouse and gave a nipple a tweak. She unzipped me, then poured some dish soap in her hand, saying

64

she'd be glad to "release my tension" which is what she did. It might not seem like it to the naysayers but it was sort of romantic.

Mrs. Fred dropped me off at the bar with a big French kiss and squealed off in her foreign-made car named a Volvo, my first ride in one. The music was so loud it was deafening me but I still felt sleepy after love when you ordinarily take a short snooze. I went to the bar and had a couple of 7 Crown doubles to wake myself up, then looked around just in time to see Shelley going out the back door with the lawyer. I felt low for a minute but I can't say I blamed her as he was cut from the same cloth as her, and I wasn't. Tarah was dancing and smooching with Dr. Fred and the others hadn't seen me yet so I left. It was the noise of the music that drove me out. I'm not used to loud noise in my life and it's the same reason I quit cutting pulp. A chainsaw is just too loud.

It was a long walk back to the motel and I was feeling low so I stopped at a few workingmen's bars along the way, also an all-night grocery store where I bought the new *Outdoor Life*. When I got back to the rooms Tarah and the doctor were fooling around on the couch. He jumped up grabbing at his clothes so I said "Peace, brother" like the radicals did way back in Chicago. I went into the bedroom, got my clothes off and started to read an article called "How to Nail a Big Swamp Buck" when I remembered the burning tent in the wilderness. It hardly seemed this could be the same day but it was, as I was to find out the next morning.

When I got up to pee at very first light Shelley and Tarah were also in the king-size bed, one on each side. You would think this would be the most exciting thing possible but I wasn't feeling too good about the ladies or myself. The world was moving too fast and I had to get my balance back. I picked up

my sport coat from where I had thrown it on a chair when I
came in and interrupted Tarah and the sawbones. There was
a gravy splotch on the sport coat which sent me lower and I
thought, B.D., you ought to wear a bib. It did warm my heart,
though, to look out the window and see my van down in the
parking lot in the dim morning light. There was also a guy
who was asleep in his car who might wake up feeling worse
than me, though that's like saying you feel great because you're
not a roadkill. It's time to take stock, I thought, which is hard
to do when you are bare naked and far from home. For some
reason, I could remember a cold October morning when
Grandpa and me got up at dawn and cut firewood all day.
When we took a break at mid-morning for breakfast, he fried
two partridges and cornmeal mush and made gravy. Late in
the afternoon the day got warm and he let me have a big glass
of cold hard cider to ease the aches of a day spent on the end
of a crosscut saw.

I went back in the bedroom, picked up my *Outdoor Life*
and sat down on a chair at the end of the bed. The room was
too warm and the girls had moved around so the top sheet
was half off. Shelley was snoring ever so little and her arm
was on Tarah's back. I looked at this page in *Outdoor Life* that
is in there every month about a sportsman's perilous adventure in a cartoon-style drawing. Usually a guy gets attacked
by a bear or rattlesnake, or charged by a wild pig or moose,
or maybe falls through the hole when ice fishing. This month
a fellow was going down a river in a rowboat, just fishing and
not knowing there was a waterfall ahead. The artist did a good
job on the guy's face as he shot over the waterfall, probably
screaming "Holy shit" and having his close call with doom,
but the person always survives the adventure or it wouldn't
make much of a cartoon.

There was a rustling from the bed and I was all slouched down so I lifted the magazine for a look. They were on their stomachs and both of their bare bottoms were showing plain as day. The room was getting lighter and if their butts were cameras it seemed like they were taking my picture. In a way I was having a stare-down with the source of life, then I thought of a weird ancient story Shelley had told me. It was an Indian story from out west about when we were first on earth. Every time a man would screw he'd bleed to death because women had sharp teeth in their articles. It wasn't until a coyote came along and pulled the teeth out that men could screw without dying and get the human race started. This is why the coyote is thought to be sacred.

Men like to say that a hard dick has no conscience, but I've never believed that as I like to think I have free will even when I'm drunk. I moved closer to them for a better look and, though I was still upset, I began to think it was time to forgive and forget. Let bygones be bygones. A bad night had passed and now it was a new day, also it was hard to think of anything more purely beautiful than those two bottoms. I got a lump in my throat and couldn't quite catch my breath. Given their behavior they could hardly turn me down. Man is not exactly built for two at once and I was going to have to keep real busy so they wouldn't lose interest. I stood there at the ready, like the Olympic diver on the Dunes TV dedicating his dive to the Lord. The first ray of sun came in the window, a sign I thought, and I went for it. I almost yelled "Geronimo" but I didn't want to startle them.

It couldn't have been better and I still felt warm all over when I returned from getting some containers of coffee for myself, also sweet rolls and Diet Pepsi for the ladies. All I can say is I did my best and we all agreed we had sweated out the worst of our hangovers. Afterwards, in the bathroom mirror, it looked like I had been saddle-soaped.

Unfortunately I may as well have gone back to a room in hell itself. Tarah was taking a shower and Shelley was on the phone and talking excitedly. When she put down the phone she started screaming at me so I couldn't even understand what she was saying. She kept saying, "I carried you, I saved you, I've been carrying you so long, you hideous dumb bastard. I even loved you, you worthless fucker, and now you did it, you're going to prison now, you asshole." The upshot was that Jerk had called about the burned tent and equipment and all of Jerkoff's "field notes." It was a shock to hear the State Police had come out to the boonies and taken my fingerprints off the vehicle where I had drawn the skull and crossbones that looked like a schmoo. It was easy as they had fingerprinted me a few months before, and my name came up right away in the burned tent accident.

I denied everything, saying that I had made the drawing in the road dust the night before outside the bar, but she wasn't having any of it. She started sobbing there on the couch and wouldn't let me comfort her, then she calmed down and became cold and mean. I had never seen her like this before and it chilled my poor heart. She told me to go out in the hall while she made a few calls and I stood out there like I was waiting for a dentist to jerk my teeth. It was all I could do to not cut and run, but there was a problem of the State Police and my slow van.

It was an hour before she came out, and by then I wasn't sad and I wasn't mad. She stood there with her hands on her hips as I studied the big girl vacuuming the hall.

"Look me straight in the eye, B.D.," she said, so I came up to her until my nose was about an inch from her forehead, then I tilted down.

"You don't love me and you never did," I said. "You just want my graveyard."

I was using a woman's wiles and it slowed her down for a few seconds, then she wanted to take a ride so off we went. She had a small bag and told me to take my toothbrush. When I hesitated she promised me she wasn't turning me in to the police, though they were looking for me. I smelled a small rat and wondered what she wanted.

I won't say it was a bad ride, because it started what I hoped was a new part of my life, but a lot of it made me sweat blood. The cool sunny air of October had cleared my head to the point I realized I could sure as hell do some time for torching their camp. Probation was supposed to make me walk the straight and narrow for three years and I had only made it four months, no matter that my heart was in the right place. I thought of my buddy David Four Feet getting killed in Jackson Prison and shivered. I did not want to die for the good cause of protecting my burial mounds, which would be like dying for the dead.

Shelley wanted to go down to Escanaba and Bark River which was only about seventy miles or so to the south. She said the ride was our "swan song" and I had promised to show her where I was brought up which would "complete the circle." I didn't know what the hell she meant by this and didn't care because a squad car had passed us on the outskirts of Marquette and this had churned up my stomach. I agreed to show her around if we could eat something first, but she said she wasn't hungry, so we stopped at a store and I ran in for a six-pack and a chunk of pickled bologna. At the counter I couldn't help but check out the place for the back door as an escape route but I was breaking my last twenty-dollar bill and the notion was hopeless.

We took back roads to get down to the old place near Bark

River. This was to avoid any Saturday traffic caused by what the tourist people call the "fall color tour" in their brochures, where Jack Frost uses his icy paintbrush to color the woods red and gold. A storm will come along and take off all the leaves overnight and the tourists who drove a long way are pissed off like it was the local people's fault. I showed Shelley a two-track where once the game warden had cornered me and David Four Feet and his brothers. We had my 1947 Dodge I'd paid fifty bucks for, and a case of beer, and we had been out shining deer. We shot a spikehorn buck for the larder, threw it in the trunk and got ourselves chased by the game warden to this two-track where the game warden stopped and waited us out. He knew the road went into a big area where there was only about forty acres of high ground surrounded by thousands of acres of swamp, and then the road dead-ended. We felt real smart so I built a fire while David and his brothers skinned and pieced out the deer. Our plan was to bury the hide and bones in the swamp, roast and eat all the meat, thus destroying the evidence. We must have eaten about ten pounds apiece and drunk all the beer. David's younger brothers got sick and wanted to go home so he had to pound them a bit. David said if the warden wanted to locate the dead deer all he'd find were turds. The trouble was we got convicted on the basis of the blood and deer hair in the trunk.

Shelley didn't think this was too funny as it betrayed an early start in the life of "petty" crime, crime that authorities kept records on and doomed the criminal to failure. I wanted to tell her to go fuck herself but then I got upset over the fact that they wrote down every little thing you did wrong. For instance, at my short trial the thing about pouring beer down the woman's neck came up, also my so-called resisting arrest when I pretended to fall on the stairs dragging the cops down

with me, even the scuffle in Montana, shining deer, everything. What chance did a fellow have to improve when they
had files to pull the rug out from under him? Especially when
I never intentionally hurt anyone. Don't Doggett, I thought
as we entered Doggett country with a potential forest fire
starting in every swale. Take your medicine and reform yourself, however that is done.

Then Shelley started laughing for no reason which lifted my
spirits, even though she was beautiful and obviously bent on
ridding herself of me. She described again what it was like to
be down near the marina in Grand Marais at dawn with the
sheriff, two deputies, and two state cops. They had all thought
this meeting place meant I was coming by water, then they
heard the roar from the hill at the far end of town. That was
me in the ice truck, cranking it up to top speed for no reason
but to make my giving up a big deal. I didn't want to putter
into Grand Marais in third gear. Shelley said the bunch of
them got off in the corner so they couldn't be run into and
watched me heading down the hill into town at sixty miles an
hour, swerving around the corner and down over the em-
bankment. My idea was to drive the ice truck into Lake Superior and half drown myself but I got bogged down in the
sand about fifty feet from the water. Even though it was barely
daylight a lot of people came out to see the show because
squad cars are rare in Grand Marais. I got to wave to Frank
and his kids in pajamas before the cops subdued me. I put up
a little tussle so the people wouldn't feel disappointed they
got up so early.

I was pretty upset at my so-called trial because I didn't even
get a jury I could explain myself to. The sharpie lawyer from
Detroit Shelley's dad got for me said we'd be better off throwing ourselves at the mercy of a judge, a notion I didn't care

for. I had plenty of friends in Munising who knew my heart was in the right place and I thought a couple of them might squeeze onto the jury. The lawyer told me just to "act like a geek which shouldn't be too hard" which upset me. I told the silly little fucker I was going to jerk his ears off which was held up as an example of my "unsoundness" to the judge, who had already thrown the book at Bob, which put him in a good mood. I could also see that the judge liked Shelley's father, probably because they were both big-deal Republicans. When Bob started yelling "Retard" at me at a hearing they just took him away. Shelley cried a lot and grasped my arm. I liked that even though at the time I suspected she had other motives, such as being a famous anthropologist. Frank wasn't too helpful as a character witness because he didn't dress too good and lipped off to the judge. Frank is his own man and doesn't like the authorities. What gave me the most trouble was convincing them I had dumped the Indian back in Lake Superior. The State Police divers even had a look but of course couldn't find anything. This is where my asshole lawyer came in handy because the police couldn't prove there was a real body before their fight with Bob. When I went into the judge's office, just the two of us, he asked me why I thought the body was my dad's and I said there was nothing to prove that it wasn't. He was plainly glad to give me probation and see me drive off with Shelley.

Now we were getting near the old homestead and I was pretty nervous. I don't know why for sure, and I began to fiddle with the buttons on the electric seats that could put you in any comfortable position. Shelley had said the seats were calfskin but when I smelled them I couldn't catch the scent of calf. I had her stop by a culvert so I could check out my old-time fishing creek. I walked downstream and felt bad that when they widened the road they had silted up the rocky creek with sand which meant trout could no longer spawn. Rather than keeping track of the likes of me the authorities might better be tending the health of their creeks, I thought.

Around a curve was another shocker. David Four Feet's house had burned down and all there was around the foundation were dry burdocks and chokecherries, and one sugar plum the bears had broken down to get at the fruit. Another quarter mile and there was our old place with David's mom bent over putting bales of straw around the foundation to insulate against the coming winter. She hadn't told me about this move when I called but she probably thought I knew. I had Shelley pull in the drive which she was glad to do as she knew this was the mother of my first love, Rose. The old woman admired Shelley's vehicle for its great big tires. In the U.P. it's the car that doesn't get stuck that gets the admiration. She pointed over about a hundred yards to the old orchard where she said Rose was picking apples with her two kids so we headed off across the bumpy field in the car. I asked Shelley if she had something I could give Rose and she said there was a nice scarf in her bag. I took the scarf out and it smelled nice with a foreign name on the corner.

"Your hair still looks like shit," is the first thing Rose said to me after all these years. She was wearing overalls and had picked four bushels to make a batch of applesauce. To me Rose looked real good though she was quite round, to be frank. I had read in the newspaper that the circle was Nature's most perfect form so that put Rose up there on the top. She introduced us to her boy Red who was called that after redskin. That's what the kids called him at school and he didn't seem to mind. Red was twelve and the little girl she called Berry was seven, though it was plain to see something was wrong with her. Berry was called that because all she knew how to do or liked to do was pick berries. Berry wrapped herself around my leg like a monkey and I had half the notion she might take a bite but she didn't. Rose told Shelley not to get drunk when she was pregnant because that's how Berry came out haywire. Red wondered if it would be okay to take a look in Shelley's Rover so she took him for a ride around the field, partly to be nice and leave me alone with Rose.

"That's the whitest woman I ever saw," Rose said when Shelley left.

"Why not? Always thought I was white myself," I said.

"You never were that white. How did you ever get such a high-class lady, B.D.?"

"A lot of women see things in me you were blind to." It was then I handed her the scarf which she shook out and tied around her neck without a word. She reached down and selected an apple, polished it against the sweater covering her big breasts and handed it to me. We looked off to where Shelley was coming back at us across the field. I was nervous but I didn't know if she was, so I bit into the apple.

"If you don't mind I'd like to stop by and visit," I said with a bit of quaver in my voice and almost choking on the apple.

"Suit yourself," she said, which wasn't much to go on, but when Shelley pulled up and Rose pried Berry off my leg Rose gave my ass a good pinch. Later at the hotel I checked out the red spot and it made me feel good.

It was at dinner that Shelley described to me what was going to happen, depending on my cooperation. We were sitting in the fancy dining room of the House of Ludington Hotel in Escanaba, and I was glad I had on my new sport coat despite the dried gravy spot. I was agitated because Shelley didn't want me to have a drink until she discussed the deal she had

74

cooked up on the phone. The upshot was that either I told her where my burial mounds were or I was facing three to five years in the prison down in Jackson for the crime of arson, added on to the other stuff.

"I'll sleep on it," I said, mostly because that was what people seemed to say when they were discussing a big deal. A man at the next table who was eating alone finished his whiskey and water, then poured himself a full glass of wine with a burbling sound. Three to five years was a long time. I couldn't remember exactly what I was doing that long ago.

"No you won't sleep on it. You'll sleep on shit. You're always sleeping on it." She was angry and sounded like her dad when he was pissed at me. "You think each day is a fresh new start, which it isn't."

"I don't get why you and your friends are always doing rundowns on people. You're always taking people apart in pieces, especially me." I felt my ears getting red. I had never been real mad at Shelley before but now she was squeezing my balls too hard. I was close to the point I had been when I poured the drink down the lady's neck in the Soo.

"I need to know your answer. People are waiting to hear. My dad and my lawyer are waiting. A State Police detective is waiting. My friends whose tent and field notes you burned up are waiting. You're going to tell me or you're going to prison. If you tell me, I'm going to help you out with some money and we'll say goodbye. Also, you can't go back to Grand Marais for one year."

"Why's that?" The man next door had finished one glass of red wine and was starting another.

"Because I can't trust you to not sabotage our field work. That's the whole deal. Take it or leave it, but tell me now. I've got to make some phone calls."

"I'll tell you what. If I don't get a drink I'm going to kick over this fucking table on your lap." I stood up as if to judge my leverage. Shelley signaled the waitress and I ordered two doubles and sat back down. There was something in her face of the school principal who used to tell me I was headed for the reform school down in Lansing, the same one who made fun of me when Rose hit me over the head with her books. One night David Four Feet and me snuck up on the principal's house and poured a couple pounds of sugar into his gas tank to generally get even.

"What do you say now?" Shelley asked as I was eating my shrimps for appetizers and sipping whiskey. She wasn't touching her soup and slid it over when I looked at it. There was nothing in the soup but beef-tasting water but it was so good I could have drunk a quart.

"I'm lost in thought over your proposition. Who is to say which of us is right? I know I could use a bottle of red wine to go with dinner."

"You are fucking driving me crazy." Now she was hissing and called the waitress over and ordered a bottle of red. The waitress knew something was wrong and brought the wine in a hurry.

"You know you got me cornered. I've been taken prisoner in the war of life. That's how I look at it. Maybe they keep the prison too warm in winter and I couldn't stand that. I'd have to hang myself with a sheet."

"You wouldn't do that," she said. Shelley can't stand the talk of suicide because she had an aunt who did herself in.

"Yes I would. You know I can't stand the hot air, and there wouldn't be any walking or fishing or trees. In fact, if you called the police right now I wouldn't be taken alive. When I got my toothbrush out of the van I also got my pistol which is in my back pocket."

"I don't believe you, but you're putting off the answer."

I reached toward my back pocket where there wasn't a pistol and she waved at me with alarm. The waitress brought my huge porterhouse and Shelley a little piece of fish.

"What's to happen to me if I can't live in Grand Marais? The son of man has no place to lay his head."

"I'd give you a thousand dollars and you could make a fresh start, maybe over this way."

"I wouldn't accept more than seven hundred," I said, which sounded like a solider figure to me than a thousand.

"Then we have a deal?"

"Of course," I said, and she got up to make her phone calls. "You're not going to eat your dinner?" I asked.

"Go ahead," she said and rushed off.

I took her plate and dumped the piece of fish alongside the steak. A portion of bird meat would have completed the circle. It wasn't exactly a happy meal but I cleaned my plate. If you live on the railroad tracks the train's going to hit you, Grandpa used to say. I had a notion to call up Frank and ask him the name of that tribal lawyer he knew over in Brimley. Maybe they could organize a welcoming party for the grave diggers, but suddenly I was tired of the whole damn thing. The steak had heated me up as beef will do, so I went outside and stood under the awning, letting the cold wind blow on me. I stood there like a statue until I got real cold, then I stood there longer. Grandpa and I used to drive past the hotel but neither of us had ever been inside. He said it was a place for the men who owned the trees, not for the ones who cut them down. Come to think of it, I was not likely to return myself.

After a while Shelley came running out as if I had made an escape. "There you are," she yelled. We took a long walk

without saying much. I had an urge to haul her into Orphan
Annie's striptease club but it didn't seem to go with the evening. There would be other times for that, I thought, if I came
back this way for a year. We took a turn down a side street so
I could show her the church that sent me off to Chicago so
many years ago. I had been sentenced to attend church by a
juvenile judge after a couple of unfortunate accidents. David
Four Feet and me found a source for black-market fireworks,
serious stuff like cherry bombs and M-80s, and there was a lot
of noise around town for a month. Before we got caught for
that we had cabled a county snowplow to a fire hydrant outside this diner, with a lot of slack so the truck would have a
head of steam before the cable came tight. Little did we know
the truck would uproot the fire hydrant and cause a flooding
problem in the middle of winter. I had to shovel city side-
walks all winter for free, and attend church where everyone
was nice and thought of me as the prodigal son.

We went back to the hotel because Shelley was cold and
tired, probably because she didn't eat her dinner. She got us
two connected rooms again with the living room having a big
flat-top piano in it. I said it was wasting money but she said
that this is where we were to have our meeting in the morning. Nice to have something to look forward to, I said, wandering around the room hunched up like I was a lot older,
which always irritates her. I admit I was a bit blue so I sat
down at the piano. Back in my church days I could play "The
Old Rugged Cross" with one finger, also "Chopsticks," but
now I didn't feel up to it despite the rare opportunity of a
piano.

Shelley tuned me in a hockey game on TV while I sat there
on the piano bench. Hockey's the only sport I was ever good
at except boxing. I suddenly got this idea I was a great piano

player whose hand had been crippled when his girlfriend had slammed it in a door, so near to greatness but yet so far. I told this to Shelley and she gave me a big hug to cheer me up and she said she had brought along my favorite nightie for our last night. This nightie is purple and smooth as satin because that's what it's made of. It clings to her and you sort of peel it off until bingo, you're there.

She went to take a shower and I sat down by the phone with an urge to call Frank and give him the sad tidings. There was a card attached to the phone that said to dial 33 for room service so that's what I did. They asked me what I'd like and since I had already eaten I wondered if they could bring me a couple of drinks. Presto, a guy was there in minutes. They let me sign my name as I only had fifteen bucks after the six-pack and pickled bologna and wasn't counting on the big payment mentioned. I took my drinks over to the piano and tried to noodle along singing my favorite country songs, but I couldn't get the piano to go with the words and, what's more, the drinks weren't making their way through the load of shrimp, fish and steak in my gut. I had just about decided to ask Shelley if she had ever loved me or was she just hanging in there for the burial mounds when she came out in the purple nightie and I didn't have the heart to. She came right over and I lifted the nightie and a lot of shower heat escaped. "It's like a blast furnace in there," I said, dropping the hem. She laughed and had a slug of my second drink. I asked if she'd mind getting up on the piano and laying out so I could sing to her. She scrambled up with no problem and lay there leaning her head on a hand. I tinkled along singing a mishmash of my favorite lines from country music, including one I made up: *"Our love was not meant to be, at least not in the long run."* She was getting tears in her eyes so I swiveled her legs around so the backs of her knees were over my shoulders and I sang, *"Yes, we have no bananas,"* and she started laughing. I stood partway up and she slid down, her butt hitting the keys in a nice way like the lost chord. We did it right there which wasn't easy.

I woke up from a bad dream where I was suffocating in a hot cabin and I couldn't walk, then I saw where I was and lightened up. The first of the morning sun was red in the east and there were black rolling clouds and snow flurries, sure sign of a coming gale. The red sun made the room pinkish and I turned to look at how Shelley's nightie was pulled up all the way under her arms. I opened the window which squeaked to cool it off.

"B.D., is something wrong?" she asked.

"Not so you would notice. Red sky in morning, sailors take warning. That's all I know."

She said "Oh" and went back to sleep. It was then I had the notion that I'd better memorize her body as another one this fine was not likely to pass my way again. I started with her face but I knew it well enough so I went down to the feet and stared at them, then the ankles and knees. I thought of the old grade school song which we used to sing to the tune of *"I'm looking over a four-leaf clover."* The dirty version went, *"I'm looking under a two-legged wonder"* but I couldn't remember the rest. Also, in the pink light her body was too lovely to be thinking of nonsense. She didn't wake up until I turned her over to memorize the other side.

"B.D., what are you doing? It's too early." She checked her watch on the nightstand and put her face in the pillow.

"I'm memorizing your body because we're going to part," I said, and she went back to sleep with another "Oh." I said I never cried but I think I was getting pretty close by the time I got the memorizing job done, also I remembered how the Chief told me to keep my feet light. Luckily other emotions took over and by the time she fully awoke she was making yodeling sounds like Judy Canova on the *Louisiana Hayride* program.

The meeting wasn't all that it was pumped up to be. I was the sailor who took the red sky as a warning and played it hard and cold as Robert Mitchum. I had had breakfast in bed for the first time since I was sick as a kid so I was in a good mood except I couldn't get a beer. I had eaten Shelley's ham and mine too, so I was a bit dry, but when I called room service they said it was state law — no beer on Sunday until noon. I asked them what kind of low-rent hellhole they were running and they apologized. It was a comfort somehow that rich folks had to wait until noon just like everyone else.

First to arrive was Shelley's lawyer fresh off a stormy ride on the morning plane from Detroit. He kissed Shelley on both cheeks, like I've seen on television, and told her her dad couldn't come because he had to do a "C-section" on an important lady. He just looked at me and sighed, deciding not to offer his hand for a shake, partly because I was staring him down like he was so much dogshit. Then came the State Police detective and the two of them whispered in the far corner while I watched snow swirling up the street which was putting a jinx on the color tour. Along came Jerk and Jerkoff with a tube of topographical maps which they spread out on the lid of the sacred piano. They glanced at me out of the corner of their eyes. I told Shelley that they had to stand over against the wall or the deal was off and I wouldn't trace a route on the map. The lawyer and the detective came over and gave me some papers to sign that said the arson charge would be resumed if I showed up in Grand Marais within a year. I was given two days to move my stuff out. I signed the papers and the detective said he'd be keeping an eye on me.

"No doubt you will because you can't find honest work," I said with a sneer. Then I went over and worked on the map with Shelley, using the lawyer's gold pen I intended to swipe. She gave me a pleading look that said "Please no tricks," but it was too late in the game for that. When I finished with the topo map she said she was surprised how close she had been several times. She waved over Jerk and Jerkoff but I yelled, "Stay in the corner, shitsuckers," so they did. For some reason I picked up the cover of the piano bench and looked at some sheet music. There was a piece by Mozart, whose name I'd heard on the NPR station out of Marquette. I took it out and sat down to play.

"A little Mozart for Sunday morning," I said, then beat the hell out of the keys. Everyone left right away except Shelley. On the way out the lawyer picked his gold pen out of my pocket and gave me the envelope of money which I didn't stop to count.

That was that. We checked out of the hotel without saying much of anything. While she warmed up her car I cleaned all the wet snow off her windows, looking at her as she sat there shivering. She wasn't built for winter. She almost ruined it by saying maybe we'd see each other again someday, but I said "I doubt it," and off she drove.

So there I stood in the Sunday snow with my toothbrush in my pocket wrapped up by Shelley in Kleenex. I felt the toothbrush and envelope of money and it was then I remembered my van was parked at the Ramada Inn up in Marquette. Worse things have happened, I thought. I'd just have to hitchhike up there. Just then a taxicab dropped off a lady at the hotel and I walked over. I asked the driver who was an old man how much was the eighty miles to Marquette, and he said things were slow so he'd make the drive for fifty bucks. I got in but before he'd start he wanted to see the color of my money just like Beatrice when I ordered a steak back in Chicago. I drew a hundred-dollar bill from the envelope and off we went. It was quite the shock when he asked me if I wasn't B.D. who he saw fight a pulp cutter over in Iron Mountain twenty-five years ago. It wasn't the biggest thing on earth but it made me feel life was holding together somehow.

We were out on the edge of town when I had the idea to stop at the supermarket and pick up a bunch of chickens, also a six-pack for my trip, to drop off at Rose's. Maybe she and her mom would cook Sunday dinner. I'd see if her boy Red might want to ride up to Marquette since he probably had never been in a taxi before. And that's what I did. A pinch and a "suit yourself" wasn't much to go on but it didn't hurt to try.

Sunset Limited

I

IN THE AFTERLIGHT of the moonset, at the time of false dawn, you could see two silhouettes standing there facing east, waiting for the train. They were a mother and a daughter, and the mother paced and shivered while the daughter stood still. It was mid-May but in the high desert of eastern Arizona such dawns can be coolish.

"I don't see why you're wearing that coat. Who's going to look at you in that coat?"

"I don't want anyone to look at me," said the mother.

"You should want someone to look at you. You said so yourself. You said so Tuesday when we did chores after dinner."

"What did I say?"

"You said, 'I'm only forty-one. I wouldn't mind going out with someone again.' Or something like that."

"I must have been drinking."

"You only had two glasses of wine. Let's sit in the truck and warm up."

"Okay, but no music. I can't listen to music when I'm trying to think."

The silhouettes moved to a pickup, pausing to listen to the staccato yelping of a group of coyotes chasing a jackrabbit.

"The rabbit's getting away," the daughter said.

"How do you know?"

"Granddad told me that when the yelping declines in frequency the rabbit is getting away. The coyotes are losing interest."

They got in the cab and for a brief moment we see their features, the daughter handsome Oriental and the mother fair-featured, dark blond, if a bit weathered in an English tweed shooting jacket and jeans. The doors close and the interior lights go out. The daughter turns the key and for a few seconds we hear a snatch of "Brown-eyed Women and Red Grenadine" before the tape deck is clicked off and the heater comes on.

"You like my music better than I did," the mother says as if almost amused.

"I'm tired of my own. You're crazy to take the train. I could have driven you to Tucson."

"The train lets me think and I didn't want you to miss school. How's your friend Bob?"

"He's just another dickhead cowboy who'll never make it out of eleventh grade."

"Such colorful language. You were in love with him last week."

Out the windshield the world was beginning to reveal itself, as if the darkness were sinking slowly into the desert floor, a landscape of cholla, saguaro, barrel cactus and greasewood out beyond the tiny wood-frame building that was the train station. You called ahead and the New Orleans–Los Angeles Sunset Limited would stop for you, and the twelve-hour ride was far more pleasant than a long drive to Tucson, than a flight to which was added the nightmare of LAX.

"You think I made love to him?" the daughter teased.

"You'd tell me if you wanted to," the mother answered, refusing the bait.

"It wasn't pleasant enough to talk about. I should have saved myself for a Cambodian cook."

"Did you really?" The mother turns and puts her hand on her daughter's on the steering wheel.

"Of course not." The daughter laughs. "He never says a thing he doesn't rehearse. He's a rerun."

Now they were silent, watching the distant headlight of the train, still miles away, bobbling like a mechanical Polyphemus. They get out of the truck and lean against the hood, an arm around each other. Now the daughter's eyes are misty with anxiety as the train draws near. The mother kisses her cheek in concern.

"I'll only be gone a few days." She tries to hold her daughter who struggles to withdraw.

"I think you should let the son-of-a-bitch rot in prison. He's not even better than nothing."

The daughter runs to the pickup, refusing to turn as her mother boards the train. The mother calls out from the platform but her voice is drowned and the train accelerates, looking somehow puny and despondent as it disappears into the immensity of the desert landscape.

In the coach Gwen did not look directly at any of the dozen or so other people who were a mixture of tourists, day passengers on a shopping trip to Tucson and a few of the growing number of eccentrics who refuse to fly. She took the first available seat and put her garment bag beside her, closing her eyes and struggling to breathe deeply. She turned to the window so that no one could see and wept about what she could not change. Gwen was extraordinarily intelligent but today she felt she was growing older without quite knowing why. It seemed to her that she had learned about everything except actual life processes, and the fact that someone she had once loved was in prison and might very well die was a quantum leap into a world as uncontrollable as aging.

Within an hour she had gathered herself back together enough to go to the dining car for breakfast. She was not by nature a self-doubter and she wondered at the mixture of mental and purely physiological causes that might occasion these steps into empty elevator shafts, uncapped wells, the quicksand near the most beautiful of burbling springs.

At breakfast she was, due to crowding, seated across from another single, an elderly man who turned out to be a retired game biologist from Louisiana on his way to visit his married daughter in Oxnard, north of Los Angeles. He reminded Gwen of her father, who was very much an outdoor man, in that his three-piece traveling suit did not fit his character. He was thin, preternaturally weathered, and his neck arose out of a shirt at least two sizes too large. He stood and bowed slightly when Gwen was seated, introduced himself, then rather shyly stared down at his plate. Soon enough, as travelers will do, she lost her resolve toward silence and they began to talk, and their talk continued through breakfast and a gin rummy game that lasted until lunch.

His name was Norbert Stuart but preferred to be addressed by his last name. He was a kindly though expert interlocutor and his curiosity about the natural world extended, as it rarely does, into human affairs. He was traveling alone because his wife back in Shreveport raised bird dogs and there were three new litters to take care of, and besides, his wife didn't care for his daughter's husband who was part Mexican ("Mezcan" he pronounced it). The fact was his wife disapproved of the very idea of California and settled for his daughter's annual Christmas trip back home. Gwen was a little startled to discover that Stuart knew her college friend Sam who studied coyotes in the Sangre de Cristo Mountains of New Mexico. Gwen hadn't seen Sam since college, almost twenty years now, but had read about him in the Sunday magazine section of the *Denver Post.*

Gwen told Stuart everything important except why she was on the train. She was voluble in a way she couldn't remember, and in a manner she couldn't have been with someone her own age. She told him about the small family ranch between Mule Junction and Guthrie to which she had retreated after a brief, unhappy marriage to a university mathematician who now owned a computer business in Albuquerque; about the Cambodian girl they had adopted and she had raised to the current age of sixteen; about her love of flying and the old Cessna 172 she owned that was temporarily grounded in need of a valve job; of the Simmental-Charolais stud bull that was the ranch's bread and butter; of her arthritic father who lived seventy miles away in Silver City because he needed dialysis twice a week, but always came to dinner on Sundays. She told him that her daughter, Sun by name, was precocious and had been recruited by colleges for early admission but had chosen to spend another year at home and graduate with her own class. Sun's hobbies were botany, livestock and Indian history.

"Maybe that's because she's Oriental and the Navajo and Apache are Athabascans who supposedly crossed the Bering

Strait from Asia, then came on down here a thousand or so years ago," Stuart suggested.

"She's too perverse for that. She prefers the Anasazi, Hopi, the Isletas and Pueblo people who came up from Mexico."

They broke off their card game after lunch so Stuart could have a nap. When Gwen returned to her seat she realized how much she wanted her life to be what she told Stuart it was. It was as if she had described the daytime but not the night. The small ranch was indeed lovely but the mortgage had been paid off by her mother who had moved back to Kansas City and remarried while Gwen was in college. There also was a modest annuity from Kansas City Power Company that, along with overgenerous child support payments from her ex-husband, allowed Gwen to stay on the ranch, though she did earn a third of their living by her wits, despite the ragged performance of the beef market. She didn't tell Stuart that her father had always been a somewhat worthless, near parody of a cowboy, and that she herself had advised her mother to leave him well before Gwen went away to the University of Colorado. Not that Gwen didn't love her father, and Sun very much loved her grandfather, just that he was never more than a dreamy affectionate cowboy with an emphasis on the "boy" who now lived in a rooming house in Silver City with his cronies, and saw some of the same girlfriends he had had during his marriage.

And this wasn't even the true heart of the night games she neglected to describe to her new friend. They had adopted Sun when Gwen discovered she was barren due to a neglected ovarian infection she'd picked up during her year in prison. Her college lover Ted, whose nickname was Zip, had an encyclopedic knowledge of all the world's injustices, and the nearest one at hand in Boulder at the time was the Vietnam War. So Zip and Gwen and the three others, Billy, Patricia and Sam — together they felt they comprised a pacifist Wild Bunch — gathered up a gallon of blood from a slaughterhouse, and a gallon of glue from a hardware store, and vandalized the local draft board office. The town was fairly liberal but the Circuit Court judge was a western conservative. Everyone's heart was broken at the sentencing, especially the parents who missed the drama and footed the legal bills.

But the heart of the darker side was that Zip had turned up on the ranch a few months ago in February looking for sanctuary. They had spent an unhappy month together in Denver after the year in prison and his appearance that blustery winter night was their first contact in twenty years. Sun had answered the door followed by their Labrador retriever who never barked because no one ever came down the road who wasn't welcome. That night the dog barked and Sun called out "Mom." Later, Sun, who was an aficionado of horror movies, said she was sure Zip was one of the "living dead." When Gwen had reached the door Zip asked if he was welcome and she nodded, then he turned and waved to a black car which drove away, fishtailing at top speed out the snowy driveway.

It took a full six weeks into early spring to make Zip well enough to leave, and then only with the considerable aid of a leftist general practitioner from Silver City, a divorced ex-boyfriend of Gwen's. Zip would only say that he had spent the past few years in Central America and any additional information might incriminate her for harboring a fugitive. He had two kinds of malaria, amoebic dysentery, the remnants of bilharzia (from Africa) and several hopeless blood parasites. He never stopped eating, using the phone behind closed doors and lecturing in general until only the Labrador would listen. When he became ambulatory he was worthless at chores.

Sun was fascinated with Zip until an angry exchange over

dinner on the matter of Native Americans whom Zip described somewhat pompously as "arch-traditional religionists beyond help." Sun said, "Oh, fuck you," and went outside to ride her sorrel mare. Finally Gwen sold two steers and bought Zip an old Chevy. He left on an early April dawn for Mexico. Within a few days Gwen received a phone bill for over a thousand dollars and a visit from three men who said they were from the FBI, though she never asked to see the identification. She let them search Zip's empty room and answered their questions because she simply didn't care. She jokingly suggested that they pay the phone bill and they said they had a copy, which seemed to be missing the point as far as she was concerned.

Another week later she received a letter (which had been previously opened) from Zip who was in a Mexican prison in Nogales, Sonora, down across the border. He had been "framed" and needed help. When Sun returned home from school that day she busied herself cleaning the remaining fingerprint powder from the walls and furniture in the guest room. Gwen announced she was flying down to Nogales the next day with their harmless small-town family lawyer.

"Mom, that guy's the biggest asshole in the history of mankind. He doesn't love you. You guys didn't even sleep together."

"How do you know?" Gwen answered lamely.

The day in Nogales had gone as badly as a day can go. The charges against Zip included the vague "inciting to riot" and the not so vague attempted murder of a Federale, the probable final sentence being in the range of fifty years. They were not allowed to see Zip himself, having insufficient money for a proper "gift." The American consul was insulting, saying that it would have been a blessing to the world had Zip never been released from prison twenty years before. Gwen did not misunderstand the coldness in the consul's eyes when he looked at her across the desk, shuffling a folder she knew held information on her past transgression.

For a few days then, through her efforts, Zip's arrest became a minor cause célèbre, with newspaper articles and a spot on NPR's *All Things Considered* called "The Last Radical." Then nothing. Gwen sat on the ranch within reach of the phone, waiting for a call from Billy, Patricia or Sam who must certainly have heard the news, but no call came. She waited a week, then called Amtrak.

After his nap Stuart sought her out with his deck of cards. Sensing her change in mood he suggested they go up to the club car for a drink. As they made their way through two passenger cars Gwen shuddered thinking of her attempt to convince Sun that Zip wasn't really all that bad but that his passion for justice made him a bit rough around the edges. Gwen had said that he was kind and quite sensitive, and had given his life and health to correct social and political ills throughout the world.

"If he's so sensitive why did he lecture me about a war that finally led to the death of my parents? I bet he never even asked who I was," Sun had said.

"Of course he did." But he hadn't, and he had also refused Gwen when she had lain down beside him, saying that he had given up sex. She wanted to say that she hadn't but his utter coldness made her timid.

"I can tell you're a young lady on a mission. I wish I was your age instead of seventy-three. Then I might be better at helping." Stuart pretended to watch her stir her whiskey and water. He took his card out of a wallet and handed it to her. "I'm still not worthless. I used to be a game warden too, and that's a rough business down in Louisiana. Call if you need me, you hear?"

She cut the cards on the table and revealed an ace of spades. There was a small consolation in this absurdity and they both smiled. She was suddenly very happy she was spending time with this old man, and reflected that the final item that put her on the train had occurred barely twenty-four hours before. She was in a butcher shop in Silver City when a thin, dark young man she remembered seeing earlier on the street entered. He said "Gwen Simpson?" and she nodded. He handed her an envelope and hastily walked out. The note read, "I've discovered I'm not getting out of here alive and will be murdered at a time convenient to the U.S. and Mexican governments. My people are unwilling or unable to help me. I still have work to do. Please contact the bunch and see if they'll help. Yrs., Zip."

As the afternoon waned Stuart and Gwen talked about mountain lions and friendship. Gwen and Sun had seen a mountain lion while riding their horses a half-dozen miles into the mountains up behind the ranch. She invited Stuart to stop by on his way home from Oxnard. He accepted with delight. He had graduated from Auburn, the class of 1935, and still went duck hunting with three of his remaining classmates who were friends.

"You are capable of making and being friends at that time in a way that you never are again," he said.

She continued shuffling the cards but was swept away by the notion that if they hadn't been sent away to prison for a year the five of them might have stayed close. Out the window the giant suburban sprawl of Los Angeles began to accumulate.

At Union Station they said goodbye and on impulse she kissed Stuart directly on the lips. Then she hailed a cab for Le Parc which was off La Cienega. Sun had suggested the hotel, having read about it in one of the travel magazines favored by bright young girls far to the interior of our dream coasts.

II

It was not his habit but Billy got up at five A.M. that morning in Pacific Palisades on the western edge of Los Angeles. He had a great deal of work to do before he commandeered a company plane and flew up to San Francisco mid-afternoon to watch his beloved Giants play a twi-night double-header. Ever since he was a tyke stumbling along the dangerous edge of a large swimming pool (followed by a black nanny) in Hillsborough near San Francisco Billy had been enamored of baseball. There is a pith, gist, saw, that we offer hapless foreign visitors to the effect that you must understand baseball to understand America. The germ of truth here is so small as to be invisible under an electron microscope (a week on an Indian reservation gives a better understanding) but baseball can reveal a great deal about a man: to wit, an adult fan invariably has a lot of boy left within him, and this was very true with Billy though on the job the boy was kept well hidden.

Before baseball Billy had liked horses but his sister, two years older, had had a bad fall from her pony resulting in a spiral fracture and a permanent, though minor, limp. The two ponies were taken away on Sunday while Billy was at his first baseball game. The sight of a merry-go-round still filled him with melancholy; when he saw his first one at five he wept because he thought the ponies had been speared through the middle. Baseball, however, stuck, and Billy's not so secret dream was to own a major league team, something that would probably have to wait until his father passed on to the heaven that awaits wealthy, petulant and ruthless men.

A garden-variety analyst could have explained to Billy that he had been destructively manipulated by his father. Only a year before, a Santa Monica marriage counselor had come close to suggesting this fact, but hadn't wanted to endanger his ample fee. Billy's (now) ex-wife knew it but the fact had worked to her advantage. Billy's daughter Rebecca, a freshman at Stanford, knew it but was an extremely kind soul and had been trying to figure out a pleasant way of talking about it.

Frankly, Billy had always been treated as somewhat of a disappointment by his father and had tended to behave like one into his late twenties. His early interests in baseball, athletics and cars made his grades suffer and his Stanford application was turned down despite his father's enormous influence in the Bay Area. His father expressed his anger by contemptuous silence and Billy sailed off to the University of Colorado with the notion that, if he wasn't smart, at least he could ski and play baseball.

Much to everyone's surprise Billy turned out to be a "late starter" and the tidal sweep of failure had reversed itself by his early thirties, and now at age forty-two, Billy was considered an unqualified success, a brilliant, albeit devious, international lawyer. The law firm begun in San Francisco by his grandfather William Creighton, a pleasant enough high school teacher trying to improve his lot, was now Creighton & Creighton and employed over a hundred lawyers in the complicated area of making it safe for American corporations to do business in foreign countries. The firm's discreet stationery listed offices in San Francisco (home), Los Angeles, Paris, London, Hong Kong, Bonn, São Paulo and Buenos Aires. Billy directed the largest branch office, Los Angeles, but his eyes were set on his homeland, San Francisco, to which he would return on his father's retirement, a few years in the offing. With his father's death would come the major league ball team and the change of the firm's name to Creighton & Creighton & Rosenthal, the latter being his sister's second husband and the real brains behind the firm's ten-year expansion phase. Billy's father was a closet anti-Semite while Billy was a closet egalitarian, bursting with pretty well concealed good will toward the world.

On the predawn ride from Pacific Palisades to Century Plaza Billy was hard at work in the back of his refurbished Checker cab (built in Kalamazoo, Michigan) which was equipped with a hot Chevy engine. (It had taken a full year for his driver, a black, former Padres outfielder, to get used to Billy's reverse snobbism.) Everyone has a flip side, a partially hidden life or at least a secret religion, and Billy was revealing his own that morning by reviewing a folder of information on Theodore Frazer, known to his few friends as Zip, Billy's roommate, friend and idol at the University of Colorado. He hadn't seen Zip in the twenty years since they were all arrested, though he had been avidly following the case in the newspapers the past few weeks.

But the media reports had quickly fizzled to nothing and then there had been a radio interview with Gwen on NPR out of Nogales that had provided some difficult moments. He had been driving his daughter Rebecca out to the airport from which she would fly to Spokane, Washington, to visit the boyfriend she had met at Stanford. The young man was a Nez Perce Indian, of all things, a fact which delighted Billy because he knew it would drive his ex-wife batty. Gwen's voice on the radio had caused him to swerve in his lane, nearly causing an accident.

At LAX he had had a short, very intense drink with Rebecca at the Ambassador Club. Rebecca was her father's confidante and knew about Gwen, Zip, Patricia and Sam, even knew what they looked like because from the time she was a small child she had been allowed into her father's secret room. When they lived in San Francisco the room had been in the attic, and when they moved to Pacific Palisades the contents had been hauled to the basement, back past the exercise and furnace rooms. It was all quite innocent and a little bit silly and to an outsider might resemble the child's urge for a nest safe from the world: a lifetime of baseball mitts hanging from a string; autographed photos of Koufax, Drysdale, Willie Mays and many others; posters; minor awards from schools; a file cabinet full of expensive IBM print-outs of research on every major league team; photos of him and his sister Marcia on ponies; a honeymoon photo of him and his ex-wife Sarah in Jamaica; and on the top shelf, photos of the wild bunch in various places, from mountain campsites to Washington marches to the streets of San Francisco. In the photos Zip always looked severe and somewhat posed, Sam invariably held a can or bottle of beer, and Gwen seemed as shy as Patricia was bold and direct. He had seen Patricia, who was a vice president of a movie studio, a few years before at a fund raiser for a senator from New Jersey. This single meeting in close to twenty years had been quite unpleasant for specific reasons that Billy didn't like to think about. Next to the photos were a few of the books he had owned in common with Zip: radical texts by Herbert Marcuse, Regis Debray, Sartre, Frantz Fanon, Paulo Freire's *Pedagogy of the Oppressed* and

the frighteningly real *Dupont Blaster's Handbook,* a detailed
manual on the use of explosives.

At the airport Rebecca had been alternately soothing and
alarming about Gwen's radio comments. "Maybe you should
try to help, Dad. But then, the way she sounded there's nothing to do."

"I've already looked into it," he lied, though he would begin the folder that evening with a call to Bonn to a trusted
employee who had been a member of the diplomatic corps.

"She sounded very sad. She sounded like she went down
there to say goodbye and they wouldn't even let her see him.
Maybe you could at least fix it so she could see him." Rebecca's favorite book had been *Wuthering Heights* and no romantic situation was too extreme for her sympathies.

"We don't do Mexico and Latin America anymore. Dad
thought we should pull out four years ago and we did."

"I love Grandpa but you know what? Grandpa doesn't have
any ethics. I think you still do, don't you?"

"Ease up. I'll try to call her this evening."

But he didn't make the call. Instead he sat in the secret
room and stared at a photo of Gwen in her hiking shorts, looking fondly at Zip who seemed to be lecturing the Rocky
Mountain landscape. At the beginning of their sophomore year
Billy had rented a fine house on the outskirts of Boulder on
the proceeds of a trust established by his grandfather. His
father would have preferred to keep him on a short string
because of the Stanford failure but his grandfather liked to
spoil him. He and Zip had met at freshman baseball tryouts
and Zip had made the cut but Billy hadn't. A month later Billy
had run into Zip between classes and was shocked to discover
that Zip had quit the freshman team. Zip had said that there
were more important things in life than baseball, a point of

view well beyond Billy's comprehension. Zip invited Billy to a picnic at the home of a radical professor where Billy found himself quite embarrassed to be a rich kid. There were stares when he unwittingly flipped a twenty into the beer collection of one-dollar bills.

That summer he had corresponded with Zip and in the fall Zip moved into the house. On a fine October afternoon while they were playing catch Gwen and Patricia rode by on horses from a rental stable down the road. Billy, who was rather swift with the ladies, invited them in for a beer and they stayed for dinner. Billy preferred Gwen while Zip was polite enough to concentrate on Patricia. Unfortunately, it was clear to Billy that both girls were drawn to Zip who already had a burgeoning reputation as a campus firebrand. The girls gradually moved in during the ensuing weeks and the four were joined by a fifth, Sam, after Billy had bailed him out of jail after an anti-war demonstration. Sam was a new sort of person for Billy, a hyperintelligent biology student from Durango, Colorado, who was also a brawler. It had often occurred to Billy that the nighttime invasion of the draft board office would have been impossible without Sam. Zip had been the master theoretician while Sam was a man of action.

That morning, as the driver drew near Century Plaza Billy was dismayed at the information he had accrued on Zip. (He would have been even more dismayed had he known that Gwen lay sleeplessly staring down her travel alarm a few miles away.) The trouble with the information on Zip was that it had been gathered from the absolute top, from contacts in the State Department and Mexican government enforcement officials, both groups well removed from the actual scene. The folder lacked what Billy thought of as "textural concertia" — the sordid, heated and grimy quality of the scene of the crime itself; the who, what and why of the veiled opposing forces that limited the information available. It had struck him over the years in dozens of trips to the firm's foreign offices that the real problem was rarely the one he had arrived to solve. He looked up from the folder and asked Fred, the driver, to repeat himself.

"I asked if I could take your ex to the airport."

"You're under no obligation. Remember, I won you in the divorce."

"She's got a lot of luggage. She always gives me a C note."

"Where's she going?" They had been apart nearly two years but Billy was still curious.

"She said Air France so it must be Paris. And I have to pick up that lady from the dress shop so I'd say this was a shopping trip."

Billy felt his wife deserved a black belt in shopping. His feelings, however, were tempered by a recent quarrel with his daughter where Rebecca had pointed out that her mother had been a relatively poor girl from Modesto and must have learned how to spend money from her husband. Rebecca was an expert in defending her parents to each other. It was true that Billy made an annual October trip to the London office to do business and to have some new suits and shirts made. In fact, everything Billy wore was handmade. It was one of the few items in his personal inventory that brought his father's total approval. Dad felt that clothes were one of the many ways to control the world around us. When Billy grew tired of these suits which ran about fifteen hundred a copy he'd give them to his driver. Once Billy had run into Fred and a girlfriend at Guido's on Santa Monica. They pretended they were strangers, laughed and shook hands because they were wearing the same suit. Guido's was an unlikely place for Billy —

a show business hangout — but the *cioppino* reminded him of San Francisco. He occasionally remarked to himself that he didn't know anyone in show business except Patricia, and one meeting in fifteen years didn't amount to much.

As the car pulled up to Century Plaza he suddenly remembered an embarrassing moment with Patricia and Sam. The wild bunch had been in San Francisco for a few days for an antiwar and a Grateful Dead concert. By Monday morning they had run out of money so Billy called his mother down in Hillsborough to see if the coast was clear (that his dad was gone). Zip and Gwen were in North Beach at an early morning meeting so Billy had taken Patricia and Sam with him. In Hillsborough he had flippantly pointed out Bing Crosby's house which stunned Patricia, and when they had reached Billy's home a few blocks away Patricia and Sam were stiff and fretful at the idea of a "mansion." Billy's mother was a kind but somewhat benumbed San Francisco socialite who had a wretched relationship with her daughter Marcia but was convinced Billy could do no wrong. She, of late, was always hungry, so the moment Billy had called she had sent the cook off to the local food emporium, Jurgensen's, to secure a lavishly weighted picnic basket for the kids' trip back to Colorado. She mistook Patricia as Billy's girlfriend and showed her around the house, inviting her to stay whenever she was shopping in San Francisco. Sam noticed Billy's red ears and patted him on the back. By the time they left Patricia clutched a Hermès scarf and it was all the mighty Sam could do to carry the picnic basket to the van. At that period all that Billy wanted to be was a run-of-the-mill revolutionary so he apologized for the household. Sam and Patricia had comforted him that no one was responsible for their parents, as Sam popped a Watney and tore a leg and thigh from a roast pheasant. Zip had assured Billy that his family's wealth had put him in a prime position to help the poor and oppressed.

The meeting with three company lawyers had begun promptly at six-thirty A.M. and ran past nine, ordinarily the beginning of the business day. The three employees pretended to be happy to meet the dawn during the three minutes of small talk that preceded the meeting, knowing full well that the schedule was to accommodate Billy's afternoon ball game.

The question at hand was how to get a large amount of currency held by an American company out of Brazil legally: the laborious solution was a shipment of Brazilian manganese to Russia, a tanker of Russian oil to France brokered by Greeks, the payment to be deposited by the Greeks in Zurich. There was nothing disturbing in the meeting to Billy except that he no longer desired the fanny of the girl who served them breakfast. He hadn't had a woman in over a year and only recently read a distressingly stupid article on "sexual burnout." During the talk about manganese it occurred to him that the last pull in the groin he had felt was when he looked at the old photo of Gwen in her hiking shorts in his secret room.

Thus it was a shocking coincidence when he heard his secretary's whispered announcement over the intercom that a Ms. Gwen Simpson was in the office. In fact, his bowels jellied as if suddenly besieged by food poisoning and he rushed to his washroom. This loss of composure was totally out of character and he did his best in front of the mirror to regain balance. He stared at an eighteenth-century painting of absurdly elongated horses he had bought in England and it didn't help. He wanted to be alone in a rowboat at the old camp in the Sierra. Where had all the blood gone that had drained from his face, he wondered.

When he walked out of the washroom he could see the alarm on his colleagues' faces.

"I haven't had a heart attack," he quipped, then asked them to excuse him for fifteen minutes. He ushered them out and crossed the reception area to where Gwen pretended to be studying a large model of a container ship on a pedestal. She glanced at him, offered her hand and looked back at the ship. Then for a few moments there was something in their meeting, an ineffable awkwardness, of two eighth graders waltzing for the first time.

"You should have called," he finally said.

"Then you could have said no."

He guided her by the elbow into his office and beyond the averted glances of the lawyers and secretary who were wondering their different thoughts about this unlikely visitor in jeans, Paul Bond boots, a lovely if antique tweed shooting jacket.

If anything Gwen and Billy were more uncomfortable in his office. They didn't pretend to be doing anything else but trying to accommodate each other's presence and it seemed impossible.

"Shouldn't we hug?" she said, then caught herself. "But then we never did hug, did we?"

"You were with my blood brother. It would have brought on thoughts of incest or worse," he joked.

"Sam was the only one brave enough. We were too stoned."

"We were going to be blood sisters and brothers but we were too stoned. Sam nicked his wrist and Patricia almost gagged. And Zip ran out of the room." Billy pulled up a chair for her, then retreated behind the safety of his desk.

"Zip never could stand blood. He couldn't even clean a fish when we were camping. That's why I don't think he tried to kill a Federale, do you? How much do you know?"

Billy drew Zip's folder from his desk, exhaling as if finally on secure ground. He still couldn't look directly into her eyes but was getting ready for another try.

"I know pretty much everything there is to know in the official sense. I'm a corporate not a criminal lawyer. I've been led to believe that Mexican law is less intricate than our own but has a heavier hand. Down there the case is considered utterly closed. Look at Zip's international rap sheet. Your cause is pretty hopeless." Billy handed her a sheet of paper which she barely looked at before she flushed and put it on the desk.

"This isn't a cause but a friend. Or maybe not. I'm not sure when a friend stops being a friend, are you?"

This brought Billy to his feet for a long look at the plaza below. From the office in San Francisco he could see the bay and the Golden Gate Bridge, which was a great deal more attractive than the white cement below him.

"The American consul showed me that sheet of paper," she continued. "I suppose I'm an innocent in these matters but nowhere does it say he was convicted of anything. It just shows where he's been and who he's been with —"

"Every insurgent and leftist terrorist group in Peru, Panama, Guatemala, southern Mexico . . . I mean, my God Gwen . . ."

"You've developed a touching belief in our government's spies. Does that go with all of this?" She remained cool as she looked around the office which could not be more expensively subdued. She smiled as lights began to blink on Billy's three phones and the intercom. "You certainly don't get a chance to be lonely."

Billy stared down at his blinking desk, picked up a phone and blew it. "No fucking calls!" he shouted. "And I mean no fucking calls!" Now all the blood was back in his face as he looked up at Gwen and finally directly into her eyes. "What do you want me to do?"

"I don't know. I do know I was at the butcher shop in town the other day and I got this." She passed Zip's note across the desk. "It looks like after things calm down he's going to be killed."

Billy looked long and hard at the note as if there were something beyond the few sentences. To his relief she stood as if to go.

"I'm going to meet Patty. I know you're busy but can I see you after work?"

He asked her to come to dinner and gave her his home address and phone number. After he escorted her out of his office and out the main door and returned to his desk he remembered he was flying up to San Francisco for a ball game. He could still catch the first game and be home by early evening. He didn't know where she was staying but would have his secretary call Patty. He slid Zip's folder back in the desk, then sat there until tears formed and he couldn't swallow.

III

When Gwen called at seven in the morning Patricia had only been asleep for two hours. When she heard Gwen's voice she thought she was back in prison and Gwen was waking her for the prebreakfast exercise period. If you didn't show up for exercise you got a demerit and no dessert with lunch. The dessert was usually awful but it was more awful to be deprived of it and have to watch everyone else eat theirs. The first two months Patty had been so depressed that Gwen had to help her bathe and dress, and after they got out Patty resented Gwen for her own weakness. Gwen's parents appeared once a month for a visit but Patty's parents never did show up from Chicago. Gwen's mother knitted Patty a wonderful sweater, and Gwen's dad, who was a cowboy and smelled of Old Spice and whiskey, gave her earrings that were tiny silver spurs. Patty had the uncomfortable feeling that Gwen's dad wanted to make love to her, but then Gwen told her that her dad was a "saddle tramp," which seemed to have a sexual connotation.

But Patty looked around her bedroom and at the phone in her hand and decided she wasn't in prison. There was also a bird at the window she had failed to identify in her newly purchased bird book. She listened to Gwen carefully — movie executives are used to early calls, usually from New York City, because of the time difference. She told Gwen she had had a difficult night but would drive by her hotel by mid-morning. Then she quickly decided that this was insufficiently warm and added that she had expected Gwen's call and looked forward to seeing her.

Patricia got up then, broke a 5 mg Valium in half and swallowed it with a swig of Evian. She tiptoed to the window and parted the shade, but her movement had alarmed the bird and it flew away, still smudgy and indeterminate. She turned off the bedside phone and remembered how Sam, coarse and unmannerly as he was, always could identify any bird they saw together. At first she thought Sam was faking it but Gwen knew enough about birds to advise her that this wasn't so. Patty's suspicious nature had done well by her in the movie business which, because of its surface extravagance, was susceptible to fraud of a thousand varieties.

Patty was the youngest of three daughters of a Chicago mill worker who would line up the girls, he thought innocently, each morning and make a mock decision on who was the prettiest. In this manner the father cursed his daughters into becoming overly competitive and feminine. Patty was the first in the entire history of the family to go to college, winning a National Merit Scholarship and choosing Colorado because her favorite girlhood book had been *Heidi* and she wanted to live among mountains. When she was sent off to prison in the middle of her junior year her parents felt a transcendent sense of betrayal, partly because they could no longer brag about "our Patty" along the row houses and at union hall social functions. They allowed Patty to disappear for seven years then, finally tracking her down for a funeral when the oldest sister died in a car accident in Galesburg. Later on, with Patty's success, the family rupture seemed unthinkable.

Patty was a little uncomfortable with the amount of money she made and tended to live well under her income. She stayed in the same bungalow she had bought thirteen years before in Sherman Oaks, which was now worth over five times its purchase price. Her only extravagances were a Porsche Carrera and the fact that she always exceeded her per diem when she traveled. Travel meant a specific loss of control and she wanted to live as comfortably as possible. It also exposed her to the sort of rich men she apparently liked to disappoint. She had had a dozen actual affairs and one failed marriage and resented the simple fact that Sam had been the love of her life. In the very recent years she had simply been too busy to be in love.

Her entire career had been spent with the largest of the studios and her mixture of femininity and abrasiveness made underlings cautious and equals very nervous. To superiors, however, Patty simply delivered the goods. She saved them from the mistakes the imperial purple is heir to, the mistakes powerful men make when they're simply acting powerful. She was instrumental in turning down projects such as *Heaven's Gate, Rhinestone* and *Ishtar*. The CEO had quipped that Patty would be rich if she had spent her career selling short on the market. Unfortunately, her reputation lay in preventing failures rather than backing successes. Her intelligence wasn't skewed politically but to problem solving. In short, Patty was unshakably reliable. The joke around the studio, which was true, was that Patty even studied and filed interoffice memos. But there was a bit more snazz and fire to her than her enemies would admit. Years before when she was still a continuity girl she had had a run-in with a bankable star. He hadn't been smoking in previous takes and had lit up on number eight after a long break. She told him to put out the cigarette and he refused, saying that he had been smoking before. His secretary, make-up girl and wardrobe boy agreed. Then the queasy director decided to agree.

"If you were smoking, then I shouldn't be working here," Patty said, walking off the set.

The producer fired her on the way out but she was rehired by the president of the studio as she was packing up the contents of her meager cubicle. He hated the fucking actor and wanted a showdown. Besides, he had stopped by earlier and remembered the actor wasn't smoking and knew the "dailies" would prove him right. The upshot continued to grow, as it were. The actor, at the urging of his agent, called her and apologized. It turned out he was also from Chicago, which she already knew, and they began going out, and continued doing so for three years, during which time he signed for two more immensely profitable films for the studio. Patty, to her advantage, was modest about taking credit, though she admitted that the actor didn't like to read so she would read a sampling of scripts to him while he was getting stoned. She actually cared for him and they had spent truly fantastic hours in bed before he had decided that cocaine was his drug of choice.

Cocaine had also been the problem the night before, she thought as she had drifted off to sleep. Patty had been responsible for getting a TV starlet cast in her first movie. The girl was lovely and talented, and though Patty had heard there had been a minor drug problem in New York, the girl had shown no signs of recent abuse. In fact, the whole problem seemed to be fading away somewhat in the movie business. Patty's private analysis of the situation was that success is an abstraction, and recently successful people don't get the jolt from their accomplishments that they had so long anticipated. Cocaine simply provided that jolt. The down side was that continual snorting over a long period of time turned the user into a spit-dribbling borderline psychotic. One morning Patty's actor boyfriend had looked at his cowboy boots and wept long and hard because the boots were getting old.

The evening before there was an after-midnight call from the starlet's boyfriend at the Sunset Marquis. He had noted that her call sheet said a driver would pick her up at five A.M. and that she was presently puffy and hysterical behind a locked bathroom door. On the way over to the hotel Patty suspected that the boyfriend would be another of the scumbag peacocks who tended to attach themselves to models and actresses. The boyfriend, however, turned out to be a rather portly middle-aged midwestern writer whose name Patty recognized, and who turned out to be quite helpful, though it took until three A.M. to get the actress asleep. By this time Patty had made a tentative screenplay deal with the writer at barely above Writers Guild scale, so it was a pretty good night though she expected a nasty call from his agent the next day. She had been a little alarmed by the way the writer drank whiskey though it didn't seem to change his behavior. When they warmed to each other she asked him why he drank so much and he said that he had no idea.

Patty might not have heard of Zip's problems, and thus would not have anticipated Gwen's call, if it hadn't been for Harold, her gay confidant and script reader. Harold read all the newspapers and had a tremendous memory, so when he had seen a small piece on Ted Frazer in the *New York Times* he clipped it. Not wanting to be a bearer of bad tidings Harold waited a full day before giving Patty a call. They had been close for a dozen years and Harold knew intimately all the details of Patty's life, including what he thought of as her thrilling revolutionary period. He had been mindful enough to call an Associated Press man he knew who supplied a great deal of extra information on Zip, much of it quite disturbing. Harold and Patty had discussed the situation at length and, quite properly he thought, Patty had decided to do nothing about getting in touch with her wild bunch.

On her way to Gwen's hotel Patty rehearsed some of the things that were going well in her life in anticipation of a potential mud bath. She was a secretly generous person to Harold who spent all of his money on books, to the two sons of her dead sister whom she was putting through the University of Illinois, and to her parents whom she had bought one of those expensive motor homes that clutter the highways of Florida and the Southwest during the winter months. That was all well and good enough, as they say in the Midwest, but the uncomfortable lump beneath her breastbone had begun to enlarge as she came closer to Le Parc. Rather than struggle with the feeling, she identified it as mixture of guilt and shame. Gwen had quite literally saved her life during her prolonged depression in prison and, after they got out, this fact repelled Patty. She, frankly, had been the weak sister and Gwen's capacity for endurance had finally angered her. But now that was so far in the past that Patty intended to apologize for not keeping in touch, if only to get rid of the baggage of guilt. She would also contribute liberally to Zip's defense fund if that was required, though the AP man had insisted that at least on the surface Zip was probably a terrorist who should be locked up forever. When she had questioned this "surface" comment the AP man said that all the information on Zip came from the U.S. and Mexican governments, and governments had dropped well below lawyers and stockbrokers on the credibility scale. She had enjoyed this comment and it now reminded her of Billy who Gwen said she was going to see this morning.

If anyone kicked in money it should be Billy. She had run into him at the Bradley fund raiser and he had been sitting with the true California fat cats. She had brought Harold along and had sent him off to eavesdrop, finding out that these men had been talking about the pros and cons of buying professional sports teams. Billy hadn't noticed her in the crowd so she had put herself in the way when he tried to disappear early. She admitted to herself that he seemed to be trying desperately to be friendly while she punished him, as subtly as possible. Her depression during the year in prison had been exacerbated by the news that had reached them that Billy had been released after three months and his charges reduced to a misdemeanor. The news hadn't upset Gwen who properly attributed it to the expensive lawyers Billy's family could afford. Sam's sentence had also been reduced upon his agreement to go to Vietnam as a medic but that was acceptable to

Patty on the basis of his claustrophobia. By then Sam was merely trading six months for three more years just to get out of a prison cell.

At the hotel the desk clerk said Gwen left word that she would be up at the small flower garden and pool on the roof. Patty knew the hotel, as she tended to put writers and young directors there who were either intimidated or bored by the grander establishments, and disliked the cruddy but pretentious nonchalance of the Château Marmont.

Gwen's back was turned and Patty's first impression was that Gwen should change hairdressers. But then Gwen glanced around, jumped to her feet and embraced Patty with the sort of unaffected radiance that is not habitual in Southern California.

"I know the story and I want to help," Patty found herself saying before freezing in hesitation. She wasn't used to throwing down her cards. "I want to do what I can." It made good sense to add this qualifier.

"You sure look wonderful. I got crow's feet from being in the sun too much." Gwen put her fingers against her temples, still beaming at Patty who began to feel uncomfortable.

"What do you expect to get out of this? I mean what's the bottom line?" They sat down and Patty assumed the role of the interrogator to avoid an oncoming sense of emotional soreness. She did not care for the immediate impression — really the same as twenty years before — that Gwen was far nobler than she herself was.

"It's easy to do nothing. It makes a lot of sense to do nothing because it's so hard to think of the right thing to do." She handed Patty Zip's note and continued. "He's asking us to help him. Maybe all we can do is go down there and say good-bye."

"I did some research with a reliable source. There's the question of whether he's worth the trip." Patty had filmed in Arizona and the thought of actually going to Nogales in the early summer appalled her. She was the sort of Nordic midwesterner who had never quite adjusted to the heat of the Southwest.

"You won't know if he's worth the trip until you see him. It's not the sort of thing anyone *wants* to do but I felt obligated to tell you."

"What did Billy have to say?"

"Pretty much the same thing you're saying. But he's looking into it. I'm going to see him later and I thought we could all have dinner."

"I don't want to see Billy. I think he sold us out. I've always thought that. I saw him four years ago by accident and he wouldn't answer my questions." Patty was flushed now and felt her anger in her stomach. She saw Gwen wince and simply didn't care.

"Billy just had better lawyers. How is it his fault his father could afford the best lawyers? Besides, what does it matter? This isn't about you or Billy or me but about a man who's going to be killed. We both used to love him, didn't we?" Now there were tears in Gwen's eyes that she wished very much weren't there. Her parents had told her when she was a little girl that it was unthinkable to cry in order to get your way.

But this evident grief had a powerful effect on Patty. She drew her chair closer to Gwen and took her hand. She really has no idea what she's doing, Patty thought. Here she is and she doesn't know what to do other than ask us to help a lost cause.

"Oh, fuck it," Patty said, "count me in for anything. What

if we didn't go and read the obituary? What would we feel like? Did you get in touch with Sam?"

"I was saving him for the last because I think of him as a sure thing. Did you ever see him?" Gwen dabbed her eyes with the cocktail napkin she took from under her glass of water. Gwen watched Patty sink into herself, then looked off to the east and the peculiar way the smog was gathering in the late morning heat. She felt confused enough to plan a drive out to the ocean in the afternoon.

"A few years after we got out of prison he wrote to me from a hospital, one of those veterans' mental wards. My parents forwarded the letter. It sounded so terrible I never wrote him back. I was terrible myself at the time and I didn't see the point in two fucked-up people getting back together. It's strange how we all thought we were so wonderful together and then it was nothing."

They made a grand effort at small talk then, as if the strain could no longer be endured. Gwen asked Patty how to get to the ocean. They actually laughed remembering a time in San Francisco when they all had driven north across the Golden Gate in Billy's van. It had taken them hours to find the ocean because they were stoned, which they only got away with because Zip was on a mattress in the back sleeping off an all-night antiwar strategy meeting.

IV

The moment Gwen had left his office Billy called the Mexican consul and asked a few questions, then set up an appointment. He had his secretary give Fred a fifteen-minute alert down in the garage out of consideration for a poker game the drivers maintained. Billy reminded himself not to ask questions about his ex-wife, then wondered if Fred was lying and Sarah was taking a boyfriend to Paris. He felt a stirring when he thought of Gwen's fanny in her jeans, the splendid shape of which had not diminished. It must be the horses. Riding horses builds fine fannies, he thought. Billy's errant and often wild sense of humor made him keep leatherbound copies of Charles Dickens's novel about the legal profession, *Bleak House*, in the office library. He occasionally handed the novel out, straight-faced, as gifts to clients he disliked. It was partly Rebecca's idea. When she was home they liked to cook together and dream up practical jokes, many of which were dangerous and insensitive, but the planning itself was the release.

On the car phone Billy called the pilots over at Burbank to tell them he'd be running late, then called his dad in San Francisco to cancel dinner plans. There was a foolish urge to tell his father he was seeing Gwen for dinner but it was unthinkable. Instead, he fibbed and said he was flying back after the first game to have dinner with a prominent L.A. socialite. At the trial his father continually referred to Billy's friends as "filthy hippies" and it grieved Billy twenty years later to remember this. On impulse he called his secretary and told her to locate Gwen's bank and wire a few grand on deposit. All this running around was obviously costing her money she could ill afford, he thought.

The meeting at the Mexican consulate was brief. The consul, Matthias Arndt-Guerrez, had been nearly a friend before the firm had stopped doing business in Mexico, and Billy still ran into him on social occasions. In the consul's private chambers it occurred again to Billy how many Mexicans of wealth and power are at least part German in ancestry. The family of

Arndt-Guerrez owned the largest brewery in Mexico, also a steel mill up in Chihuahua. Billy could, in any event, expect Matthias to be discreet in this matter. After a few pleasantries, they got directly to the point.

"Your college chum is a bad apple," Matthias said, "but then you are aware of that."

"I only need to know if he's actually in danger of being murdered and what his probable sentence will be."

"Fifty years, which means twenty with good behavior. He's in bad health so that is also a death sentence. As far as being murdered I'm not sure. The international left, at least the Mexican and Central American groups, consider Mr. Frazer a well-intentioned pest, an old-style Don Quixote radical, you know what I mean? An altruistic ideologue scarcely near the left power structure. In Cuba he was confined to lecturing schoolchildren and cane-cutting crews. He was given a bicycle rather than a car, an accurate gauge of the esteem in which he was held. The right wings of a half-dozen countries wish him dead but he is one among thousands they would like to exterminate. I'm a little uncertain of his standing in Mexico. Like your own country, one arm of our government frequently does not know what the other arm is doing. There are also billions of dollars in electronics and fruit-and-vegetable export businesses in the Nogales area. Labor organizers are not popular, perhaps fatally unpopular. That's about it."

"Are you neglecting another factor we're both thinking about?" Billy had a sharp ear for things left out of explanations. He always advised corporations against allowing "spooks" to be placed in their foreign operations, though this advice was frequently not taken.

"Of course our respective governments tend to lose enthusiasm for their respective constitutions. This is what you mean, no doubt. I wouldn't be surprised, since this is a border matter, if your government is involved in Mr. Frazer's imprisonment."

Back in the car Billy made another call, this time to Patricia's office to make sure she was there. Her secretary was evasive, trying to interpret the nature of the call, but Billy didn't want a turn-down so said he was a personal friend, Bob, in town from London, and discovered that Patty was due at the studio momentarily.

The pleasure from this minor subterfuge was brief. There was a traffic tie-up on Hollywood Freeway near the Barham exit and Fred brought Billy's attention to something quite unpleasant: a tall and pathetically thin man with very long hair was standing nude on the balcony of an apartment house playing with himself.

"Maybe he's waiting for the right model of car to get off," Fred joked. "That's it. He's waiting for a blue Lamborghini."

Billy watched the man stroking himself and thought, inaccurately, that this couldn't happen in the Bay Area. He glanced around and saw that other drivers, also stuck in the traffic, were watching. An older woman was laughing. Perhaps that was the right attitude but Billy didn't quite have it in him. The truth was that Billy was beginning to delaminate. Everyone started beeping at the naked man and Billy slumped down in the seat and rubbed his face, then opened his briefcase in a panic for something to do.

"That's a real weird way to show the world you're lonely," Fred said, accelerating violently as the traffic loosened up.

Patty's office turned out to be a large back-lot bungalow, manned by a brisk English secretary whose efficiency on the phone Billy admired. He had been made to wait for a few minutes at the gate, and now he waited further, remembering the full dimensions of Patricia when she was cold and angry. Then she was standing at the door and he followed her into her office, a cavernous room, nicely if eccentrically decorated with paintings, bibelots of the best sort, framed movie posters and a few photographs.

There was the kind of silent face-off that both of them were good at, and Billy might possibly have won had he not seen a naked man jerking off on a balcony.

"What are we going to do?" He nearly blurted it out.

Patricia gestured him to the sofa but continued leaning against her desk, clearly the superior position.

"I'm not sure I like your first person plural. I'm not sure I want to be *we*, in other words. I still have a very distinct feeling that you sold us out," she said.

"That was clear to me the last time. Try to enlarge your heart, though, and think about what we're going to do about Zip."

"Zip's cause sounds lost. But I think we should try to do what Gwen asks us." There was not a trace of warmth in her voice. "How does that sound to you?"

Billy nodded in agreement, trying to retreat into the day before when the problem did not dominate his life. Deep within him a torment that had been thoroughly rationalized and put to sleep began to grow.

"You think I tipped off the police. The draft board had an alarm system. Whatever that means to you now. I don't think it really matters if we like each other, and if we're going to do anything for Zip, that should be clear to both of us. Agreed?"

It was Patty's turn to nod. She walked over to the sofa and offered her hand. Billy stood and shook it, desperate for escape.

"Can you bring Gwen over? She'd probably get lost. I might

be running a little late so seven would be fine." As he headed for the door his heart cringed a bit waiting for something else.

"Are we only going to do something because we couldn't bear ourselves if we didn't?" Patricia's question was almost plaintive.

Billy leaned against the door jamb thinking that she was right on the money. "There's something to that. When I was a kid I used to have nightmares about the electric chair. I told my granddad who was the only one I could actually talk to at the time. He said if you're going to spend your life worrying about the electric chair you've already been electrocuted." Billy paused, seeing that Patricia was eager to say something.

"Actually, when I saw her I thought she simply had no idea what she was up against. To be honest, she took care of me in prison so I owe her whatever. So it's not like I'm being a sucker for Zip's latest fuck-up. It's for her."

V

Gwen was walking the beach up near Trancas. If she had looked up she might have seen Billy's jet heading out over the ocean before turning north. Gwen was so direct that people frequently interpreted her singularity as being simple-minded. It was more than a mannerism — her mother had been the same way. This characteristic encouraged people to help Gwen even when she didn't need help. She was a very hard person to lie to because she never lied herself. She would have been appalled had she known that the willingness to help evinced by Billy and Patricia was for her rather than Zip. This ingenuousness made Gwen less seductive than she should have been for her level of attractiveness, since sexuality is, at best, an indirect art. She was vaguely aware of it all and supposed it came from a solitary childhood on the ranch near Mule Creek, population zero. When she was a physically advanced thirteen-year-old a cowboy at the local rodeo had said, "I'd like to stick it in you," to which Gwen had replied, "You would, would you? I think that's a strange thing to say to someone you don't even know." This quality tended to keep men, young and old, at a distance.

After a walk she fell asleep on the beach, awaking startled at the path of the sun. The ocean had aroused her and she wished that she could knock thirty years off her train mate Stuart's age. In the parking lot she was approached by a youngish beach bum in the dirty remnant of a tropical suit. He asked for a buck or two for food and she opened her purse, looking at him in alarm.

"My God, what are you doing to yourself?"

"My wife left me. So I've been having a few drinks for a year."

"There are plenty of fish in the ocean, if you'll allow me to say something stupid. Start taking care of yourself. This is all I can afford," she said, handing him ten dollars.

"I love you," he called as she drove out of the parking lot.

Gwen was delayed by rush-hour traffic and reached the small lobby of Le Parc at the same time Patty did. For some reason the specific density had lifted a bit. Patty had brought a wrapped present plus a bottle of champagne and while they waited for the elevator she joked about Billy's visit. Two sallow rock musicians at the desk glowered at Gwen and Patty in a parody of lust, and Patty gave them the finger as the elevator door closed. By the time they reached Gwen's room they were laughing hysterically. Patty iced the champagne and Gwen opened her present which was the loveliest blouse imaginable. Gwen remembered that she had packed along the article from the *Denver Post* about Sam to show Billy and Patty, and found it in her suitcase, failing to notice that the mention of it froze Patty in her chair. Then Gwen went off for a shower leaving Patty to stare at "Coyote Man Sticks to His Mountains" and a large photo of Sam as feral as the beast he studied.

Meanwhile, up in San Francisco, Billy sat drinking far too much with two cronies at the Washington Square Bar & Grill. The first game at Candlestick had been rained out as a scoreless tie in the fifth inning. Now he sat there waiting for a call from the airport to say that the fog had lifted and they had been assigned a take-off time and position. His two cronies were aging and alcohol-weathered preppies (one was an otiose sports columnist) and over drinks they had been cruising and flipping through subjects ranging from the bear market, to baseball, to the threat of AIDS, which they did not feel threatened by. They had repeatedly questioned Billy's melancholy mood until he had somewhat blearily admitted that his "dearest old friend" was on the eve of his execution in old Mexico. This was a real show stopper in that rarely, if ever, did anyone in the social position of the three actually know someone who'd been executed — or murdered, for that matter. The announcement was so extreme that Billy had even shocked himself. When the two cronies recovered enough to ask questions Billy limited himself to:

"Let's just say he was a great shortstop who got mixed up with the wrong crowd south of the border."

When the call came from the airport Billy was not in the best of shape.

Gwen and Patty pulled up in front of Billy's house in Pacific Palisades just at twilight. Gwen felt a little intimidated by the neighborhood, but Patty's nonchalance and the shared bottle of champagne soothed her. They were met at the door by a black man in a baseball cap whose hands were covered with flour. This was definitely not what they were expecting. The black man said his name was Fred and that Billy had been delayed by the weather in San Francisco. They followed Fred through the hall — Gwen thought the home was lovely while Patty thought it was far too "House Beautiful." There was a modest amount of disarray to show that it was the home of a divorced man.

At the door to the kitchen they were met by a young woman whose hands were also covered with flour.

"I'm Rebecca, the designated daughter. I hope you're not expecting too much lucidity. He called from a bar and sounded a bit fluffy. This is Jack Blackhorse." A rather dark Native American came in from the backyard dressed in chinos and a polo shirt. He was somber and rather good looking.

Rebecca and Fred were making pasta and Fred asked Jack Blackhorse to make drinks for the ladies, explaining it was taboo for "redskins" to touch spaghetti. Jack made drinks and told Gwen and Patricia he had five older sisters and never learned to cook, and that he was from the Nez Perce reservation up near Colville, Washington.

"I've eaten the so-called collard greens of your people," Jack said to Fred. "I always thought rhubarb leaves were poisonous."

"At least we take the fur off our meat before we eat it,"

Fred replied. "One more game and then I got to go to the airport."

Fred and Jack went over to the breakfast nook and resumed a backgammon game.

Gwen and Patricia were a little off balance. Rebecca noted this as she drank from a glass of red wine, then stirred a huge skillet of meatballs in marinara sauce.

"Don't mind them. They carry on like this whenever Jack visits. We better have a few drinks in defense. This is Dad's favorite dish. I make the meatballs with a mixture of veal, pork, beef and lots of garlic. Billy doesn't seem like a garlic person, does he? I'm real honored to meet two original members of the wild bunch. I went down to his room in the basement and got this." She picked a book off the counter. It was Frantz Fanon's *Wretched of the Earth,* signed by all of them, with a photo of the five on a Rocky Mountain camping trip.

"Oh, Jesus," said Patty.

"Oh, my God," said Gwen, turning away in embarrassment.

When Billy finally arrived he went through a marvelous charade of pretending not to be drunk, and might have fooled an outsider. He took Gwen and Patricia off to the den for a "meeting," telling them he had retained the best lawyer in Mexico to look after Zip. (He actually hadn't done so but would take care of it in the morning.) He would also make sure that Zip was isolated from the other prisoners for the time being, thus out of harm's way. Gwen suggested that it might be helpful if they all went down to Nogales and looked the situation over, and maybe they'd have time Memorial Day weekend which was the following week. This plan made Patricia and Billy uncomfortable but they were eager to agree. Then Gwen

said she had called home and there was a message from the
bank that someone had put money in her account. She paused,
glancing from Billy to Patricia. She said this would enable her
to get a valve job so they could fly her Cessna to Nogales from
the ranch, cutting the trip to less than an hour.

Later, when Gwen was helping Rebecca put dinner on the
table, Patricia took Billy aside.

"Do you have any doubts? Do you think we can really do
anything for Zip?" She hesitated to ask.

"At best we might make some sort of difference. At worst
it's a picnic, a class reunion, a funeral with no corpse."

There was an awkward but funny moment at dinner when
Rebecca baited her father into talking about AIDS, then nudged
Jack Blackhorse under the table.

"All you ex-liberals from the sixties like the presence of AIDS
because it keeps your kids from screwing around like you did,"
Jack said.

This elicited gasps and dropped silver from Billy, Gwen
and Patricia. Rebecca began laughing at her practical joke.
Jack pointed at Rebecca. "She put me up to it."

VI

Early the next morning Gwen was back on the train with a
slight hangover and the scent of garlic still on her skin. She
could not have hoped to accomplish more than she had in two
days. All the improbable tensions of the trip on the way out
had dissipated, and she read a mystery novel about the Nav-
ajos called *Listening Woman* that Sun had loaned her. She
drifted in and out of sleep all day, and in conscious periods

thought of how best to approach Sam. She had left the *Denver Post* article with Patty but had written down the particulars of Sam's location in the Sangre de Cristos. It was up between Galina and Lindrith in the Sante Fe National Forest which was rough country, she knew, because she had taken Sun up into the area to see Chaco Canyon, the Anasazi settlement.

Then it was twilight and her daughter was waiting for her in the pickup. They hugged and watched the train disappear to the east, then they turned west and studied the sunset which served to remind Gwen why she lived where she did. The smell of saguaro flowers in the air was so clear one's depth perception was doubled: the shadows were the homes of thousands of ghosts, for this was the homeland of Cochise and Geronimo. It was a little-admitted fact of history that Sun pointed out to her, that many Mescalero Apache families rode their horses pell-mell off the tops of mesas rather than submit to us.

Very early the next morning Gwen drove north from the ranch on Arizona 666 on her way to see Sam. The evening with Sun had been a little difficult due to her dislike of Zip and Gwen's efforts on his behalf. Sun, however, looked forward to houseguests, to seeing her mother's college friends she had heard so much about. Living that far out in the country they talked about everything there was to talk about, then they read. On Saturdays they drove to town and shopped for groceries, had lunch, visited friends, spent an hour at the library, had dinner and went to the movies. On Saturdays a neighbor stopped by to do the chores in exchange for their doing his chores on Sundays. It was a matter of feeding the penned bulls and any other penned cattle, checking irrigation head-gates and making sure no stock had gotten through the fences. The most intense periods of labor for Gwen and Sun were during haying when the irrigated alfalfa was cut, bailed and stacked, but the second crop wasn't due until mid-June. The real pleasure of the evening for Gwen was to call the airport mechanic and have him start a rush job on the valves of the Cessna. Gwen had inherited this passion for flying from her mother. Her dad had steadfastly refused to have anything to do with the old Cessna except to ridicule it.

It was indeed ironic that Sam, studying coyotes in the mountain fastness of northern New Mexico, would have an infinitely better idea of what could happen in Nogales than Gwen, Patty or Billy. It wasn't because he was smarter — in terms of sheer intelligence Patty, by common consent, led the five. She could practically dictate their term papers. Sam's exhaustive knowledge of Sonora came about because the mountain terrain he loved in New Mexico became snowbound by November and then he would move his coyote operations down to Sahuaripa, about two hundred miles east of Hermosillo. Sam spoke fluent, idiomatic Spanish — the language of the poor rather than the educated. In the winter he relied on vaqueros for additional information on coyotes. The vaqueros treated him with a mixture of amusement and respect. The younger ones thought he was crazy, but the older ranch hands tended, with their more profound native roots, to have respect for both the beasts and a man who would spend his life with them.

Sam's other advantage, which was the equal of the first, came about by accident. An ex–Black Panther, a chopper gunner who died at Khe Sanh, had given Sam a small poem to live by, a poem that supposedly derived from the "Sarmouni Brotherhood," whatever that was — Sam hadn't asked.

He simply carried the poem in his wallet as a reminder and corrective. It read, modestly enough:

> There is no God but Reality.
> To seek Him elsewhere
> Is the action of the Fall.

His reverence for this little poem did not mean that Sam delimited reality in the manner of the true believer whose blinders came in a thousand colors, rather that he studied what appeared to be "there" rather than what he wished to be there. To a degree that is incomprehensible to the individual, our lives are pretty much lived in air-locked compartments — Patricia had the movie business, Billy was in international law, Gwen lived the life of the marginal rancher, while Sam could only survive in emptiness, in the dimension of stillness that wilderness offered.

In sharp contrast to the hordes who had been attracted to the ecological movement, Sam disliked the attitude of moral superiority above all else. It was a bit simplistic but Sam was a victim, survivor and student of war. One merely had to tip open the *Britannica* to discover that between the years 1912 and 1945 the Germans had destroyed a hundred million lives out of a basic assumption of moral superiority. And this was only the most notorious example that could be extrapolated in every direction in human history, including our own extermination of over a hundred Native American cultures, up through Vietnam, and perhaps Nicaragua in the future. Sam no longer thought these thoughts that had formed his life; they had become cellular, and he dwelt among the wildlife attempting to survive as they had. Part of the ethos, the soul history, of American capitalism was to destroy absolutely everything that wasn't immediately useful. Sam's high school history teacher in Durango, Colorado, liked to quote General Philip Sheridan: "To destroy the Sioux you must destroy his living commissary, the buffalo. Only then will our plains and prairies be safe for the speckled cattle and the festive cowboy."

Sam had literally walked off the war. After five months in prison, a clinical depression and the loss of a quarter of his body weight, Sam was sprung through the efforts of his father, a high school superintendent in Durango, and his draft board. The local opinion was that Sam had got mixed up in the wrong crowd up in Boulder. In a classic "out of the frying pan, into the fire" move Sam became a Green Beret medic and a student of the languages of Vietnam and Cambodia. After three years and dozens of experiences that would remain unspeakable he received a medical discharge after he tried to duct-tape back together some children who had been blown to pieces. With his ample muster-out pay he spent three years walking around western Wyoming and Montana, then finished his education at University of Oregon, taking a master's in game biology.

The first object of Sam's study was the grizzly bear but after a half-dozen years in Montana this particular field of game biology had become overfull of researchers and very contentious. His career with the Department of the Interior had effectively ended at a conference on grizzlies in Missoula when he had lashed out at his superiors for using the drug phencyclidine hydrochloride to stun bears to remove them from an area or to attach telemetric collars. A problem grizzly who had been stunned a half-dozen times with the drug had recently devoured a camper in Yellowstone. Game biologists could be rather otherworldly but Sam knew that the street name for phencyclidine was angel dust. Any critter that had received six massive doses of this drug was liable to be irascible and psychotic. Sam said this at the Missoula conference, adding unwisely that he had used the drug himself in the old days and it had put him in a fighting mood. He recommended they stick with alpha-chloralose which wasn't as effective and thus a little dangerous to those who administered it, but this would properly reduce the number of game biologists. This was a man clearly not destined for promotion.

Sam resigned and went home to tend to his mother who was dying of stomach cancer. She was in a great deal of pain so Sam would make the long drive from Durango to Denver, score heroin and shoot her up to supplement her more ortho- dox medicine. After he buried her and consoled his father he began a guide service, taking mostly bird watchers and stu- dents of Indian lore into the back country north of Durango, and to Mesa Verde and Chaco Canyon.

It was after one of these trips guiding an elderly man and his wife from Chicago that he received an offer in the mail from the couple announcing that they had been auditioning him. They had a family foundation and wished to underwrite an exhaustive study of the coyote, and would Sam consider it, and if so, prepare a budget? They were alarmed and surprised by the smallness of his demands, but then were led to under- stand on their successive summer trips that there were advan- tages to "traveling light" when studying this critter. Later Sam discovered that these people were relatives of the man who had underwritten Frank Waters's monumental ten-year study of the Hopi Indian.

The late May afternoon Gwen showed up on his mountain- side Sam was repairing his telemetric receiver and charging his battery packs with a portable generator. He was also brooding about his shortcomings, the main one of which was alcohol. Once a month he would come off the mountain to get supplies in Gallup or Farmington. He would find a Mexican, Navajo or Zuñi girl to make love to, then get very drunk for the next twenty-four hours, sleeping it off in the back of his old Studebaker pickup. This behavior was becoming tiresome to him. He had checked out the psychiatric literature on recluses like himself — hermits, prospectors, solitary explorers — and knew that a great deal of time in solitude tended to blur the peripheries. Reality is perceptual and consensual and after thirty days alone you could forget where your skin left off and the world began. Then you emerged for supplies and forgot how to behave partly because you never really knew how in the first place.

From his box canyon up the mountain Sam could see across a gently sloping alpine meadow, to a steadily descending forest, down to a broad scrubby plateau full of sage and mesquite. There, in a grove of cottonwoods beside a creek was the trailhead and the end of a narrow gravel road maintained by the Forest Service, a three-hour hike if you were in good shape. You would have to be a rock climber or some sort of intense survivalist to approach Sam without his knowing it. His closest neighbors were ranchers of Spanish descent, distant children of Cortez, and they provided, being hostile, yet another buffer to this domain which was public in name only. As a victim of war Sam liked to cover his back and flanks, plus he possessed a level of alertness and attention he seemed to have gathered from the creature he studied.

Thus it was he noticed the curl of dust made by a car on the gravel of the Forest Service road and set up his spotting scope determining it was a single figure without a pack, thus someone on an errand. This mystified him, as no one was due for two more months unless it meant his father was ill. After an hour the figure disappeared into the forest, and then in another hour the figure emerged at the edge of the alpine meadow. Now he could see it was a light-haired woman in a green shirt and khaki trousers, he hoped not a graduate student snooping into his research. When Gwen's features became clear Sam drew in his breath sharply, swore with pleasure and began to pace. In the old days they had been buddies, and he always felt Gwen, with her rural background, understood him better than the rest. His brain, in the fashion of a computer, clicked off the reasons for her arrival, and he accurately guessed that something had gone awry with Zip. He skittered around briefly trying to straighten up his campsite, gave up and ran down to greet her.

They spent the first hour filling each other in and a number of disturbing factors arose. Sam had received several letters from Zip over the years and they always arrived having been opened. Zip had wanted Sam to use his military experience by coming down to Guatemala and helping blow up a dam, thus flooding out a military base. Other than having thought it was a naïve way to communicate such a plan, Sam had written back to say his killing days were over, and that though he couldn't do much for himself or other people he could try to make the world a better place for coyotes. This point of view had brought forth a truly nasty harangue from Zip to which Sam hadn't answered.

What bothered Gwen was that Sam had yet to comment on the chances of their freeing Zip, reducing his sentence, saving him from the death Zip felt was imminent. She was hoping that Sam's experience with Mexico might reflect some encouragement that he, thus far, had been unwilling to offer. She began to repeat all the details of the case but he waved her words away.

"It's like the States. If you have a great deal of money and first-rate legal help your chances improve immeasurably. We seem to have that much. But just like here it depends on how badly anyone wants to keep you in prison or kill you. And we don't know who this 'anyone' is."

They picked some dandelion greens to cook as a side dish to go with Sam's humble salt pork, pinto beans and *chiletepines* concoction. While they were eating Gwen was startled to hear Sam's telemetric receiver begin beeping.

"Turn slowly. She's up there on that small rock ledge. She's number seventy-one but I call her Sister. Every day at lunchtime she checks me out though she never has accepted any food except a jackrabbit I snared. Her ears are up and she's nervous because you're here. Before she had a litter of pups a few weeks ago she'd sit over under that tree."

"Why do you suppose she watches you?" Gwen had swiveled and caught the dun-colored shape of the coyote up on the ledge.

"She hunted all night and slept all morning. Now she's rested, bored and curious. They're a lot like dogs and people in that they all have different personalities. She's just the most inquisitive one I've studied."

After lunch they bathed in a spring-fed rock pool and made further plans. Sam would locate a sheepherder friend to keep an eye on his camp, then would drive down to Gwen's on the Thursday before Memorial Day weekend. Gwen sat on a rock, wrapped in a towel, having found the cold water nearly unendurable. She had noted that Sam had avoided the subject of Patty whenever Gwen had mentioned her. Now he talked about all of his half years in Mexico, a country her own great author, Octavio Paz, had called "the labyrinth of solitude." Sam said if you stepped outside the ordinary tourist framework in Mexico, the country became the closest thing to the void an American could know.

At mid-afternoon she watched the passage of the sun and said she'd have to go though she didn't want to. He insisted on joining her on the three-hour hike back to the car. She tried to refuse because it meant he'd have to walk back up the mountain in the dark. This seemed to puzzle him a moment as if he'd run into a vacuum, but then he said that all of his work took place at night because that was when his "critters" were most active.

At the bottom of the hill in the twilight he touched Gwen's arm, then cupped his hands around his mouth and made a succession of long yelping howls that echoed down the canyon. Within a few seconds there were several answers, and he took her hand and kissed it in parting, heading across the plateau before she could respond. He can be awfully pleasant, she thought, for someone who has given up on the human race.

VII

It's time to pause a moment at the beginning of the last and longest chapter of our fable. Ever since he first popped out of the egg man has been weeping. When John Milton presented his argument for *Paradise Lost* he said, "Of man's first disobedience / and the fruit of that forbidden tree, I sing . . ." and hardly anyone ever finishes the poem. It's all part of the old school of "nobody gets out of here alive," the reflection, whether in mirror, lake or coffee cup, most often vanishing in seconds, that something is terribly wrong. This, after all, is a world where it took the Catholic Church over forty years to issue a "position paper" on why the Church did nothing in particular to interfere in the Holocaust. Jeremiah spoke in jeremiads and still makes rather good reading for strong stomachs.

There's a lovely ranchero song out of Sonora with a refrain that goes, "Two horses, two friends, two guns." You don't need to be a student of doom to figure this out. If you're not careful you can go to sleep in America and wake up in a foreign country. Sonora is full of the unpardonable beauty of desolation, a starving province that funnels its people into the sweatshops of cities like Nogales. They seem unafraid, these peons in Yankee clothing, because they know that the past is all we have, and it's what we're going to get more of. In the memory of their grandparents this is still the country where the men of Porfirio Díaz slaughtered tens of thousands of rebellious peasants. So when our four fly south to the border for a mere hour, they are still a lawyer, a v.p. in the movie business, a ranch woman, a student of coyotes, a heady brew of incomprehension. To give up, to abandon Ted Frazer, a.k.a. Zip, finally would be to abandon their own pasts, to say that the vibrancy of the time they spent together, no matter that it ended badly, meant nothing, or meant an insufficient amount to divert the courses of their lives for a few days. Within the mythology of our culture back to the early explorers, the mountain men, the Indian fighters, the cowboys, through a half-dozen wars, the notion of the primacy of friendship runs like a national spinal column. The fact that it was more talked about than adhered to does not make it less a motivation. Most often, no one threw themselves on that live grenade to save their friends.

Because of Zip's winter visit only Gwen actually knew the man they were trying to save. And at this point she alone had left her own element to effect the rescue. Billy, Patricia and Sam remembered a golden boy whom everyone liked — eloquent, kind, a born leader, the sort of half-manic goofy who spends his life pushing our tired ideologies forward. They would have been less enthused about the man Gwen knew: a fatigued gadfly rather than a revolutionary, a man so obsessed with injustice that it had destroyed him, reduced him to an embittered paranoid who tended to be ignored and avoided by his fellow revolutionaries. The authorities who still might wish to pursue him had forgotten that it had been well over a decade since there was anything meaningful on his record.

In the eyes of Sun, Friday was a strange and fascinating day, one of the best days, in fact, of her entire life. Her mother had stayed up late the night before, making potato salad and waiting for Sam, whom Sun had found curled up in his sleeping bag on the front lawn when she got up at daylight. Their Labrador was sleeping with Sam, and Sun had run into the house to get him a cup of coffee. Gwen came out in her robe and he told her his truck had broken down and he had hitchhiked the last fifty miles. Sun was entranced because Sam spoke to her teasingly in Khmer, a language she hadn't heard since she was adopted at age five.

After breakfast she and Sam helped Gwen untether and push out the Cessna from the lean-to pole shed that doubled as a cattle shelter in bad weather, then watched her take off from the grass strip for the airport in Safford to pick up Billy and Patricia. Sun showed Sam around the ranch, riding double on the John Deere tractor because the gears were acting up on the pickup. They were intense and voluble from the beginning and she buried him in questions about coyotes, then about Native Americans of which he knew a great deal. She jumped in the pen and showed off their prime Simmental-Charolais bull, warning him not to follow as the bull only tolerated her and the dog, and even disliked Gwen. Theirs was the immediate relationship of a very bright girl who discovers a long-lost uncle who is also bright and imaginative.

They pulled the hydraulic jack out from the tool shed and Sam began working on the transmission of the pickup with Sun passing the wrenches. She felt a wave of melancholy that her mother hadn't married someone this nifty. She wasn't at all surprised when Gwen's Cessna came sweeping back down the canyon and Sam didn't emerge from under the truck — Sun knew that Sam and Patricia had been a hot item and Sam was probably in some mental pain about her arrival as he pulled the gears.

The Cessna taxied up. The bull bellowed and the dog barked as they always did. Sun walked over, immediately nonplused that Billy and Patricia looked like a "weekend wear" ad in *Vogue* magazine. She had never met such people despite a number of stays in Albuquerque and Tucson. Sun owned the built-in shit detector of the intelligent teenager but found them both likable, despite Billy's apparent nervousness and the fact that Patty folded her arms after they shook hands.

They walked over to where Sam's feet were sticking out from under the truck. Billy said he had brought a case of Anchor Steam Beer from the coast, and Sam wiggled out, stood, and they embraced, leaving a grease smear on Billy's sweater. Then Sam and Patty looked at each other, and Sun, being a closet romantic, felt tears rise. The two of them just couldn't seem to say a thing. Gwen and Billy backed away pretending to be interested in the bull, while Sun walked over to lug in the two huge, expensive-looking suitcases. Sun glanced back and saw that Patty was now hugging herself as if to break her own ribs, but Sam had come closer and they had begun to stroll down the driveway.

Sun spent the day trying to cover all the bases at once. When the four of them would split up for a while in separate twos she would become frantic and undecided where to eavesdrop, even join in the talk when it seemed provident. She listened most attentively at the kitchen table when Billy filled them all in on the latest developments of the case. A new lawyer was working on getting them visiting privileges to see Zip and it looked good. The Mexican lawyer who was supposedly very important was already running into unspecified political resistance which he hadn't anticipated. When Patty and Gwen walked off Sun wanted to stay with the men but was too shy. She followed the women out into the yard and Gwen told Patty an embarrassing story about how, a few years back, she had nicknamed Sun "Screen Gems" because Sun read movie and gossip magazines. Sun remonstrated that she had left all of that behind along with heavy-metal rock groups. Then Patty invited her to come out for a week in the summer so Patty could show her how movies were actually made. This was an overwhelming invitation to Sun who thanked Patty and wandered off to think it all over.

Billy called out from the house and Sun went in to tune the satellite dish to the San Francisco Giants game. Sam drank beer on the couch and dozed. Billy had a strangely familiar way of talking to her but then Sun remembered that Gwen had said Billy had a nineteen-year-old daughter. He was curious about Sun's elaborate stereo equipment and the desk computer over in the corner. She blushed when she explained they were gifts from her father who was in business in Albuquerque. She loved her father, but a month a year with him was more than enough as that part of New Mexico was dreary, and so were all of his friends in the electronics business. Sam yawned at the ball game on television and suggested they go horseback riding which delighted Sun. She was a little surprised to see how he rode, and they stayed overlong in the hills so she could show him some coyote dens.

When they got back to the ranch house Billy was grilling chicken and Gwen and Patty were setting up the picnic table in the backyard. Sun ran upstairs and set up two speakers at the windows of her room so she could play some tapes she had made of what she called "mother's music" for the picnic. She hadn't fully admitted it but she had come to prefer it over that of her own generation. Sun selected a tape that began with the Allman Brothers, B. B. King, then an Otis Redding–Carla Thomas duet, Janis Joplin's "Get It While You Can" and Grace Slick singing "White Rabbit." She adjusted the volume and ran back downstairs, checking out the kitchen window for a reaction. The four of them stood there so still, Sun thought, as if they were getting their pictures taken.

The dinner vacillated between giddiness, melancholy, silence, laughter. Sun thought they were drinking too fast for the long haul, including her mother. Patricia wasn't sure she could bear the music but was voted down. Sam roared with laughter at Grace Slick.

"I always sort of liked that song but I never understood what the fuck it was about. Remember when we'd drop a few tabs of acid and just listen to music as if it actually meant something? It was a religion, wasn't it?"

This statement started a mostly good-natured quarrel. Then Sun interrupted with a question that turned out to be inept and almost disastrous. "If you guys are so smart, and I think you are, how come you got caught in the first place?"

It was a show stopper but Sam tried to save the situation by
jumping up and doing an elaborate pantomime of the raid on
the draft board. Gwen and Billy were the lookouts while Patty
held the flashlight for Zip and Sam who busied themselves
pouring glue and cow's blood into the files. Patty had dropped
the flashlight and when the police bullhorn came on they all
ran into each other in the dark hallway. Billy maintained boozily
that they must have tripped an alarm. Then Patty became
angry and said that Billy's house might have been bugged in
the planning stages, or someone had to have tipped the cops
off. Gwen led Patty away to calm her down, and Sun ran into
the house and upstairs to her room, embarrassed to have pre-
cipitated the quarrel. She turned off the music and reread an
article about Brazilian Indians in *Natural History*. Billy and
Sam yelled up for more music so she turned it back on. It was
easy for Sun to see that something unpleasant was going on
between Billy and Patricia.

Sun dozed off then, having snuck two beers and a swig of
Gwen's martini. She awoke with a start when the long tape
was finished. She got up to get a glass of water from the upstairs bathroom. Out the window, and just at the edge of the
yard light, she could see Patty standing in a blue robe above
Sam in his sleeping bag. His hand reached out and grabbed
her ankle and Patty stooped down and kissed him. Then his
hands drew up her robe and Sun looked away thinking, Jesus,
these folks have got out of hand. She started down the stairs
but heard Billy and Gwen talking so she stopped.

"We'll leave at dawn. The cool air will give us more lift."
Gwen said.

"You're still trying to get me off the hook just like the old
days."

"I always thought of you as a good-hearted noodler. A good-
looking noodler. A sexy noodler."

"Thanks. Give me a break. Kiss me good night."

"Absolutely not." Gwen laughed, moving to the upstairs door behind which Sun fled.

At dawn she bid them all goodbye with relief, then watched as Gwen made a pass over the ranch, dipping the wings in farewell. Sun, quite naturally, wondered if she'd ever see them all together again.

When Sam finally got back to his mountain in late June and thought the whole thing over he felt that it might have worked if it had taken longer. Even the hot hours when nothing had happened had whirred past with the speed of the ubiquitous ceiling fans, which only translated hot stillness into hot breeze.

The flight down was violently rough from a rare late May thunderstorm and their mutual hangovers misfocused every word said. When the sun came out Billy, who sat in front with Gwen, asked for his sunglasses in the kit bag at Patty's feet. When she opened the bag the sunglasses nestled on top stacks of neat thatches of hundred-dollar bills. She exchanged glances with Sam and a little while later she became airsick. When they landed at the Nogales Airport and before they split up as per plan, everyone became irritated at Sam's use of military terminology. Billy and Gwen would go to the house loaned to Billy and owned by the family of the Mexican consul in L.A. Sam and Patty would also stay on the American side of Nogales but would spend their afternoon across the border doing reconnaissance. No one liked the word "reconnaissance" because it made the world seem unnecessarily dangerous.

An hour later Sam and Patty were sitting in a sidewalk *cantina*, listening to the oldest guitarist in the world and eyeing the police who emerged from the federal building across the street. They had driven around for an hour to get what Sam called "the lay of the land," another term which irritated Patty. He explained that right-living Mexicans from the interior called Nogales and other border towns *"poso del mundo,"* which loosely translated as asshole of the country. On the way from the airport she had noticed the miles of fruit-and-vegetable warehouses, a billion-dollar local business, and on the tour Sam showed her the enormous American-owned electronics complex where scab wages were about five bucks a day. Sam had said that down here mere survival took the heart out of a man's life. She said what about women, and he said everybody. Humankind.

At the *cantina* it got rougher. He watched the federal building and drank margaritas while she drank *agua minerale* from a bottle.

"Would you screw a cop to help out Zip?" he asked.

"I'd have to think that one over."

"Gwen did. After she got out of prison she screwed a cop at Zip's request so he could find out what happened. It was Billy's girlfriend Sarah, the one he eventually married. She overheard us and called Billy's dad who made a deal for a misdemeanor so Billy could practice law. But the cops insisted the plan go through so they could nail Zip and the rest of us, but mostly Zip. I'm telling you this so you'll lay off Billy. This won't work if you keep ragging him, so don't say a fucking thing. I know you suspected it."

Patty tried to pretend she was shocked but she wasn't. It all fell into place, confirming her suspicions.

"So we're helping him redeem himself?" she asked.

"You know that's bullshit. We would have come along just for the excuse of seeing each other again."

His smile was so warm that she tried to feel warm too. Only she didn't. Or not quite. Because she used to be a continuity girl she noticed the same American in Bermuda shorts, Hawaiian shirt and baseball cap pass them twice in ten minutes on a motor scooter. She started to say something but Sam had noticed too, and the American was glancing back from a stoplight. On the way back to their motel on the Arizona side the customs man took overlong passing them through.

Gwen didn't like the villa where she was staying with Billy. It adjoined the border fence but was stuck grandly in a thicket of cottonwood, flowering bushes and planted bamboo. She felt tiny sitting on the sofa of the three-story living room. It was the most foreign house she had ever been in but Billy simply paced around, ignoring the room and waiting for the lawyer. There was a two-ton orb of lapis lazuli in the hall and every bit of space was crammed with colonial and native antiques and artifacts, and ersatz revolutionary posters from the time of Morelos. Billy said the house was owned by the art dealer cousin of the Mexican consul.

Gwen was about to repeat her complaint about their lodging when an enormous thug strode through the front door followed by a small, dapper Mexican lawyer in the kind of suit Billy wore. The thug told them in broken English to keep their door locked and disappeared. The lawyer introduced himself, kissed Gwen's hand and asked Billy to pass along respects to his old friend Billy's father. The lawyer's English was perfect except for fractured idioms, telling Billy he was "barking up the wrong bush" coming to the aid of a horrible person, and that he should go home.

"Is that it? Then you folks did a real shitty job." Billy said. "What did you carry in that alligator briefcase all the way from Mexico City, your lunch?"

Gwen was startled by this cold side of Billy which she had

never seen before. The lawyer merely smiled and said that Billy was a hard man like his father. Then he opened his brief-case and rattled off his progress on the case, adding many absolutely new details. Zip and two other revolutionaries had been pursued to a canyon west of Nogales by a Federale cap-tain and two soldiers. The Federale had been forced to shoot one of the revolutionaries and Zip had attacked him. The other revolutionary escaped. A puzzling fact was that the testimony of one of the soldiers had stated that an American had accom-panied the Federale and kicked Zip in the spine so that they had to carry the prisoner. The lawyer said this fact had been removed from later testimony but he had paid plenty for the earlier records. He had also arranged for them to visit Zip any morning they wished. Afternoons would cost extra.

"Why didn't they tell me this three weeks ago?" Gwen asked, but they ignored her.

Billy was pleased with the new items in the case but the lawyer was discouraging. The prosecutor would make Zip seem more dangerous, to justify the shooting of the revolutionary. And the presence of the American inferred that the two coun-tries' intelligence networks might have been involved, which made it all very messy indeed. The United States was justifi-ably paranoid about a possible Communist revolution in Mex-ico, according to the lawyer who announced he was right wing but then business was business. He felt that Zip, despite his distant past, had become a harmless nitwit who was being pursued because certain as yet unknown authorities had noth-ing better to do at the moment.

When the lawyer left Billy and Gwen sat there for a while as if poleaxed. Then Billy discovered the liquor cabinet, made her a drink and got himself a beer from the refrigerator. Gwen was so bleak that Billy gave her a hug, assuring her that they

were going to kick ass, but there was the sense the warm air
was water and they were drowning.

It was on the verge of getting a little difficult back at the motel. Patty was propped up in bed in a bra and half-slip looking
at a number of scripts she had brought along. Sam paced around
shirtless in hiking shorts taking an occasional swig from a bottle of *bacanora mescal*. He was apparently trying to think well
beyond the world of coyotes.

"Why are you reading that shit? Try to think about what
we're doing."

"It's not shit, it's my homework. You ever been to Russia?
I have and that's what this place reminds me of. I haven't
learned enough about it to think. Actually, it occurred to me
that Zip was supposedly trying to organize workers. Why don't
we try to get hold of some union people."

"That's what I mean! That's a fucking good idea. What else
you got hidden in that big brain?"

"I was wondering why you never tried to see me when you
came home."

"You said after the trial that I ruined your life. I also wrote
from the goofy ward and you never answered."

"That's not trying very hard."

"It's a helluva lot more than you did which is nothing." Sam
began sorting through his large backpack as if looking for
something to do. He drew out two leather-wrapped packages
and took out a 9 mm Walther pistol and a sawed-off Remington 12-gauge known in the trade as an "alley sweeper." He
poured Hoppe gun oil on a rag and began cleaning the weapons. Patty looked up from her script, shocked and speechless.
Sam took another swig of *mescal*, then noticed that the blood
had drained from her face.

"I don't like guns either. I never use them. I just have them in the hills because there're some hunting types that don't like me. But you got to have weapons if the other side has them, and they sure as hell do around here."

Patty's reaction was to totally pack up her things and get dressed within a few minutes. He was too surprised to remonstrate. At the door, suitcase in hand, she said to offer Gwen and Billy her apologies, and Zip if they saw him, but it was too late in life for her to go back to prison because of a "fucking lunatic."

Late in the afternoon Billy went with the lawyer to visit an old friend of the lawyer's, a mogul in the produce business who owned a hundred semis and a dozen warehouses. The meeting took place in Jorge's office, an elaborate eyrie up in the corner of a vast warehouse. Jorge and the lawyer chatted about their *chicas de casas* (mistresses) before getting down to business. The lawyer asked Jorge to put in a good word with the judge in Zip's behalf. Jorge knew the case and made a show of outrage over being asked to help a terrorist. Then the lawyer said that Billy had any number of politicians in the bag and if the U.S. decided to re-embargo Mexican produce Billy might be quite helpful. This idea did a good deal toward calming Jorge down, though he now pretended to be noncommittal. He smiled at Billy and said, "The intrigue and viciousness of our politics is impossible for an American to understand. Your graft is child's play. A judge or politician here is capable of a double double cross, a triple cross. But perhaps I could make an inquiry."

Thinking it might be a morale gesture Gwen and Billy dressed up and strolled over to the Mexican side of the border for dinner. She dressed in lavender, he in a white tropical suit, a well-heeled couple bowed to in deference as they walked through customs. The American on the motor scooter stared at them from another stall, apparently knowing who they were. A block past customs Billy nodded to Sam who stood in front of a *cantina* across the street. Sam made an elaborate "who knows?" gesture and Gwen was irritated at the charade.

"This is appalling, isn't it? We don't know what we're doing."

"Calm down, you've got the first-day blues."

"You forget I was down here before. I heard you on the phone with the newspapers. It must be maddening to spend your life spieling that sort of bullshit."

"It's a living. It's also the way the world works when you're not down on the farm."

"That's not worth resenting."

They stopped on the street in front of the Coronado Restaurant, a little tremulous in their mutual refusal not to continue the quarrel.

"People who went to college are usually better at saying awful things." Gwen laughed.

"We're still getting over our hangovers." Billy glanced at a blue sedan wedging its way into a parking place across the street. No one got out.

All through a wonderful dinner of Guaymas shrimp and roasted loin of lamb they talked affably, almost giddily, of their absurd college camping trips. Zip had had a specious theory that the wilderness caused clear thinking, though only Sam actually knew how to camp. Gwen remembered as they drank a Montrachet and a Chambertin that Billy wasn't on a budget. Billy reminded Gwen that on their last camping trip he had disastrously hauled along Sarah.

"She got blisters and cried a lot," Gwen said.

"There was no place to shop in the mountains." Billy was watching a burly man who had entered a few minutes before and was drinking at the bar. Their waiter who was an elegant old fellow stared at this man from the shadows. The man, who looked vaguely familiar to Billy, wore a suit that would have looked somewhat well tailored years ago but had been worn to bagginess. Suddenly the man bustled to their table.

"Billy Creighton! What a thrill to run into you down here. I heard your American Bar Association speech in D.C. last winter. It was on the taxation complications of owning a professional sports team, wasn't it? And Gwen, are you still ranching? Great food here, right? One thing about my job is I've eaten my way around the world a dozen times. I'm Virgil Atkins."

The man sat down with authority and rattled on until Billy and Gwen were bug-eyed. Atkins said he had heard that they had flown down in Gwen's Cessna and that Sam and Patty were here too, but Patty had taken a cab all the way to Tucson. The last detail startled Billy and Gwen.

"Who the fuck are you?" Billy said, signaling for the check. "We don't have to listen to this."

"I'm here to watch your scumbag friend get put away for life, you might say. I've seen him in Guatemala, Costa Rica, Panama, wherever. Now he's finished and I suspect you're here to say goodbye. Nothing more, I hope, for your sake."

"You're here to make sure it happens, aren't you?" Gwen was flushed with anger.

"You're a tough one, Gwen. You take a train to L.A. and talk to one of our guys all the way out. He's a good rummy player, isn't he? But you don't really tell him anything. Then you sucker all your soft-core friends into helping you try to spring your terrorist. But now the Mexicans got him without me lifting a hand."

Billy stood as the waiter brought the check. He turned his back, deciding to ignore Atkins until he collected himself.

"We don't have to talk to you unless you identify yourself," Gwen said rather lamely.

"You don't have to talk to me at all. It's a free country. I'm just letting you know you're out of your depth. I'm just reminding you that the President and Congress mandated that we pre-empt terrorists." Atkins got up, shaking his head at the idea of their innocence, and bustled out.

The old waiter came over with Billy's change and a bottle of brandy with two glasses. "You look like you're needing this. Tell your friend at the motel to meet me tomorrow at the Blue Parrot Bar at five in the afternoon."

Billy and Gwen nodded, drank their brandy and decided they weren't going to panic or be pushed around. They looked as if they meant it.

Early the next morning Patty came back to the motel from Tucson via another expensive cab ride. She had decided she couldn't leave until she at least said goodbye to Zip. She sat on a chair by the motel swimming pool and mentally prepared her lines for Sam, who, meanwhile, was watching her from the window of the motel coffee shop. He walked out and up behind where she sat, leaning down and kissing her hair. She took his hand and said nothing.

"I missed you a lot," he said.

They turned with surprise as Billy pulled up in a Hertz sedan, looking as though he had slept on his face. He told them to pack up their stuff because everyone in the world, especially Washington, knew they were there so they may as well move in together.

Afterwards, none of them could admit how truly pathetic their first visit to Zip turned out to be. They were escorted into a dank room in the federal building, empty except for five chairs and Zip, who was standing against the wall with a single ray of sun on his face. Patty couldn't help but think that the bastard had even arranged the lighting.

Zip said he had been kicked in the spine and couldn't sit down. He was cold and questioned whether it was a set-up because they had been set up before, hadn't they? He told them to go home immediately because it was better that he be murdered for the cause. Gwen interrupted and asked him why he had sent a note demanding that they come down. Zip grinned maniacally and pointed at a totally concealed bug in the ceiling which could have been imaginary. Then Billy asked if he had attacked the Federale and Zip laughed. No, he had never been capable of attacking anyone. How could he jump a Federale with a smoking gun when an American had already kicked him in the spine. He was to receive a fifty-year sentence and most probably be murdered for lecturing workers outside an American-owned electronics plant. He told them to go and not come back.

It was then that Patty said, "Fuck you, you didn't even say hello." Zip hobbled over rather histrionically and shook hands with each of them, wearing a look so cold that all of them cringed.

Gwen and Patricia were trying to recover by looking at the flowers that edged the patio behind the villa. Patty was paranoid enough to wonder if the gardener with the hoe and rake was really a gardener.

"Zip was always such a cold-hearted son-of-a-bitch on most levels," Patty said.

Gwen nodded in half agreement, then rambled on about how an obsession with injustice can be self-destructive. She had read about a black novelist in South Africa who said he wasn't going to let the ten years he had spent in prison ruin his enjoyment of life. Patty wasn't really listening and both of them could hear the rising anger in Billy's voice through the open patio doors. They drifted over until they could see where the lawyer was trying to calm down Billy. Two stringers from the *Wall Street Journal* and *Forbes* were getting up to leave.

"You have to understand, Mr. Creighton, that your story of Frazer sounds like one of a dozen conspiracy stories any reporter gets per week. It's either mutilated cattle, the return of Lee Harvey Oswald, the AMA's suppression of cancer cures. An arrest for an unlawful labor speech isn't financial news."

The *Forbes* man remained silent but nodded in agreement at the *Journal* writer's condescension.

"Take a fucking hike," is all Billy would say. He had begun to feel that the world had been thrown in his lap. After the stringers hurried out Billy asked the lawyer if he felt the American-owned-business community had anything to do with it. The lawyer said he had checked that out while they were visiting Zip. It was an unlikely contention as there was an infinite supply of cheap labor. When they discussed it both the lawyer and Billy had been a little surprised at the blatancy of Virgil Atkins at the Coronado Restaurant. Atkins's behavior might have been an act to throw them off, but the lawyer had another idea. The mistakes of the FBI and CIA had been newsworthy in recent years; perhaps these men were as tired and underpaid as revolutionaries like Zip. If Atkins was really important at age fifty-three, what would he be doing around Nogales snooping after a third-rate radical?

When the lawyer left Patty asked Billy how the lawyer knew that Atkins was fifty-three and Billy shook his head wearily. Gwen found this quite amusing and reminded Patty of a game they used to play in prison where they would collect everything irrational that had happened to them during the week and act it out on Sunday as if it were theater.

"Perhaps all the lawyers and spies in Mexico are fifty-three," Gwen said.

"The gardener just left. He's also a fifty-three-year-old spy and goes to law school at night," Patty added. "And this place is just barely important enough for Zip to rot in jail."

Sam was making his way through the Parajito Hill district, formerly the *zona* of prostitution. He used rapid-fire Spanish to ask an old woman who was selling black velvet paintings where the Blue Parrot Bar was. She told him he was handsome and the bar was only five blocks down the street. Sam was unused to being told he was handsome and was busy feeling good about it when he heard the scooter. That fucker must be real dumb, Sam thought, or maybe he thinks I'm dumb, or maybe he doesn't care. Sam waited for the scooter to pass in his direction. He reversed himself and ran up the hill on a side street, then left down an alley of shacks. A plump, ragged woman was hanging up clothes and Sam gave her twenty bucks for her clothesline. He tied one end to a post, then crossed the alley with the other end, ducking behind a car without tires and holding this most elementary of snares. This was how Zuñi boys tripped mule deer they had frightened through a narrow canyon neck, he thought. Within a minute the scooter came shooting down the alley and Sam necktied the American. He waved at the woman who stood watching from the door of her shack, stepped over the squirming body and headed back down the hill toward the Blue Parrot Bar.

When Sam reached the bar he was met by the huge thug who had served as the bodyguard for the lawyer, though Sam didn't know it. Waiting for him was the waiter who served Gwen and Billy at the Coronado and the gardener Sam recognized from the villa. It turned out they were the leaders of the local labor movement which they admitted was rather weak, albeit enthusiastic. The waiter explained that they had viewed Zip as an utter nuisance whose efforts had been counterproductive. They didn't want a revolution, just better wages. However, the fact that Zip was going to receive a long sentence for a minor offense and a trumped-up charge was bad for the morale of the local workers who thought he was wonderful, if crazy. The long sentence would come from a collusion between American interests and a crooked judge. It was that simple, or so they said. And that was why they forged Zip's handwriting and sent a messenger to Gwen in hopes of getting some help. It seemed to them that things were going well in that their rich friend had power and was causing a problem. If the problem got big enough the Mexicans would get rid of it because everyone in Nogales knew the case wouldn't bear scrutiny. The rest of the meeting was spent in planning even bigger problems for the authorities. Sam said that Billy would be glad to make a large contribution to the union. The gardener said they would gladly accept it though it wasn't necessary. On his way home Sam liked the way things were getting less vague in favor of something down and dirty.

There was a certain amount of comic relief in the evening, except for Billy who had arranged for one of the firm's planes to bring down the sportswriter friend he had been drinking with at the Washington Square Bar & Grill in San Francisco. The sportswriter had entered in a hound's-tooth jacket and a Giants cap just as Patty and Gwen went off for groceries. The man and Billy exchanged a clumsy high-five.

"Sending the floozies away before little Bobby gets a shot at 'em? Vegas says it's three-to-one we do it this year, baby. It's the Series, I shit you not. What a faboola plane you got, Billy. Just me, a pastrami and three brewskies and I'm in old Mexico."

"This is actually the American side of the border." Billy wanted to calm the asshole down a bit as the speech patterns were suddenly repugnant given the present situation.

"Shoot it to me, stud. I got to start back in an hour."

By the time Gwen and Patty returned with the groceries Billy was dictating a column for the sportswriter to use in the following morning's edition. This deception was costing Billy a red Corvette he no longer used and Rebecca scorned, plus a management position when Billy bought a franchise, a carrot in the future that could obviously be withdrawn.

Sam was in the kitchen mixing drinks when Gwen and Patty returned. Sam rolled his eyes and gestured toward the living room. Gwen and Patty tiptoed to the door and listened to Billy's voice which affected that of a radio announcer:

"There once was a boy named Ted Frazer from Denver, Colorado. He was a great Little League shortstop so they called him Zip. After Little League he played American Legion sandlot and won a scholarship to University of Colorado. The Detroit Tigers wanted him to try out. Let's just say that Zip could have gone to the top, to the limit, but something began to bother him when he played the Mexican kids from the barrio. They weren't getting the fair shake from life that Zip was. Zip tried to help them. Remember, this was the sixties and the world had developed a short fuse. Zip began to see a world bigger than baseball out there, a much bigger game."

"That's great, Billy, but is it true?" The sportswriter's voice had become humbler.

"Of course it's true, but there's a lot more. Turn the fucking Dictaphone back on." Billy continued with speculations on how neither the Mexican officials nor the American-owned sweatshops were interested in Zip's imprisonment. The word along the border was that the force behind the persecution was clandestine American officials, especially a low-grade bureaucrat named Virgil Atkins. America, not Mexico, was sentencing Zip to fifty years, a death sentence.

"Jesus, I can't use names. How do I end it? What do you want?"

"For every sports fan, for every one of your readers, to pick up their phones immediately and call their senators, congressmen and the President. We have to work fast. Tell them it's the ninth inning."

Patty and Gwen began laughing as they made dinner and Sam swept by them with the fresh load of drinks. Patty whispered that they should act as if they were in mourning. Gwen searched through her purse for a couple of tapes Sun had loaned her, then squeezed her eyes and thought of her favorite dog which had been run over in her childhood. Patty was amazed to see how readily Gwen made tears come to her eyes.

In the living room Gwen was introduced to the sportswriter as the soon-to-be widow. The sportswriter gave her a hug and said he would give the old college try to springing her hubby. Gwen let her tears flow freely on his lapel. Patty and Sam brought out two large platters of hot dogs, hamburgers and warmed-up pizza.

"Everything I never got to eat until I went to college," Billy explained with delight to the sportswriter as he walked him to the door.

A little later, while they were still eating and listening to Chuck Berry, Sam spread out a large city map of Nogales on both sides of the border, pointing out the locations of the federal building and the bypass used by the hundreds of produce semis. Now they were all very sober and exhausted.

"I was thinking about when we got those green and white Dexedrine spansules in San Francisco and danced for two days straight. Patty went off somewhere to try to meet Richard Brautigan, remember that?" Billy was half asleep in his reverie.

"He shot himself two years ago," Patty said. "I don't know why. I heard he drank too much." She couldn't help but glance at Sam.

"Why not is the point you have to work on. Look at Sam here. All he needs are coyotes." Gwen took one of three *jalapeños* Sam had in his glass of *mescal.*

"We are heroes of reduced expectations, aren't we? I've been keeping the world safe for business for twenty years." Billy got up as "Maybelline" came on, grabbed Gwen and began dancing. "But I was a bitching dancer, wasn't I?"

Never one to let up, Patty ignored Billy and Gwen, and zeroed in on Sam, asking how he kept in touch.

"I don't. I've stepped aside and let the whole shit monsoon go right on by me."

"That's what I mean. Everyone is out nature walking, jogging, climbing mountains, rafting rivers, perfecting their bodies. Nobody cares about blacks or Chicanos. You'd think they'd at least care about Native Americans, the Indians."

"But I'm only good at animals," Sam interrupted. "Your business can handle the rest."

"You motherfucker," Patty hissed, but her heart wasn't in it. She drew him to his feet and they danced to a slow blues number.

Just after daylight Sam and Gwen were at the Nogales Airport revving up the Cessna for a reconnaissance, which had become an acceptable word. Neither had been able to sleep after five A.M. when the phone had begun ringing with the appearance of the San Francisco morning edition. They were all drinking their bleary coffee when a call had come and Billy had said, "Good morning, Dad." Then a pause and: "I don't give a shit anymore, Dad. This is something I have to do." This had sent Patty back up to her room and Gwen and Sam off to the airport. Billy hung up on his father when the lawyer arrived to go to the hearing where they would petition for a stay of sentence. He had never hung up on his father before and on the way to the federal building he felt utterly unnerved by his own behavior.

When they were shown into the chambers by the bailiff the judge merely nodded at them and reburied his head in legal papers. This pleased Billy as it meant the judge had already received some highly placed phone calls in regard to the mess caused by the San Francisco paper. Also, the chambers were rather crummy, Billy thought, and the presence of so important a lawyer from Mexico City must have put the man on edge. Then the bailiff showed in Virgil Atkins and Billy couldn't help but say, "What the fuck's he doing here?"

The judge looked up and spoke, averting his eyes from both Billy and Virgil Atkins. "Mr. Atkins is from your embassy in Mexico City. He must attend to make sure Mr. Frazer is entitled to certain rights as an American citizen." Billy comprehended the intent if not the precise meaning of the judge's Spanish.

The bailiff explained that Zip had refused to leave his cell, claiming that the judge was a mere tool and running dog of the American oppressors. The judge laughed at this, saying he hadn't heard the expression "running dog" since his student days.

The hearing was informal but only the judge and lawyer were allowed to speak. The lawyer went through an involved litany of reasons to exonerate Zip, or at least lessen the charges to simple "lecturing in public without a permit." The lawyer's trump card was his announced intention to subpoena the soldiers, one of whom had stated that Zip had been supine and hadn't made any effort to attack the Federale or resist arrest. Both of the soldiers had also stated that an American had been present at Zip's capture. The judge interrupted to say that none of this was in the official records, and the lawyer responded by waving his sheaf of papers. The judge still refused to stay his intended sentence of fifty years, the announcement of which was a mere formality. If the lawyer wished to appeal there might be another hearing in several years, in that the courts were awash with serious drug cases. And that was that. The hearing was over.

Out in the hall Billy's ears burned as the lawyer explained that they would win, but it would probably take three to four years, just as it might in America with a "bought" or hanging judge. He had recently flown to Houston to help a wealthy Mexican youth who had been sentenced to a hundred years for possession of a pound of marijuana in his college dormitory room.

"Is he out on bond?" Billy asked.

"Of course," the lawyer said.

"Well Zip isn't, and he can't be, so your system sucks."

At this point Atkins caught up with them, having obviously tarried to speak to the judge. He was a bit breathless.

"I was telexed your sports column, Creighton. I see you're trying to play hardball. This is out of your league."

Billy stood there for a full minute wondering which way to go, then remembered his father's dictum that when you're at the summit of your anger, the most effective way to go is to act laconic and bored. He spoke in barely more than a whisper so that Virgil Atkins had to lean toward him.

"I'm not sure what league you're speaking of, Mr. Atkins. You'll find to your regret that you played the bully the other night. I had it on good authority this morning that your employer is pulling you back home like Pinocchio on a fucking string. Good luck in Newfoundland."

On the way to the car the lawyer asked if this was true and Billy said it might be, that in a job that demanded invisibility Atkins had lost his cool and gone public.

Gwen and Sam were at three thousand feet out over the stupefying San Raphael Valley south of the Huachuca Mountains forty miles east of Nogales, a location favored by John Ford. Sam pointed out the Green Cattle Company, a Spanish land-grant ranch which owned four hundred thousand acres along the border. North of there Sam located a smaller place on the map given him by the waiter and gardener, and Gwen nosed the Cessna down onto a grass strip. An old couple rushed out of a substantial ranch house and the four of them pushed the plane into a pole barn waiting with open doors. The old woman shook hands with them and laughed, saying that though they were Republicans they were also Christian and had been involved in the sanctuary movement for years. Her husband stood nervously beside a station wagon, waiting to take Sam and Gwen back to town.

Patty was sitting on the patio with a script in her lap chatting with the president of her studio on the phone. She had been watching the new gardener who wore a neck brace and seemed incompetent in that he merely repeated the same flower beds the other gardener had worked on the day before. He also looked like a mestizo rather than a campesino and was admirably muscled. When Billy returned from the hearing with the bad news Patty mentioned the gardener in the neck brace which disturbed Billy further. Sam had told him about the rope-and-scooter incident in the alley, but the two of them decided not to mention it to Gwen and Patty.

The no-longer-very-wild four were having a snack and getting ready to go visit Zip when Billy's father, William Creighton Sr., arrived with an aide-de-camp. To say this further exacerbated a depressed atmosphere is the most dainty of euphemisms. Patty, Gwen and Sam quickly passed him on the way out to the car. Rather than simply ignore them, Creighton Sr. pretended he didn't see them. He waved away the aide and looked around the room before fixing his eyes on his son.

"You're traveling nicely these days. I tried to get Rebecca to come along but she said for her to do so would be a cheap shot. There's no point in my insisting that you come back with me, is there?"

"No, sir. It's not looking very good and I have to hang in there."

"As you know, I could no longer deal with Mexican irrationality. Right now I'm interested in minimizing any damage to the firm you might be doing in politicizing on the home front. I have answered questions by saying you're trying to save a college friend's neck which has passed muster so far."

"I don't think I'm doing any irreparable damage. It's no longer the old-boy network unless you're a defense contractor." Billy had the temerity to glance at his watch. His father reddened then sighed.

"Of course I'm angry but that's beside the point. What can I do to get you out of this goddamned mess as quickly as possible?"

"I'm not in a goddamned mess. Zip is. Like the morning paper said, make a few phone calls. I'm sure you've got the call-through numbers. I'll leave here when I get him out."

"You won't settle for anything less?"

"No, sir. And it's not the rest of them, Dad. It's me. I'm running the show. It's my idea."

Creighton Sr. obviously wanted to shake his son's hand as a modest gesture, but the thought disturbed him. "Goodbye for now, Billy," he said, wheeling and walking out the front door. For some reason he waved and smiled at Gwen, Patty and Sam who were standing against the car waiting for Billy.

"How can you be our age and still let your friend's father intimidate you?" asked Patty of no one in particular.

It was to be the most confusing afternoon and evening of any in their lives except, perhaps, when they were arrested at the draft board in 1968. On the way to the federal building Sam had to take over the driving because Billy had suffered an apparent short circuit, sweating and shaking and mumbling. It was very disturbing to the rest of them, making them realize how much they had been depending on his almost flippant stability.

Their confusion redoubled when they saw that the normally busy street in front of the federal building was empty and had been cordoned off. They were readily waved through which reminded them how visible they were. The same Federale captain was near the door, barking at his men, some sort of storm trooper who gave the arriving four a look of withering contempt. Inside the front door Sam questioned a security man who had been friendly on their first visit. The man said there was to be a demonstration for "Señor Ted Frazer," also the people were very angry because Rudolfo had been murdered. Sam knew that Rudolfo was their gardener and one of the two men he had met with at the Blue Parrot, but when Gwen questioned him on what the security man said, Sam only shrugged.

They were escorted into the same visiting room and Zip could not have been more captious and irritating, alternately embracing and upbraiding them. He had heard, via the jail grapevine, that there was to be a demonstration in his honor which gave him a manic and inappropriate sense of his own power. This contrasted with his weeping over Rudolfo whom he had known for a decade and was very important in the "movement." Rudolfo had been in the Oriente province with Castro, and had escaped the jungles of Bolivia when his friend Che Guevara was murdered. This information made the four a little concerned about who they were dealing with, as if their collective reality had become exponentially distorted.

Billy made a vain attempt to bring Zip back to earth by telling him it might be three years before their appeal was successful. It didn't work. Instead, Zip's craziness was drawing Billy ineluctably into itself, so that Billy's movements around the room were birdlike rather than decisive as he tried to follow what Zip was saying. Patty, Gwen and Sam were powerless and stiff in their chairs. Zip said that you were allowed to make love in Mexican jails but he didn't feel up to it today, then he made a series of inane puns on the idea of being "purged" by his own country. He almost calmed the room and himself down by making a little speech on how he had failed to become great. Gwen had heard the speech before and went to Zip to console him which caused Zip to shoot off on another bughouse tangent. It was Billy's howl, finally, that cleared the air.

"I have to ask your forgiveness. I have to confess something . . . so listen." It was curious because everyone knew what he wanted to confess and didn't want to hear it, but Billy didn't know they knew.

Zip embraced Billy who was mouthing words that couldn't be heard. "Nonsense," Zip said. "I don't want to hear it and besides I know everything. You came down here and we're brothers again, aren't we? That's what's important."

Rather than Gwen or Patty, Sam began crying at this point. Then Gwen and Patty tried to comfort Sam, but were interrupted by the guard who said the prisoner had to be put away because of the demonstration. Zip was quickly led off and the rest of them were guided out to the office area which was noisy from the streets below. The guard told them they would have to stay until the demonstration was over. The atmosphere was more than a little festive with clerks and guards hanging out the windows waving to those below. Sam took a pair of binoculars from a desk top and scanned the crowd, focusing on the captain of the Federales, Virgil Atkins and the American in the neck brace who were standing together in the doorway of a store. Sam called Billy over but Billy was nearly comatose and was being tended and consoled by Gwen. Patty stood alone in the corner, frozen with anxiety.

The bailiff from the judge's office rushed in and gestured at Billy to come along, then in a stream of Spanish tried to explain himself. Sam came up and told Billy he had to go meet with the judge. Gwen and Sam tried to accompany Billy but were pushed back rudely by the bailiff.

It was the kind of meeting in the judge's chambers that none of those attending felt comfortable with for even a second. The judge sat at the head of a conference table, looking out over the waiter, Jorge the fruit-and-vegetable tycoon, the lawyer, Billy and a fresh spook who ineptly tried to "get the ball rolling." The new spook's name was Michael Straithwaite, and he spoke with a Virginian accent, explaining he was replacing Virgil Atkins who was being reassigned. He went on to say that the current situation was being misrepresented by the press and knee-jerk liberals . . .

Curiously enough, no one else at the table paid any attention to Straithwaite. Billy was still confused and the lawyer whispered that he had been ready to take a plane but something had happened in Mexico City. Then a truly nasty quarrel started between the waiter and Jorge, who had a hundred trucks tied up by pickets at the bypass. Jorge said if a single tomato rotted he would tear the heart out of the waiter. The judge tried to quiet them with a string of inanities about the gravity of the situation.

"Fuck your situation, Ernesto," Jorge yelled at the judge. "You have always had this problem that you want to go to bed with the Americans and still wake up a Mexican. What are the fucking Americans paying you?"

Straithwaite leapt to his feet to say he resented the insinuation, having comprehended the Spanish. Billy, who was coming alive, accurately deduced that Straithwaite was a spook of a much higher order than Virgil Atkins. The judge gaveled the table senseless and announced that Mr. Theodore Frazer was a piece of Yankee vermin who was to be banished forever from Mexico, on pain of the immediate resumption of the fifty-year sentence. There would also be a fine and court costs of fifty thousand dollars, at which point everyone glanced at Billy. Billy numbly gave the thumbs-up sign. The lawyer asked when the prisoner could be taken across the border and the judge said after a day or two of paperwork. Straithwaite rushed off, presumably to a phone, after he said that he was happy that a difficult situation had been resolved. When the lawyer led Billy off down the hall Billy was stunned enough not to notice that Jorge and the waiter were chatting amiably.

It would have been wonderful if the whole thing had ended right there, but it didn't. It almost never does except in the sporting contests. Maybe that's why they're so popular.

By the time the four of them arrived home in mid-afternoon they felt peeled like the many peeled throats of Cerberus, and not quite in the mood to celebrate. They mostly sat around in their separate silences trying to believe they had won. Sam made an enormous pitcher of margaritas but the ice had melted before more than a few inches were gone. There were a lot of calls from journalists until Billy unplugged the phone, then replugged it to give Rebecca and his dad the good news. Gwen called Sun, and Patty and Sam sort of wished they had someone to call. They ordered a dinner to be delivered but it stayed in paper bags on the table. They filtered in and out of the showers and tried to get interested in television. They listened to *A Prairie Home Companion* on the radio but it seemed too remote and innocent. Patricia found a station that was featuring a tribute to Miles Davis, and that music seemed to fit the mood.

The only serious discussion of the evening was brought about by Sam's attempts to get the rest of them to leave for home the first thing in the morning. He felt and said that he was best suited to be Zip's escort back to America and wherever he wanted to go. Perhaps he would take Zip to the mountains to cool him off and build up his health. Sam's real reason was his view of life as a grave and terrifying approximation. In short, he expected something could go wrong and knew that it could better be handled by someone working solo.

But no one agreed. "Man is nostalgia and a search for communion," or so said Octavio Paz of *Labyrinth* fame. There was a natural impulse after all they had been through to want to stay around for the good part.

Meanwhile, at a hotel in Nogales, Sonora, that looked shabby on the outside but offered pleasant accommodations, a meeting was taking place. Virgil Atkins is having a drink or two while Michael Straithwaite, in a Haspel drip-dry suit, is admiring his own cordovans and drinking bottled water. Straithwaite tries to console Atkins using the metaphor of a game, "Win some, lose some," which works with most men in a state of extreme disappointment. But not Atkins who recites all the ways and places he's tried to nail Zip over the years, only to lose him again, plus all the government money it took to arrange the fifty-year sentence.

"Washington says to let it go and move on." Straithwaite is bored by Atkins's whining and is on the verge of telling him he blew it.

"I didn't hear you say that. As far as I'm concerned Frazer's still on the list."

There's a noise at the door and Atkins lets in the American in the neck brace and the captain of the Federales. Straithwaite stands and nods at Atkins. "Virge, I didn't see these guys. Good luck."

When Straithwaite left he felt a certain tightness in his ass that made him want to propel himself across the border to America. If the room was bugged, he had covered his tracks.

The linen closet Straithwaite passed in the hall held a diminutive Mexican bellhop with a listening device and a tape recorder. The conversation between Atkins, the captain and the American was disturbing indeed. The bellhop waited un-

til they were safely off to dinner, then left in search of his
leader, the waiter, who in turn made his way to the judge's
house and replayed the tape.

The visit of the judge and waiter to the villa confirmed Sam's
grim intuition but pushed Gwen, Patty and Billy toward the
lip of hysteria. It wasn't the fact that Atkins and the American
had said they knew where the Cessna was stored but that the
American argued for letting them get airborne before blowing
the plane to pieces with three AK-47s, destroying the evidence. The captain agreed and Atkins said nothing. The captain also stated that he was sure it would be at least two days
before Zip was released because the judge was going to Tucson to play golf with a cousin the following day.

   In the discussion that ensued the judge pointed out it would
be impossible to get the authorities to arrest an American spy
and a captain of the Federales. The waiter nodded and said
he had somewhat anticipated the problem. Could the prisoner be released to Sam at five A.M. the following morning?
The judge agreed and left the house. Billy asked the waiter
if the judge could be trusted. The waiter said yes, because
the judge hated the captain who had intercepted a narcotics
bribe due the judge. Also the judge's career would be finished if Zip was murdered. The waiter's plan was extremely
simple, in fact, using the well-traveled and successful route
he had established for the sanctuary refugees from Central
America.

Up in their bedroom Sam quickly checked the shotgun and
pistol while Patty was still in the bathroom, not wanting to
offend her. He loaded both, turned and found her standing at
the door in the kind of nightgown that made him smile. She
didn't want to be obviously upset so she ignored the guns.

What she wanted to know was if he was going to come see her when it was all over. He thought it was a better idea if she came to see him as he had been noticeably unsuccessful in terms of booze when he visited cities.

"Is that an actual invitation?"

"Of course. We're just getting to know each other. Maybe we're lucky we like each other. Most people don't." Now he was beginning to blush, a trait she had always found endearing.

"Remember when I used to make you sing a song if you wanted to sleep with me?" She sat on his lap but the feeling was more melancholy than erotic.

"I don't remember any lyrics but I could make some up," he said.

Billy paces in his room in his pajama bottoms, sweating and watching a ball game on ESPN. The set is small, black-and-white, and the sound is off. Billy has the feeling that the outside world is just like that. He looks up at the wall at a primitive eighteenth-century crucifix. He lights a cigarette and begins to genuflect but recovers his senses. He opens the door and looks out into the dark hallway and at a yellow slice of light coming from Gwen's door. She enters the light and opens the door, wearing the kind of old robe that no one wears if they intend to sleep with someone else.

"Do you want me to come over there?" she asks.

Yeah. Come on over. We'll tell jokes." His voice cracks down into a whisper.

In his room she sits on the edge of the bed as he continues to sweat and pace. He turns off the TV and abruptly turns it back on. He can almost hear the noises in his head, and the anguish is palpable.

"I don't look very sexy, do I?" she asks.

"You look wonderful . . ." Then he begins to speak in a

maddening rush, continuing the confession he had tried to make to Zip and all of them that morning. He says Sarah overheard us and called my dad who convinced me we were wrong and we talked to the FBI in Denver. They said go through with it, and soon.

But Gwen stops him. She says she had always known because Zip asked her to make love to a policeman to find out. Billy sits down beside her but can't stop weeping at first, and when he does, their embrace becomes that of a disconsolate brother and sister.

Just before daylight Sam trotted across the patio, scaled the wall and got into the back of a waiting flat rack truck full of muskmelons. The truck pulled away as he drew the tarp over him. The truck made its way over the border to an alley behind the federal building where Zip stood with two security men and the very nervous judge. The security men boosted Zip up into the truck with Sam pulling at the other end. Zip's breath hissed through his teeth from the pain of his back injury.

The truck continued east, gaining elevation into the relatively peopleless area of large, arid *fincas*. Then it was on a narrow mountain road, among canyons and pines, the home of mountain lions and coyotes, driving into the rising sun. The truck pulled laboriously off onto a two-track for a hundred yards. The waiter emerges from a thicket leading two horses as Sam and the driver help Zip to the ground. Sam pulls his dop kit from his pack and gives Zip a pain pill. The waiter points off to the north and down the mountain to the San Raphael Valley in the distance. Sam embraces the waiter and he and Zip mount their horses and they are off on the slow decline through the forest.

*

It was still barely light when Billy, Gwen and Patty loaded their Hertz car and were off through Nogales to Route 89 which ran north to Tucson, seventy miles distant. It was their very bad luck that the captain had drunk a great deal the night before with Atkins and the American, and was just emerging from a diner and a restorative bowl of *menudo*. Now he would read the paper and go back to bed. As he got into his car he looked up and saw Billy driving past with the two women. The captain followed, and patched through on the radio to Atkins's room where the American answered. The American said it had to be a decoy and told the captain to meet him on a plateau a few miles behind the village of Patagonia.

Only, Gwen and Patty went through the charade of driving to the Tucson Airport, turning into the Hertz office, going in the terminal and renting an Avis. Then they headed back south toward Patagonia and the narrow blacktop that led to the San Raphael Valley.

By the time the captain drove up the narrow dirt road south of Patagonia the American was already there with a helicopter he had borrowed from the DEA. The American looked fresh as a daisy, and had set up a spotting scope to scan the road miles below them. The American checked out the captain on the use of the AK-47 which the captain resented even though he was unfamiliar with the weapon.

"How can you be so sure?" the captain asked, adjusting the spotting scope. The American had predicted that Billy and the two women would appear on the valley road within an hour and a half.

"Look at it this way. It's our only option and the probability is high that it's their only option."

*

Sam and Zip had crossed the border and were resting in a clump of greasewood and cholla. Sam glassed the old couple's ranch, relieved that they had gone and everything looked good. When he had called after the waiter left the night before, the old woman had said, "God bless you," and he had said, "I hope so." Zip sat on the ground, his senses dulled by the Percodan, but he was smiling. They remounted and headed for the ranch.

The American was looking through the scope and said, "There they are." The captain took a quick look and said it was a different car, which drew a contemptuous look from the American who stowed a .270 Weatherby beside the AK-47s.

"I want the plane at least fifty feet off the ground. Correct?"

"Correct," said the captain.

Sam helps Zip down from the horse and leads him into the pole barn beside Gwen's Cessna where he slumps, asleep against the wall. Sam permits himself a smile, walks back outside, slapping the horses on the ass and sending them back to Mexico. Sam looks off to the north and sees Billy's car approaching, followed by a brown cloud of dust.

Billy, Gwen and Patty rush to help Sam push the Cessna out of the pole barn. They look at each other and then at Zip in a state of profound foolishness.

"We fucked up. There's not enough room," Sam says.

"We can make it without the luggage." Gwen starts the engine and Billy and Sam load Zip into the back with Patty, bow to each other until Sam starts to push Billy into the plane. It is then that Sam hears the sound that so hideously dominated three years of his life. The chopper is sweeping along the ground toward the back of the ranch house — "on the deck," they call it. Sam yells, "Get out of here," and grabs his alley sweeper but Gwen is paralyzed at the controls. Sam runs toward the landed chopper and blows the captain sprawling as he jumps out. The American calmly sights through the scope of his .270 and fires a shot into Sam's knee. Sam drops the shotgun and clutches his knee, crawling in a circle.

Billy runs openly to Sam and drags him back to the plane as if the American didn't exist. The American ignores them as he calmly sets up two of the AK-47s on tripods.

"What the fuck is he doing?" Billy screams as he loads Sam into the plane.

"He's waiting until we're airborne." Sam hands the pistol to Billy as Gwen tries to stanch Sam's bleeding with her scarf.

"I don't know how to work this." Billy holds the pistol down and Sam reaches out and flicks the safety. Billy fires a shot into the ground and looks up at them. "Please go. We shouldn't all die. I'll see you or not. Please."

The plane begins to taxi as Billy sprints around the back of the barn, eyeing the American from the corner as the American tries to keep track of both Billy and the plane. Then Billy runs out and gets one shot off before the AK-47 blows him along the ground like a wind-driven leaf. The American's hands try to pretend he is fine as they swivel the rifle back toward the plane lifting off in the distance. Then the hands lift toward the blood gouting from the wound in the American's throat.

It is too much for us to presume, in that no one has reliably returned from death, but the winter sparrows that fluttered back into the yard now that the excitement had passed might have thought, if sparrows indeed thought, that there was a trace of a smile on Billy's face.

The Woman Lit
by Fireflies

SHE HAD NOT yet accepted as real the quiver in her stomach and the slight green dot of pain in the middle of her head that signaled an incipient migraine. Her husband on the car seat beside her punched in a tape called *Tracking the Blues* which contained no black music, but rather the witless drone of a weekly financial lecture sent from New York City. This particular tape was seven days stale and had been played three times on their trip, but Donald repeated it to get "fair value" for his money. The tape, not incidentally, replaced Stravinsky's *Histoire du Soldat* from an Iowa City FM station, a piece she always enjoyed.

"Do you mind, darling?" he asked.

"Not at all, dear," she replied, partly because the pain clinic she had attended in Arizona that spring had emphasized giving up resistance to outside phenomena at the possible onset of a migraine under the notion you wanted to starve rather than feed the affliction. For instance, she shouldn't have been driving — sitting with her eyes closed listening to music would have been helpful, but she drove to avoid reading to him, which is what he required when he drove. An additional, insurmountable problem was that his car, an Audi 5000, was low-slung and the early August corn beside Interstate 80 in Iowa presented itself as a dense green wall. She preferred the higher vantage of her own nine-year-old Toyota Land Cruiser, a functional clumsy old machine that she and her beloved friend Zilpha used on their outings, or so they called them, which were somewhat famous in their neighborhood in Bloomfield Hills, a suburb of Detroit.

Clare would be fifty in another week, Donald was fifty-one and eager to get on with life, a matter about which she had mixed feelings. They had just been visiting their daughter Laurel, who at twenty-nine was a veterinarian married to a veterinarian, the both of them ministering to horses and cattle in a clinic outside of Sioux City, Iowa, up near the Nebraska border. The visit had been cut short two days by a quarrel between Laurel and Donald. On the way home they were to spend the weekend with Donald Jr., who at twenty-seven was a commodities market whiz in Chicago.

"I love you, Mom, but I can't understand why you don't leave that asshole," Laurel had said.

"Please, Laurel, he's your father."

"In name only," she had replied, and then they kissed goodbye as they always did, with Clare's heart giving a breathless wrench at separation.

A specific giddiness began to overtake her when she thought of the goodbye. *This is the way, after all, I've spent my life,* she thought. You could not fault Donald for being Donald, any more than you could fault Laurel for being the same as she was at three years, a cantankerous little girl with a sure though general sense of mission, a personality so specific as to be sometimes offensive.

"The overloaded leverages are coming home to roost," Donald brayed so loud she applied the brakes. She quickly reset the cruise control at a modest seventy considering that most cars passed her at that speed. The week before at the club she attempted a witticism about how all the lives saved by the Mothers Against Drunk Driving were being lost to the raising of the speed limit. The luncheon ladies were used to Clare and let the quip pass, but not a new member who found it "dreadfully morbid." Suddenly it occurred to her that Donald didn't feel really good about making money unless others were losing theirs, which made it all, to her mind, a silly game to spend your life on rather than the grave process with which he was totally obsessed.

An ever so slight tremor of head pain made her dismiss the thought about Donald and money as true but banal. She forced her thoughts back to a pleasant morning with Laurel, spent hiking on some bluffs above the Missouri River. Laurel had discovered a rattlesnake that had difficulty getting out of their way because of a huge lump in its belly — no doubt, Laurel said, from swallowing a gopher. They both laughed when Laurel added, "Poor thing, also poor gopher." The laughter was nervous relief. The first hour of their walk had been spent lifting Clare's confusion over a pamphlet an anti-vivisectionist neighbor had given her concerning a doctor down south who, on a defense contract, had shot several thousand cats in the head for research. Laurel habitually defended the scientific community but this one puzzled her, as the brain of a cat was dissimilar enough to that of a human as to make the research appear useless. She did not tell Clare that it would have made more sense to shoot several thousand dogs, or better yet chimpanzees, though the latter were very expensive. The purpose of the research, of course, was to better treat head wounds in soldiers. Then Clare had brought up another item that she had brooded about for two years without mentioning. Laurel had sent her an article from *Orion Nature Quarterly*, by a Spanish fellow, Lopez, called "The Passing Wisdom of Birds," in which the author described Cortez's vengeful burning of the aviaries in Mexico City in the sixteenth century. Clare loved birds and cats and could easily overlook the fact that Cortez had destroyed the city and murdered hundreds of thousands of citizens — that was to be expected — but the burning of Montezuma's aviaries seemed to stand for something far more grotesque and the image of the conflagration passed through her mind daily. So she had asked Laurel, a scant fifteen minutes before they saw the gorged rattlesnake, why she had sent the article, and Laurel had said, "People who love each other try to explain themselves to each other. I wanted you to see again why I work with animals. I can't stand people. Now it's your turn to explain yourself to me." That, as they say, was that, until the poor snake appeared as a convenience, almost a stage prop if it weren't for the immensity of the sky above and the wide, brown Missouri River below them.

Back on Interstate 80 she wondered why they bothered teaching us the things they did — the grandeur, sweep and intricacies of civilization at its best — when there was little enough to do with the knowledge. Clare's criticisms of the human condition were sharp but basically mid-range and items like Cortez and the birds shifted her off balance as did, to a lesser degree, the three thousand holes in the heads of three thousand cats. Now she tried to reduce the growing pain by an act of will, dimming the fluttery green energy to a pinpoint if only for a moment as she had been taught to do in Arizona. There was a sign for a rest stop in ten miles and it was 2:50

which meant she would beat the phone call by a minute. The tape about blue chip stocks had mercifully finished but now Donald was whistling "The Colonel Bogey March" and tapping out the rhythm on the cellular car phone, anticipatory to his daily broker call. His lips pursed and the whistling and tapping stopped as he made a notation in red pencil on the day's *Wall Street Journal*.

"I'm going to have to stop while you phone. I'm not feeling all that well," she said, stiffening at his possible reaction.

"Fine, honey. We've got time to kill." Donald glanced at his watch. "There's room for your nappy in Davenport."

She never understood quite how "nap" became "nappy" but had always judged an inquiry as not quite worthwhile. She looked at him with a longing close to homesickness that the troubled at heart feel for those who treat the world as their lovely private apple. Donald was a passably good man, or so everyone thought, a citizen so apparently solid that, as a club jokester had said, he could throw a successful fund raiser for a crack dealer. A business associate had organized a dinner for ten at a hotel in Davenport, which Donald looked forward to as an orphan would his first circus. He was being especially tender because Clare was the daughter of one of the founding partners of the accounting firm which had branches throughout the Midwest, and the Davenport office was doing especially well. The Davenport people would be thrilled to meet Clare. It would be all bows by the men and curtsies by the ladies. He had even alerted them about Clare's taste in wine which he thought a wasteful vice she had inherited from her mother. Frequently, he noted, the wine on a dinner bill equaled the price of the food, and when he picked up a case of Meursault or Chambertin at the wine store he liked to joke out loud: "Here goes three shares of General Motors." The old clerk at the wine store invariably smiled his mask of a smile knowing it was Clare's money in the first place, a point which would appall Clare herself in that she was so fair-minded as to be frequently rendered immobile.

But not now. She eased the car into the rest stop, slowing to a creep for fear of hitting the children darting in and out of campers and cars in the crowded parking area. Across a green swath semis were parked with the muffled drone of their engines at rest only at destinations. One of the semis held squealing pigs in metal-slatted layers while another was full of silent cattle. Clare got out, taking the leather and canvas Buitoni bag Donald had bought her on their trip to Florence. At the time she could not believe his brusque affability translated so well. They had dined nearly every evening with Italians he had met in his tours of brokerage offices, several times in their homes, allowing Clare a look into the life of Florence never allowed the ordinary tourist. Donald waved at her with the other hand on the phone, antsy to make his daily call. She watched him dial, then walked toward the Iowa Welcome Center and the adjoining bathrooms, her head beginning to thrum in the noisy heat. It occurred to her that the tourists all looked blowzy and fatigued because they were headed back east at the end of their vacations.

When she thought about it later Clare was surprised again by how clear and cool her painful mind had felt. Every human and object, the landscape itself, had the distinct outlines found in a coloring book before the crayons are applied. The green wall of the cornfield behind the Welcome Center became luminous and of surpassing loveliness. She turned and walked back toward Donald in the car but he was in his brokerage trance, his clipped business voice saying, "But what the hell happened to Isomet?"

In the bathroom stall she checked her bag for certain items: Donald Jr.'s Boy Scout compass she used on hikes with Zilpha, a small can of cranberry juice, the addresses of three orphan children she wrote to and helped support in Santo Domingo, Mexico and Costa Rica; in a leather packet was her passport and a copy of the new translation of the *Tao Te Ching* given to her by a counselor at the pain clinic, and at the bottom, and most important, was the tan beret she had bought thirty years before on Rue St.-Jacques and had never worn. As a comparative literature senior at Michigan State she was to spend a year studying in Paris which lasted only three weeks when her father died and the family sent her boyfriend Donald to fetch her home. At the time Donald was her act of rebellion, a left-wing political science major who wore lumberjack shirts, the only son in a working-class family from Flint, who intended to be a writer or labor leader. On dates they read John Dos Passos's *U.S.A.* trilogy aloud to each other. Curiously her father had rather liked Donald, and perhaps this was foresight into the man Donald would become. So each morning for three weeks in her tiny *pension* Clare would look at her beret but was too timid to put it on.

Now in the toilet stall she finally put on the beret and laughed softly to herself. It was so easy. For luck she also slipped on a conch pearl ring Zilpha had given her in March as a remembrance. Among her last words had been "We never got around to the Amazon," a trip they had planned since they were girls when they were convinced they'd discover a pleasanter civilization somewhere in the jungle. Clare took out a Cafergot pill, then put it back, preferring pain-ridden consciousness. She tried to remember something René Char had written, "Blank blank blank the legitimate fruits of daring," but the growing pain blinded her memory. The note itself was simple enough: "I am in a small red car driving east. My husband has been abusing me. Do not believe anything he says. Call my daughter." She added Laurel's number, wrote "To The Police" on the envelope and stuck it to the side of the stall with a postage stamp. She noted that someone had scratched "Bob is cute" with a sharp object on the paint and she smiled with the confusion of female and male.

Behind the Welcome Center a small boy walking the family dog held Clare's bag as she climbed the fence which was more difficult than she anticipated. She wobbled and the wire cut into the soles of her tennis shoes. On the other side she lost a few moments explaining to the boy why he couldn't go along, but then the dog started barking and she hurried off down between two corn rows, toward the interior, wherever that might be.

Within a scant five minutes Clare would have liked to turn around, had turning around not already become so improbable. A hundred yards into the cornfield the beret made her feel silly so she took it off and stuffed it into her bag. The moment the hat came off the pain became so excruciating she fell to her hands and knees and retched up her lunch of iced tea and a club sandwich. The pain was such that she could not balance herself on her hands and knees, but pushed her legs backward until she lay on her stomach. She closed her eyes a moment but the world became bright red and whirling. There was the slightest memory of a pain lesson but it was too abstract to be of much use: the secret was to maintain your equilibrium in the face of incomprehension, as pain, finally, could not be understood.

At eye level she looked at the way the roots of the corn broke up the earth. She tried to let go of her brain which it

now seemed would boil over with its brew of knots and hack-
ings, clots, soft lumps against sharp hot stones. She rolled
over onto her back. By the time the sun made its way down
through the tassels, leaves and stalks, it was weak and liquid.
There was a crow call so close it startled her, the bird flapping
low over her row, then twisting, darting back for another look,
squawking loudly in warning at the intruder, then a third pass
up the row out of curiosity. She had never been so close to a
crow, she thought, and tried closing her eyes a moment to
rehearse crows from the past. The red storm had somewhat
subsided and she saw the open mouth of a rooster at her
grandmother's, and herself as a child stooping near the rooster as he swelled his throat, craned his neck outward and
crowed as if he could not stop himself. As a child she had liked
cellars because they frightened her, and now she longed for a
cool, black cellar with a rooster for company, for her grandmother's dog whom the rooster pretended to chase though he
kept a safe distance, as if he and the dog had agreed upon a
reasonable pace for the dog to walk away. Grandfather told
her that the rooster felt the whole world was after his hens,
and that was all he thought about.

Now she heard a siren, but only gradually understood the
sound, from back toward the rest stop. She scrambled to her
feet and they moved off quickly down the row as if informed
by their own panic. The siren became louder, then stopped
abruptly. She continued to run, holding her hands and the
bag up against the slapping of the leaves. There was an image
of Donald explaining himself to the police, who she hoped
would call Laurel despite Donald's usual cagey aplomb. But
then Donald passed away with her breathlessness and her flayed
brain began to play the rest of the Stravinsky Donald had
truncated, then she tripped on a clod of earth and fell sprawl-

ing in a bare row where the corn turned direction. Now she was far enough from Route 80 so that she no longer could hear the trucks, only the crows, as the one had become five, and she twisted her neck for a look as they passed over, apparently discussing her. Perhaps the police could see the birds far out in the cornfield and guess that she was there, but she hoped they would believe the "small red car driving east." The sun was warm in the narrow clearing and she moved her upper body into the shade. She drew out the cranberry juice, drank it, then looked at the Boy Scout compass, deciding to head west along the wider row after a rest. She curled up, noting the earth smelled like a damp board after rain, then more heat. She looked at a dirty hand and thought idly with a smile, despite the pain, that for the first time in her life she did not know where her next shower was coming from.

Clare slept for a few minutes but was startled awake by her first dream in several months. She was a girl again, out in her rowboat on Burt Lake, and Dr. Roth was on the dock calling out and asking her why she had died. That was all there was to the dream and then she awoke. The pain had localized toward the right side of her head and within it Dr. Roth continued to call after she woke up. Clare was difficult to push off balance and ignored the phenomenon which was not unlike certain other symptoms of classic migraines. Besides, she liked Dr. Roth very much; he was not only her doctor and confidant, up to a point, but also had been Zilpha's doctor. Dreams are no respecter of time and Dr. Roth couldn't have been more than a child when Clare was a girl in a rowboat. She turned over and thought, at the very least, she had her first dream since Zilpha died, and then two weeks later when Clare's dog died her sleep had become even blacker. The dream wasn't ominous to Clare: death simply didn't hold her interest, but there was the nagging angle of Dr. Roth who Clare at the very moment realized she had been in love with for a brief period.

This recognition jolted her to her feet and she continued to head west, wondering if "maize" and "maze" were somehow connected. She normally walked a great deal because she was essentially claustrophobic and walking made the world appear larger. The fact that the field offered no variation was moot. Dr. Roth's lighthearted question meant something different to her than might appear. Once, when they had a drink after a library board meeting, he had said that most of his patients were already dead, and life herself was merely a technicality that allowed them to get up in the morning to collect a paycheck. They shared this sort of acerbic wit that made them both somewhat mistrusted in what are known as the better circles. The characteristic was harder on Dr. Roth than on Clare because this sharp wit, added to his slowness to write unnecessary prescriptions, limited his practice to those who desired honesty in medicine.

But on another evening after another library board meeting, when they had had to deal with a group of evangelical nitwits who wanted *The Catcher in the Rye* and *Slaughterhouse Five* banned from public consumption, Dr. Roth had looked up from his melancholy brandy and said, "You should be careful. You've lived your life with the kind of will that could later cause a lot of problems."

"I know it," she had said. But she didn't know it; the statement only brought forth the familiar feeling of an unpleasant truth.

That was half a year ago and the morning after, when she heard Donald pull out of the driveway she began to weep, an act so strange to her she couldn't pinpoint the event that had made her weep before. A few weeks later both Zilpha and Clare's dog had been diagnosed, Zilpha with lung and the dog with fibroid cancer.

Down toward the end of the row the greenness narrowed and blurred, and then there seemed to be a line of taller greenery. Her pace quickened in wan hope for a change of view, but she slowed down as the pain redeveloped with the swiftness of pace, though luckily enough the pain had moved to the left side of the head where it was more confinable. On the left side Clare could reduce the pain to a diffuse green light, then work consciously on reducing the dimensions of the light. The only side effect was that her sense of time became utterly jumbled, which was vertiginous but preferable to the pain. During one of these seizures, and at this particular state, the best she could do was to remember to feed the dog. Out in the field all that was required was to walk a straight line.

In fact, she thought she was moving within the heart of time. Normally she stood aside and lived on her comments to herself on what was happening to her, but when the pain moved to the left she moved inside herself, and this had the virtue of being novel within the framework of suffering. The pain was always a moment behind her as if she stood on the platform of a caboose watching the world go away. There was a sudden impulse to pray but she found the act embarrassing because, of course, she could *see* herself praying. As a child up near Petoskey on summer vacation her parents had allowed her to go to Daily Vacation Bible School with the maid's daughter. The maid was a mixed-blood Chippewa but her religion was Evangelical. Clare's parents had once discovered their daughter out in the garage praying over a three-legged cat that lived in the neighborhood. This was viewed as highly amusing and became part of a repertoire of "Clare stories" her parents shared with their friends during the rites of the martini hour. Now, to her surprise, this made Clare angry. What was the point of being angry at her parents for something that happened forty years ago, but then what was so funny about a child pray ing for a three-legged cat? In defiance she dropped to her knees but couldn't think of anything to say so got up again. Dr. Roth should see her now. He liked to think that, all efforts of the glitz media to the contrary, life is Dickensian, and that pathos is invariably the morning's leading news item. Clare with dusty knees and a verbless prayer would, no doubt, amuse him.

It had taken Dr. Roth several years to set Clare straight over the fact that Donald was an anti-Semite, albeit a quiet one. Clare had invited Dr. Roth and his wife to a large dinner party and late in a rather boozy evening Dr. Roth had made an acid but very funny comment about Richard Nixon which everyone had laughed at but Donald, to whom Nixon was an object of reverence. "Golly, but you guys can be smartasses," Donald had said, and the table had become so quiet that Zilpha had plunged courageously ahead with a lame joke. When everyone left Clare was instantly furious, partly at herself for letting the first incident pass. Years before, they had been visiting friends in Palm Beach with the real purpose of the trip being to pick up the dog from other friends. They had all eaten dinner at the Everglades Club and their host had proudly announced that the club was off limits to Jews. Clare had merely said that she found the fact odd just twenty-five years after World War II and let it drop, though the comment put everyone on edge. Before bedtime Donald had said something critical about her dinner behavior, admitting quite pompously that he agreed with the club policy. She had only looked at him and said, "I see." Next morning the joy of picking up the yellow Labrador, who was being given away for littering the pristine lawn with stray coconuts and palm fronds, made her overlook the issue.

Curiously, Dr. Roth was remote and analytical on the subject of anti-Semitism. He had grown up in Ann Arbor in a sheltered academic family, and after medical school had married a Jewish girl from Memphis whose family had been in the country from well before the Civil War. His experience was limited to a number of minor incidents similar to the one with Donald. He tried to tease his way out of Clare's questions by saying that being Jewish couldn't be as bad as being a manic depressive or a woman, and his wife was all three. When Clare insisted, he finally admitted that his own Jewish experience could be likened to her acute migraine, not in the degree of pain but in the utter uncertainty of when something unpleasant was going to occur. The incident could be a small item in the paper, say an inept political statement, or the recent suicide of one of his favorite authors, Primo Levi. The condition of being Jewish bred a perpetual wariness shared by all minorities, and the wariness tended to become an irksome cliché in life unless one was careful. The true burden of awareness had been carried by his parents' generation where the threat was all too specific.

One late afternoon over drinks he said something that disturbed Clare, to the effect that they shared an economic condition that was out of sync, and definitely out of sympathy with ninety-nine point ninety-nine percent of the rest of the world, and they had to walk an extremely narrow line not to die from being rich freaks. He asked how Clare and Donald got their home and she said it had been a wedding gift from her mother. Dr. Roth said his own home had come from his father-in-law on the same occasion, and when had either of them given more than nominal consideration to the purchase of anything — food, clothing, wine, books, cars, vacations? He said he would have gone mad long ago without the single day a week he spent as a volunteer at Detroit Receiving, a hospital that serviced the black ghetto and the poorest whites. Then he noticed a hurt look quickly pass across her face before she could conceal it.

"What about me?" she said.

"Oh, your reading in unpleasant areas and your migraines keep the tips of your toes in the real world."

"That's not very much, is it?"

"It's usually enough. Our sort doesn't need a great deal of consciousness to get by. Most often sending a check will do."

"I'm not leaving this shitheel fern bar on that sour note." She signaled the waiter for another glass of wine. Clare swore on the order of once a year. "This can't be another monkey occasion." She was referring to a benefit ball they had attended, the purpose of which was to raise money for new accommodations for the chimpanzees at the Detroit Zoo. Donald was in Atlanta for a few days and Dr. Roth's wife had entered a manic shopping phase that could best be resolved in New York City. Zilpha had only recently died and Dr. Roth thought it important for Clare to get out of the house. Unfortunately they were seated at a table with two self-important General Motors executives whose wives ignored everyone, and an exhausted neurosurgeon whose wife obviously wanted to be at a zippier table. Despite a normal aversion for talking shop in front of laymen, Dr. Roth and the neurosurgeon began some heavy-hearted joking on the effects of crack cocaine on the nervous system of newborn infants, the neurosurgeon's punch line forcing everyone to drink hard and fast.

"We're going to have to look at Detroit as a vast rookery for psychotics," the man said.

"What's a rookery?" a GM wife asked.

"A breeding ground. Our dominant product is psychosis. It's moved ahead of automobiles."

"That doesn't speak well for the future of the work force," an executive huffed.

"Not unless you're producing worker-tested automatic rifles," Dr. Roth quipped.

That evening had been effectively deadened and in the shitheel fern bar they tried to work themselves out of the hole that they had dug.

"I'm tired. Can't you look in your catalogue of piths and gists?" Dr. Roth was referring to a ledger Clare had started at the university and continued to the present where she recorded passages of literature she cherished. Dr. Roth had been amazed at Clare's ledger, the range was boggling, all recorded in a neat, almost lapidary script, from Aeschylus down to E. M. Cioran, with a preponderance coming from the early modernist period in world literature from 1880 to 1920. Her intended but never finished senior honors thesis was to be on Apollinaire and there were many translated quotes, but her temperament seemed to have been most captured by Rilke. Dr. Roth's own sense of balance had been disturbed when he came across Yeats's notion to the effect that life was a long preparation for something that never occurred.

"My piths and gists don't work since Zilpha and Sammy died." Sammy was the name of the female Labrador. In an instant Clare relived Dr. Roth's stricken look when he had stopped by late one afternoon for a drink and found her and Zilpha listening to the Beethoven "Last Quartets" while Zilpha held the fat, stinking, cancerous Sammy on her lap, smooching with the dog, hugging its bulk to her breast, both of them within a month of death.

"I'm thinking hard," Dr. Roth said. "Let's not come to this

place again. It's full of binge shoppers trying to sedate themselves. Now, I know you have an aversion to anything Oriental as being too passive, even though you're utterly passive yourself. A Wayne State University student suffering from obvious malnutrition said it to me. The general notion is that the only use for today is today. The only reality you are ever going to get is the ordinary one you make for yourself. In other words, there's no big breakthrough."

"That's awfully grim. Does that mean there's no Christmas on earth? And what does he do with the information?"

"The 'he' is a 'she.' I gave her ten bucks and made her promise she'd go eat a good meal. Then I loaded her up with vitamin samples. I don't know what she does with this information. I only know she doesn't take care of herself."

"Can I make a donation?" Clare had become nervous.

"Not at the moment. Perhaps later when a donation doesn't mean you're delaying doing something about yourself."

"When you say 'doing something about yourself' it sounds like psychobabble. You know the big section in Borders Bookstore that covers self-improvement."

"Pathology can only be imaginative up to a certain point. If you like, I'll work on the sentence."

Clare found herself nearly at the end of the row and presented with a barrier she hadn't allowed herself to comprehend while thinking about Dr. Roth. It was a dense thicket, apparently as impenetrable as any of the topiary hedges she had seen in England and France. The thicket grew into the cornfield so she couldn't turn right or left. She stepped back twenty feet for a better view and thought she could make out the top of a cottonwood; as her breathing calmed she was sure she heard flowing water, then she remembered that a mile or so before they reached the rest stop there had been a creek or river named after a cow — Guernsey, she thought. Her watch said that had been over two hours ago which didn't seem possible. A creek crossed at seventy miles an hour in a split second doesn't look threatening, but now she felt tears welling up. She had expected a barnyard and farmhouse at the end of the row, and now the compass said that was a possibility only in a southerly direction since north was the interstate. Millions of women merely leave their husbands; why had she fled? She swallowed with difficulty, wishing she had saved some of the cranberry juice, then looked up at the thunderheads, their edges lined with silver from the descending sun. She sat down and made traceries in the dirt with the compass bracket. She had an impulse to discuss the situation with Zilpha but she felt that would further loosen her tenuous grip. Laurel was a better choice.

"Laurel, you little bitch, this is partly your idea. What do I do now?" There was an urge to be angry, cheap, vulgar.

"You could have waited until Davenport and taken a cab to the airport when Dad was in the shower." This was so like Laurel who was matter-of-fact even in the cradle.

"I knew the pain was coming and I lost my good sense." The pain was increasing a bit with the tinge of self-pity so she stiffened up. At the clinic one of the first lessons was never to adopt a "why me?" attitude which might precipitate a collapse.

"You know very well your good sense is bullshit. Remember when I came home from college years ago and said that you act as if you're living three feet from yourself? You were angry but it's true."

"I suppose so, but let's get back to the situation right now. I'm sitting here in the dirt and I don't know what to do. Like most people I'm only prepared for the life I've already lived, none of which included this sort of thing." Clare remained cool with this admission. On all the trips she had made to beautiful places with Zilpha they had never camped out, though twice they had bought a lot of expensive equipment that was donated to the Boy Scouts on return. Laurel and her husband had backpacked everywhere, even in the winter on cross-country skis.

"For Christ's sake, Mother, you're going to have to toughen up. You said you read that book on camping I sent. You're going to have to get some water in your system to avoid hypo-thermia. You know that from a lifetime of tennis which I always thought was a waste of time. You might have to go back to the rest stop for water."

"I refuse. It looks like it's going to rain. My bag is canvas so maybe I could catch some water."

"It's important that you crawl into that thicket to stay dry. No matter how warm it is now, if you get wet you'll be cold by nightfall. Don't drink any water from that creek unless you find a way to boil it. If you get desperate, don't forget why you're doing this. I'd say you're in for a long night unless you're willing to hoof it back to the interstate. I hope you'll come to spend a few months with us."

"That's kind of you but I have my heart set on Paris."

"That's silly of you. Paris isn't the same as it was thirty years ago. You'll be disappointed."

"I don't care. I've passed through a few times since and I don't care if I'm disappointed."

Clare signed off on the phantom conversation with a wave at the oncoming thunderheads that had begun to rumble. She rechecked the edge of the thicket, noting that there were narrow breaks and holes that raccoon and perhaps deer made. She crawled in a small opening in the greenery and looked upward, seeing enough of the sky to know it would still be wet in a hard rain. She remembered with a smile something she had overheard her gay decorator say on the phone, to the effect that his friend should fasten his seat belt because it was going to be a bumpy night. President Reagan had also liked to quote from the movies. Then she recalled as a child at Thanksgiving time on her grandparents' farm how she liked to make small caves in dried corn that had been stacked in shocks. She felt this memory comprised her first bright idea of the day other than leaving Donald, and she busied herself uprooting the green stalks which came up easily, and which she layered on top of the thicket. It was easy so she erred on the side of excess until, when she crawled into the thicket hole, there was a large area that blocked out the sky. If she hadn't been so thirsty she would have been happy in the choice. She emptied out the bag containing her small purse, compass, address book, the beret, the empty juice can (she didn't want to litter), and the passport. It had been Zilpha's notion that the act of taking your passport with you everywhere added drama to life. She arranged these objects like talismans, then scooted back out and spread the bag's mouth open.

The thunder deepened in its volume and she looked up to see lightning shattering the sky like luminous tree roots. The thunderclap that followed had a sharp edge as if the sky were being torn, and the wind came up suddenly so that the leaves down the row were pale and flapping. Clare backed into her makeshift cave with a feeling that things were well in hand, at least for the moment, but the torrent that followed, brief as it was, cast her behavior in a fresh light. When she gave birth to Laurel that early May so long ago she could hear a cloudburst beyond the walls and windows of the delivery room, and there was a tinge of déjà vu in the present rain. *I had two*

*children and lived with a man nearly thirty years. I don't
seem to have a real idea what occurred to me. Maybe nobody
does, or just a few.*

The driving rain splattered mud upward and formed pud-
dles in the opening, but she was dry and warm and drowsy,
the remnants of pain merely diffuse and endurable. She froze
then, startled at the slightest movement to her left, but then
saw it was only a cottontail, the same kind of rabbit that made
her put chicken wire around her herb garden back home. The
rabbit studied Clare from half a dozen feet away, then continued feeding on wild clover shoots, but with its ears alertly
erect and its nose trying to determine if Clare presented a
danger. Within its ears on the pinkish lobes wood ticks dotted
the flesh, gorging on blood. Clare counted seven. She and the
rabbit stared at each other so long that Clare didn't notice that
the rain had stopped and the water caught by her bag was
both being absorbed and draining slowly out. The rabbit's ears
stiffened for an instant at the sound of a cock pheasant crowing
from the direction of the creek, followed by the sharp clear
notes of red-winged blackbirds. There was a new dimension
of stillness in all of this and Clare felt somehow heartened that
the rabbit didn't feel in danger, much less know what a human was. She stayed absolutely quiet, breathing soundlessly
and not even blinking her eyes for fear the rabbit would leave
her alone. Laurel should see her now, she thought, well within
her body, moving gracefully in the heart of time, but then the
rabbit hopped off for reasons of its own. The message was dim
but Laurel seemed to be asking a question.

"Mother, what about the water?"

Clare scrambled out, her hands skidding in the fresh mud.
"Oh fuck!" she yelled, for the first time in her life. The bag
was soaked but nearly empty with scarcely a gulp left down

in a corner. She pressed her face into it for fear of losing any of the precious water, which tasted a little of the sunscreen lotion that had leaked there years ago.

How dumb. There was the sense that she was stuck in a children's story of enormous dimensions, one of those old Europeans out of *The Book House: Ramona fled, watching the barbarians destroy the village, hiding herself behind a tree on the edge of the dark forest.* Clare supposed that even if she did make her way back to the rest stop and drop a quarter in the pay phone the world could never repair itself. With a smile she imagined Donald's umbrage when the police asked him if he had abused his wife. And did he know who might own the red car traveling east? It was she who had set fire to the village before running into the dark forest, and now the consequences enlarged themselves as the sun reappeared casting a golden late afternoon light off the tassels. She was a free woman but would gladly have traded anything for a quart of cold water. Donald was also free to go home and soothe his wounds with his Bing Crosby collection that he liked to tell visitors "was known far and wide," at least among other collectors. Clare was not a bully, though, and raised in her mind some of Donald's good points: he was, surprisingly, a relentless lover; he had taken Laurel and Donald Jr. everywhere, from Disneyland to Busch Gardens, the Smithsonian, and the Museum of Natural History in New York (while Clare was at the Whitney), to Detroit Pistons games, to the Lions, to the Red Wings, to their corporate box for the Detroit Tigers, while Clare stayed home and read or went on outings with Zilpha. Donald loved the life outside the mind and slept like a rock, though he had recently surprised her with a first edition of *Tar* to round out her Sherwood Anderson collection. And last Christmas he had managed to find Faulkner's book of poems A *Green Bough*,

which, she overheard him telling a friend, cost him "an arm
and a leg."

Clare cleaned the drying mud off her hands with a sharp
stone and tried not to think of water. Perhaps the beginning
of the end had been five years ago just after Donald Jr. had
graduated from the University of Michigan. Clare and Zilpha,
on whim, had been late additions to a list of matrons who
wished to go on a Detroit Institute of Arts tour of the mu-
seums of Moscow and Leningrad. Zilpha's visa had come in
ten days but Clare's had never arrived despite repeated phone
calls from her travel agent to Washington, and they had missed
the trip. Zilpha's husband, whom Donald loathed, was a big-
time liberal dope lawyer, and through the intercession of a
black congressman he discovered that Donald had jinxed the
visa with a phone call to a friend in the State Department, the
sort of favor that is due a major Republican fund raiser like
Donald. When Clare confronted him he had affected a minor
breakdown, saying he couldn't have borne up under the strain
of his beloved wife's visiting the "evil empire." Untypically,
Clare thought of shooting him while he slept, but instead she
and Zilpha went off to Costa Rica to visit one of the children
whose survival the brochure and a letter said she sponsored.
This trip had also made Donald frantic despite the assurances
of his State Department friend that Costa Rica was "as safe as
Switzerland."

Clare was beginning to feel the mild dizziness brought on
by hypothermia, a lightness in the head from her extreme
thirst; vomiting plus the long hot walk had pushed her to the
edge of tolerance, and though the late afternoon sun was cooling she found it unendurable. Back in her green cave she felt
she was due another reassuring message from Laurel when
her eyes lit on the cranberry juice can. The camping book said

to boil suspicious water for fifteen minutes. Of course. She grabbed the can and scrambled on her hands and knees through the dense thicket toward what she thought of as the distant sound of water, much increased after the cloudburst. Unfortunately the Guernsey was less than twenty feet distant and Clare nearly catapulted down the slick, muddy bank into the sluggish, dark brown water, an inadvertent baptism by immersion, but she came up waist deep and laughing. The world that had been so narrowed by her physical and mental anguish became quite suddenly larger as she filled the cranberry juice can, resisting the strong temptation to drink the water straight.

Half an hour later Clare had the water bubbling away, the can stuck in a small mound of dirt and the fire crackling around it, with the dry grass and reed stalks kindling the dampish sticks found beneath the cottonwood tree. To extend her patience to the advised fifteen minutes she looked at her only book, the *Tao Te Ching*, for a few minutes but she was far too excited about the boiling muddy water to concentrate. The counselor at the pain clinic had told her that if she adapted all the principles of the volume to her life she could very well be cured of her migraines. Dr. Roth had not been sanguine on this prospect, saying that if she were Pope John XXIII or Martin Buber or Saint Theresa she would also be free of the disease. Clare carried the book along, though she had a childish aversion to Orientals, because the translator was the same as that of her favorite volume of Rilke, *The Sonnets to Orpheus*. The aversion had been occasioned by her father's service as a major during World War II, though he never got beyond Washington, D.C. One day Clare stayed home from kindergarten in order to ride along with her mother when she took her dad to the train station. He had been home on leave for only a few days when he was called back to Washington, and both of her parents had wept at the station. After the train pulled away her mother had told her that "he's off to fight Tojo." Clare knew that Tojo chopped the heads off American soldiers and she was terribly frightened at the idea of a headless father.

At the clinic in Arizona she had become friendly with a wheat farmer from Fort Dodge, Kansas, who was suffering a spinal defect, the accompanying spasms of which could strike him to the ground at any time. When they had all been given the *Tao* one evening at dinner he had been irritable, but in the morning he assured Clare that the "secrets" of the book might save them. She was startled at this statement because Frank, the farmer, was critical of their counselor whom he referred to as a "goofy bastard," partly because the counselor wore an earring. Frank had also been outspoken against an Italian from Albany with a bone disease who had told Clare at the dinner table that she had "nice stems." Frank had fairly shouted at the Italian to mind his language. A plump woman from Pasadena had piped up that there was nothing dirty about good legs, and the table had agreed, with Frank leaving in a huff before dessert. After that, despite the heat, Clare had worn slacks rather than hiking shorts.

She carefully eased the can out of the mound of dirt with her handkerchief, managing to burn the tip of a finger which she ignored. Now she had to wait for the water to cool sufficiently and glanced to the west at the setting sun, guessing that she had another hour of daylight. She hoped to do at least three more of the six-ounce cans, plus an extra for the night, before dark, and the sure thought of removing this manic thirst made her feel giddy. It was so utterly ordinary, this thirst, that it returned her solidly to earth, the only concern being for immediate comfort.

"Laurel, I'm doing rather well considering. I was just wondering if there were rattlesnakes around here."

"That's unlikely. They prefer rocky hillsides where they can find rodents. I heard there are a few moccasins in the southern part of the state but they'd be a rarity and you're well up in the middle. The main problem might be mosquitoes."

"I've already noticed that. At what point does the daughter become the mother?"

"You're not ready for that. I bet you still get a few passes."

"Perhaps. I certainly don't want to talk about it to my daughter."

"Back in high school my friends and I used to wonder if you and Zilpha had some boyfriends stashed on your outings. We thought you two were so thrilling."

"Everyone suspected that we might have gentleman friends, and it was fun to let them think so. It used to drive your father a bit crazy, and I'd say, 'But dear, you go on business trips at least once a month and I don't wonder about you.'"

"You never suspected him?"

"I didn't really care."

"Then why did you hold on so long?"

"I had my friends, my books, dogs, garden, my children. Why does a husband have to be the absolute center of a married woman's life?"

"I don't know but they always are. Actually, I know you're the center of his life, with making money a close second."

"Are you suddenly getting warm about your father?"

"No, it was only an observation."

"I'm the center like a prized possession. Remember when I wouldn't go to any more fund raisers after I was introduced as a 'prominent Republican wife,' with no name attached. It seemed to stand for something quite out of focus."

"That was funny, also sad. I'm sure you were sorely missed. Dad always liked to pretend we had more money than we did. I mean, we had plenty so why pretend? Kevin pointed out my trust would have grown as much in a savings account as it did under Dad's care."

"Was Kevin upset?"

"Not at all. It's just Dad always treats him as if as a veterinarian he has his head in the clouds, when if you pull a difficult calf or help a mare drop a foal it's pretty realistic."

"Businessmen would be utterly destroyed if they didn't think they were the most practical men on earth. Lawyers tend to be that way too. Zilpha's husband used to say that a lawyer was society's proctologist. Sadly, that was the only charming thing he ever said."

"You miss her terribly, don't you? And Sammy too?"

"More than I dreamed possible. Strangely, I couldn't have done this if they had still been with me. It was a pleasure to give so much to them because I loved them. Then they were gone and I had to do something. I just tasted my hot water. It's somewhere between truck stop coffee and the average veal glacé in a Detroit restaurant, the kind where they slip in a bouillon cube. I'd better get busy now."

"Keep me posted. Remember, you don't have to spend the night. There's still time to make it back to the highway if you hurry."

"No thanks, dear."

Clare finished her first can of water with pleasure, spitting out a bit of grit that had accumulated at the bottom and setting out for the next. It was similar to weeding her large herb garden because she didn't think about anything except what she was doing, though thoughts might float easily in and out. The difference was that she didn't try to hold on to the thoughts so that the bad ones disappeared on their own accord.

On the third trip, when her thirst was somewhat abated and the sun was beginning to set, she made her way down the riverbank searching for more wood. Just past the single cottonwood tree there was a large branch she tugged away from clinging vines as if she had found the mother lode. If she could keep a small fire going she wouldn't miss a flashlight so much. If you're going to leave your husband, take a flashlight. That was about as sensible as the rules could get for the time being. A movement in the vines startled her and an opossum scurried out, looked at Clare and flopped over in fake death. She had seen this twice before in her garden back home and it was difficult not to draw certain parallels, amusing ones, though if you played dead long enough the act of coming back to life was questionable. Of the seven women who had been in her tennis group (the A class) a decade ago, four had been divorced in the past few years and none of them were doing very well, but then it was so easy to be smug about her own passivity, the way she let the years float gently by, relying on Zilpha's natural ebullience, two long walks a day with Sammy, hours of reading and cooking, the latter more for herself than for Donald who ate everything she cooked him with equal gusto.

Back at the campsite she coaxed the dwindling fire back to life, broke up the branches and put the sticks in a neat pile, stooping there, impatient for the water to boil. There was a reassuring chatter of birds but she guessed there was at most only a half hour of daylight. She put down a layer of corn leaves, then pulled enough dry marsh grass to cover them, to protect her sleep from the ground's dampness. She took off her skirt and blouse, hung them on a stick and held the clothes over the fire to draw out the slight amount of moisture left from her river plunge. It was a balmy night, but with nothing to wrap herself in but her own arms she was sure she would be cold by morning.

It was so strange to stand there nearly naked, feeling the smoke and heat purl up her body, with just enough darkness to make her legs and tummy golden. She felt good enough for the moment not to have to think of herself as an admirable person. If Zilpha had been there she would have been smoking the cigarettes that killed her. It had been her nature to defy everything, just as many intelligent men drink themselves to death. Right up until the last day Zilpha had said she had no regrets about dying, and on the last day she had only joked, "I'm not absolutely sure this is a good idea. Too bad I can't call and let you know." With her husband her eyes had brimmed with tears and she had merely shook her head. It was by common consent the lousiest marriage in the neighborhood and everyone wondered why they bothered to hang on.

Clare stuck her clothes stake in the ground and decided once again to make sense out of the *Tao*, especially a single line Frank had thought was so wonderful. The line was disappointingly sparse: "Thus whoever is stiff and inflexible / is a disciple of death." Frank had said that he'd spent thirty years being angry at the United States Department of Agriculture over grain prices and all of that energy had been wasted, and the anger had vastly accelerated his back problems. Clare and Frank had been talking in the shade of an enormous boulder; hiding, in fact, from the counselor who was being especially captious and unnerving that day, or so they thought. The twelve of them were being led on a "meditation hike" and were supposed to be dispersed in a boulder-strewn valley to sit alone and concentrate on a double-faced question: "Do you want to live?" and, simply enough, "Who dies?" There was also an admonition to keep alert for rattlesnakes. To break up the obvious tedium and anguish of the questions, Frank and Clare, through hand signals, had met behind the boulder for a chat.

"What the hell does that hippie mean? Suicide's not Christian."

"It's not supposed to be something to get angry about," Clare said without a good deal of conviction. "He says that our bodies are quarreling with themselves and that makes them hard to heal. He's not the USDA. They don't wear earrings."

Frank smiled, then developed a stricken look so Clare massaged his back and shoulders. Clare had seen one of his seizures the first day of the clinic and had doubted that she could handle one behind the boulder. He had twisted on the floor of the dining area and at one point his entire weight was supported by his heels and the back of his head, his trunk thrusting upward. Now his back softened from iron to clay under her hands and they embraced for a moment but he began weeping after he kissed her. At the time she wished she had the gumption to seduce him despite the consequences, whatever they might be. After that incident Frank was embarrassed when talking to her, as if he had behaved badly, and she didn't know how to tell him otherwise. At the end of the clinic Frank's wife picked him up and she looked overplump and spiteful to Clare.

Back at the fire Clare felt the warm smoking clothes and decided she wasn't inflexible, at least compared to Donald, but maybe that was one thing wrong with marriage, or smallish social settings, where the comparisons were so limited. Her brother felt he never drank more than his three best friends, but the four of them had all nearly drunk themselves to death, and were at present all leading lights in the AA for the Detroit area. The sheer taffy in self-awareness exhausted her. Saying that you were no more inflexible than your husband was small-minded dogshit, and she laughed out loud. She wanted more life, not *Robert's Rules of Order*. Crossing a fence was certainly a start, a flexible one at that. It occurred to Clare that while Zilpha swore occasionally, and Laurel repeatedly, she had never learned how. "Fuck you, Donald, you jerkoff," she whispered to the gathering dark, but the oath was froth. "Jerk-off" was what the boys who worked at the neighborhood gas station called each other. They always glanced down at her legs while they were doing the windshield. If she was wearing a tennis skirt they did an especially good job at the wind-shield. Quite suddenly a blush rose to Clare's face as she thought of Zilpha's son Michael. It had been an unforgivable mistake, and constituted her only secret from Zilpha.

"It's okay, Mother. It was the right thing to do."

"No it wasn't. I was never so ashamed of myself. How did you know?"

"Michael told me way back when. I think it was four years ago, right after it happened. He called to say he was going to ask you to run away to New York with him. He wondered if I thought it was a good idea." Laurel and Michael had been close since childhood, an unlikely pair, with Michael as obsessed with art as Laurel was with the life sciences.

"How absurd. It was stupid of me to let it go that far. I must have been sleepwalking." Clare put on her warm, smoky clothes in defense. The clothes felt wonderful against her skin.

"I doubt that. The last thing I ever felt when I was making love was asleep."

"You're simple-minded if you think I'm going to talk to you about it."

"Suit yourself. What I'm trying to say is that your night is going to be long enough without feeling guilty about something so innocent. If you get hungry just roll a couple of ears of that field corn in that wet clay and lay them at the edge of the fire. By the time the clay dries and hardens the corn will be ready. Not great, but better than nothing. I love you. Good night."

"I love you. You didn't tell anyone, did you?"

"Of course not. And I doubt Michael will ever write his memoirs."

"Thanks. Good night."

Clare picked two ears of corn and rolled them in the remains of a mud puddle until they were covered with a thickish layer of clay. It was a messy business and she dried her hands before the fire until she could flake off the clay. Perhaps Laurel was right. She felt guilt because she had pretended she only made love to Michael to get out of an uncomfortable situation, but then Michael was as removed from a rapist as could be imagined. A modest "no" would have pushed him over. Also, it was soon after Donald's nasty interference in her Russian trip, but she recognized that was only a minuscule part of it. In fact, Donald hadn't been given a thought.

"Be honest with yourself," Laurel chimed in from the dark.

"Why? Okay, then. At the moment Michael reminded me of a young English instructor I studied with as a freshman. I knew we both wanted to make love but there were rules against it and besides we were too shy. When I came back as a sophomore I found out he had committed suicide that summer in New York City. Every time I got a crush on someone, they moved to New York. I chose badly."

"Did he leave a note?"

"Not that I know of. Once we had coffee at a cafeteria and he gave me some bad advice. He told me that literature was so rich with possibility that I could safely ignore life itself. I asked him why Pasternak had said that despite all appearances, it took a lot of volume to fill a life. He told me Pasternak's reputation had been discounted by the higher critics. Two of his colleagues passed our table and one of them winked at him as if I were his bimbo."

"Which is what you wanted to be."

"You might say that. When I met your father I made sure he didn't get away."

"I know all about that one. It fails to interest. Anyway, Michael said you only had that single event. As they say, don't sweat it. I made love to him once myself when we were fourteen. We smoked a marijuana cigarette, drank some wine and did it. We decided afterwards that we wouldn't let it ruin our friendship. Actually we fell asleep and Zilpha caught us. She broke out laughing and closed the door."

"So I heard. We didn't come to any conclusions when we discussed it."

"You two never had any secrets, did you?"

"I never told her I made love to her son. It still bothers me."

"Oh, for Christ's sake, Mother. The corn should be roasted by now."

"Good night, dear."

"Keep in touch if you get lonely."

"I will."

Clare tapped the baked clay with her knuckles to no effect, then used a stone to break it. The green shucks steamed on the night air and she waited for them to cool. What had happened one day was that she and Zilpha were supposed to help Michael pack up to move to New York after a morning tennis game. Zilpha looked terrible, having spent the night arguing with her husband, plus she had a summer cold, so Clare volunteered to go solo on the packing chores. She went straight to his studio apartment from the tennis game and found him untypically organized. Michael had given all of his furniture to friends, and he wandered around the apartment stuffing what he called simply his "art" into portfolios, wearing pajamas which was all he ever wore unless it was absolutely necessary to wear clothes. If the trip was to the grocery store or to his mother's house he'd slip a raincoat over the pajamas.

Clare began by disassembling some large unstretched frames Michael, more than anyone she had ever met, had no abilities outside of his imagination, nor was he interested in any. Michael and his father had given up on each other in his early teens, and he kept his doting mother at an affectionate distance. He developed a few friendships among other burgeoning artists at Cranbrook, and he and Laurel kept close though she went to Country Day, but Michael had been considered pretentious and unlikable in the neighborhood. He had not been at the club since his fourteenth birthday when he took off his clothes and pissed in the fireplace. He was flunked out of Rhode Island School of Design for a total lack of interest, spent a year in Paris and Florence, then came home for a few years in Detroit where his paintings caused a minor rage in the art community. The paintings were a bit of a puzzle to Clare because Michael painted only what he called "the insides of things": animals, engines, clouds, trees, women. For a year or so on his return from Europe Clare and Michael had become close again, just as they were when he was young. She helped him hang his paintings at several galleries, bought not a few of them and had lunch with him at least once a week at a restaurant that indulged him his pajamas. Donald didn't begrudge the time she spent with Michael, never referring to

him as anything but "the poor little bugger," though Michael
was of average size. Of course he seemed a bit effeminate, but
then Donald and his cronies were sure that all men but themselves betrayed gay tendencies, even professional hockey
players. This was a mystery to Clare when she listened to
their after-dinner jokes. Sadly to her, Michael sensed charity
in her continued purchase of paintings and began to keep her
at a distance. Only in the last few weeks before his move to
New York had they become quite friendly again.

That day in the dull, humid heat of a Detroit July Michael
surprised her with her favorite wine, a Château d'Yquem,
saying that he wished he had swiped it from his father but he
had bought it himself. They drank the wine on the floor, her
back against the wall, but Michael sprawled in front of her.
He told her about a recent adventure with a lovely black girl
who had decided he was too crazy and went back to her mu-
sician. He was a bit sad about that and said so. The wine was
nearly gone and they had lapsed into silence when he looked
at her strangely.

"I'm finding you quite exciting," he said.

"I'm the same person I've always been."

"That's not what I mean."

"Michael, I don't believe that. You're teasing me." She
blushed deeply, unable to look at his eyes. "You shouldn't
tease about such things."

"I'm not teasing."

He put a hand around her ankle and she let a leg straighten
out. His other hand covered the crotch of his pajamas where
it was obvious that he wasn't teasing. She closed her eyes and
said, "Oh, well," with her ears buzzing. He made love to her
quickly there on the floor and she was embarrassed at her
excitement. Afterwards, they stood in the kitchen apologizing

to each other in miserable half sentences, then went back into the main room where she tried to think of a graceful way to pick up her panties on the bare floor. They stood there for a few minutes, then he embraced her strongly and they took off everything and made love for quite a long time, ending with exhaustion, then laughter. He yelped when she put hydrogen peroxide on his raw knees.

The ear of corn was much better than Clare had reason to expect, lacking sweetness but full-flavored. It was now dark but a three-quarter moon was rising, a cream-colored globe barely above the horizon. A full moon would have been too dramatic, she reflected. One of the grandest times ever with her father had been a long walk one night in the summer during a full moon up near their cottage on Burt Lake. They had taken the long way through a virgin oak forest down to a Chippewa graveyard near the lake, and her father, who was inventive for an accountant, made up new variations on the Robin Hood stories. When they reached the white picket fence of the cemetery she clutched his hand tightly as they looked out over the crosses at the sheen of the moon on the lake. At this juncture her father always tried to spook her by saying in a whisper, "Perhaps there'll be a message from the spirit world," but this time when he finished they heard from far out on the lake the tremulous wail of a loon as if it had been arranged. He clutched her hand as hard as she did his, then they laughed at their fright and made unsuccessful loon imitations.

Clare considered saving the second ear for morning, then thought why bother, since she was surrounded by virtually millions of them. The idea that she probably wouldn't have married Donald if her father hadn't died was less interesting at the moment than Robin Hood. Michael had sent her a book of poems called *Roots and Branches* by Robert Duncan, whom she had never heard of; the poems were splendid though difficult, and now she could remember an entire passage she had copied in her ledger:

> Robin Hood in the greenwood outside
> Christendom faces peril as if it were a friend.
> Foremost we admire the outlaw
> who has the strength of his own
> lawfulness. How we loved him
> in childhood and hoped to abide by his code
> that took life as its law!

The day after her lovemaking with Michael she and Zilpha had a final lunch with him, then a trip to the airport. It was an unsuccessful event with the only lighter moments provided by the memory of the time the three of them had packed a picnic basket to search for Michael's car which he had "misplaced" a week before. They had driven all the way to Zug Island near Wyandotte to consult an actual Gypsy fortune teller who, startlingly enough, had pinpointed the lost car within a block of Wayne State University. It seemed terribly funny when they had arrived at the car and found the tires were gone.

At the restaurant Zilpha went off to the bathroom and Michael suggested, half seriously, that they get rid of her and make love in the airport parking lot. Clare became angry and said, "Never again," and Michael paled. He was quite hopeless and she didn't hear from him again for several years until his mother's funeral, where he looked harsh, thin, hardened, which she supposed was part of living in New York. They were both weeping over Zilpha when they embraced, and Mi-

chael pinched her bottom and whispered, "I'm willing when
you are." She stepped back sensing the kind of humor that
arises out of grief, but no, he wasn't kidding.

Clare stirred the fire and wondered if her diminished pile of
sticks would last, but then even the slightest of fires would
suffice to leaven the balmy night. She feared the dissociation
of waking up in the middle of the night to total blackness,
though the moon should be a modest compensation. She rear-
ranged the wood where she could reach it from her green
cave, and firmed some dirt around her can of water so she
wouldn't inadvertently tip it over. She wished she felt a little
stronger when she curled up for sleep and thought again of
the notion of prayer, but she lacked the solace of a religion
that does not depend on ignoring the human condition. When
she prayed as a child God's face in her mind was similar to
her father's — the graying hair, the furrowed brow, the essentially kind look that was still not interested in trivialities.
Her childhood prayer from Sunday school was simple enough:
"Now I lay me down to sleep, I pray the Lord my soul to
keep. If I should die before I wake, I pray the Lord my soul
to take." Curled there on her bed of leaves and grass, Clare
thought this prayer lacked a great deal in terms of reassur-
ance. She didn't want the Lord to take her soul in the night;
she wanted to go to Europe without having to listen to Donald's incessant business prattle. In the nave of Notre-Dame
he had whispered, "Remind me to make a call," as if he ever
forgot. In the Uffizi he couldn't stop saying, "I wonder what
this would bring at Parke-Bernet."

The world itself was a marketing possibility. Before he had
played his *Tracking the Blues* tape today in the car he had
interrupted a favorite Stravinsky passage by saying that local

acreage was recovering from the 1985 downturn, though Donald Jr. had said pork bellies had the flutters but would really firm up by Labor Day. A signal announcement had been that the black walnut tree in their backyard was worth seven thousand bucks as furniture veneer, and that walnut tree thieves were circulating the Midwest waiting for the innocent to go on vacation. Curiously enough, Donald didn't mind when she asked him to write a large check for the American Indian College Fund or the NAACP, two of her favorite charities, saying something to the effect that "those folks got the wrong end of the stick," as if all American history had been a business deal. Maybe it was. Donald had tried to hedge at her support of the Nature Conservancy and Greenpeace because he felt the bird watchers and "little old ladies in tennis shoes" were cramping certain resort complexes in northern Michigan that were otherwise good investment potentials. Clare reminded him that if she wasn't already a little old lady in tennis shoes, it could clearly be seen on the horizon.

But how could you blame Donald for so fulsomely taking on the colors of the workaday world? Perhaps the lines were drawn more clearly than she had ever thought, and that was why she lay curled in a thicket staring at the weak light of a cottonwood fire. One autumn afternoon when she was helping her father comb burrs out of the long hair of their English setters she had asked him why the Bible said it was easier for a camel to get through the eye of a needle than for a rich man to enter heaven. He treated the question gravely and said that if all your mind is full of is money you become crazy, and that insane people live in a private hell without even knowing it, and that insane rich people created a hell for a lot of other people without knowing or caring about it. As simplistic as this seemed Clare still essentially believed it. Her father said

215

it and he looked like God, though he had done a lot of bad things to her without knowing it. He couldn't have done them on purpose.

Clare sat up as a lump had begun to form beneath her breastbone at the first indication of certain childhood memories. She put a fresh stick on the fire and watched its brief, feverish blaze. She always read herself to sleep and the absence of this routine was haunting. She would have read the footnotes in the *Tao* if there had been enough light. She studied a book of matches from a truck-stop restaurant in Illinois called R Place where they had stopped for lunch on the way out. The restaurant gave a special award and inscribed the name on a plaque of anyone who could eat a four-pound hamburger. The waitress had told Clare that the meat patty was only a little over three pounds but the bun and all the fixings brought the weight up to an even four. For some reason this disgusted Donald who thought the idea "lowlife." The waitress pointed out a burly trucker on the other side of the room who was on his way to victory. Clare excused herself to wash her hands and passed by the trucker on the way to the bathroom, though the trucker was well out of the way. She paused at the table.

"I hope you manage. It looks wonderful," she said.

"You look pretty damn good yourself. I'd give you a bite but I'd be disqualified."

She waved and passed on, wondering if the man had a wife and what she looked like.

Now she reached out and put her beret on tight for extra comfort. She took off her watch and stowed it in the bag thinking if she kept looking at it time itself would swallow her. It was extraordinary that at one moment she could be thinking of making love to Michael on the floor and at the next she was

trying to devise a prayer appropriate to the situation. Back to
the basics, she joked: religion, fucking and Dad at the cemetery.

When and if she emerged her friends and acquaintances
back in the neighborhood were bound to prate "nervous
breakdown" or "depression" during countless phone calls and
lunches. One of the favorite local psychiatrists was an ardent
pill pusher in his efforts to remove any socially embarrassing
symptoms. The probable cause in her case would be obvious
to all — the deaths of Zilpha and Sammy — but her marriage, which was considered to be improbably solid, would
not be questioned. The same psychiatrist had offered nothing
when she had gone to him, troubled about Donald Jr.'s apparent lack of morals in school. He seduced innocent, homely
girls and kept a tally, cheated wherever possible on school
work, plagiarized term papers and, as a school leader, made
problems for teachers who didn't give him good grades. The
psychiatrist had dismissed all of this as Donald Jr.'s effort to
take short cuts into his father's world, and when sufficient
negative reinforcement came from his "peer group" the behavior would cease. Unfortunately for this theory Donald Jr.
continued to be widely admired as charming and capable. His
SATs were too mediocre to get him into an Ivy League college, which his father hoped for, but strings were pulled and
he was accepted at University of Michigan where he became
the president of his fraternity. Donald Jr. had always been
impeccably dressed, even for a trip to the 7-Eleven, while
Laurel, who had gone to Northwestern, was a slob, drank beer
and smoked marijuana, and graduated summa cum laude. She
had also been the best student in her class at Michigan State's
veterinary school, neither of which honors made more than a
cursory dent in her father's consciousness.

There was a rustling in the thicket off to the left and Clare's pulse quickened, but then a barred owl called from the cottonwood and Clare supposed the other creatures were making adjustments to keep out of the owl's way. At one time Donald Jr.'s character had been puzzling because she was blinded by the fact that he had been a much more loving child than Laurel, helping Clare in the garden, arranging his Audubon cards, building bird houses, acting as a deft little "sous chef" when she cooked. It was as if during puberty he woke up, looked around and decided to become a child of his time.

Clare wriggled closer to the opening for a look at the moon and stars, then sat up and stuffed her bag with dry grass for a pillow. This camping had its moments but she was claustrophobic enough to dread tents, elevators and theater lines, and the stars and moon were a tonic after the dark lid of her thicket. There was still the slightest twinge of pain in her left lobe and she monitored the size of the speck of green light. She heard a strain of Monteverdi, then a bar of *The Firebird,* and the light diminished. With Laurel the light was steady but the images of Donald and Donald Jr. increased it. She searched for good memories to control her fear of another attack.

When they were first married and Donald had just entered the firm as an assistant office manager he still wore his lumberjack shirts in the evening and on weekends. He hadn't finished his senior thesis, an essay, ironically enough, on Thorstein Veblen's *Theory of the Leisure Class,* so through the long winter of the pregnancy Clare had actually written most of the thesis. She thought Donald talked brilliantly but didn't write well, while she was shy but wrote well, if a little too carefully. Some of Donald's politically active friends from Michigan State were back in the Detroit area and they all met at least once a week. Donald would regale them with stories about the "bourgeoisie" at work and in the neighborhood near their Birmingham apartment.

Clare's mother had busied herself in her grief by drinking even more than usual and shopping for a perfect home for her daughter. Clare's brother Ted, younger by five years, was in his junior year at Kent, a prep school in Connecticut, his fourth in four years. When her mother had finally found the home, she and Clare had spent a great deal of time overseeing the redecorating. Clare was unconcerned and felt the project was good therapy for her mother. Meanwhile she and Donald and their scrubby friends ate at inexpensive Polish, Italian, Chinese and Greek restaurants, and went to the wonderful movies of those times: all of Bergman, Fellini and the early Antonioni. They marched with other civil rights protesters, hand in hand with blacks, and listened religiously each Sunday morning to the wild-eyed sermons of the Reverend C. L. Franklin, Aretha's father. They actually shook hands with the great man himself, Martin Luther King. He had said to Donald, "Keep up the good work, brother," and Donald had beamed. Like so many others they had been paralyzed with fear by the Cuban missile crisis. Clare had been reading William Faulkner's *The Reivers* when she heard on WJR that President Kennedy had been shot in Dallas. Donald rushed home from work and they wept together, glued to the icy, catatonic replays on television.

One evening, before they had moved into the house, all of their friends had come over for dinner and to listen to blues and jazz records on their new stereo. Donald discoursed on Charlie Parker, Muddy Waters, B. B. King and the primitive discs recorded by Alan Lomax, before carefully putting the needle on the record. Among their favorites were Forest City Joe singing "Chevrolet" and Vera Hall's "Can't You Hear That

Wild Ox Moan." Clare thought that perhaps that evening had been the beginning of the end. Laurel had been sick with a cold, and Clare at the time was a distinctly amateur cook. Hearing of the party, her mother had volunteered to send over a little something from the club. Two waiters showed up at 8 P.M. sharp when the guests were groggy from Gallo burgundy and famished to despair. Clare went into the bathroom, embarrassed to the point of tears when the food arrived. She primped herself, wiped away her tears, blew her nose and emerged when she heard the shouts of joy from the other room. There were only ten of them but her mother had sent over a huge prime rib roast, a Smithfield ham, side dishes including six dozen oysters, a mixed case of French wine and two cases of imported beer. Their friends were utterly thrilled with the food, without a single negative comment. They ate, drank, danced and laughed, and at the bleary end of the party Clare wrapped up ample packages of leftovers for each of the guests.

In the morning they had the first serious argument of their marriage, over, oddly enough, a novel by James Baldwin and a profile of Malcolm X in a Detroit newspaper. A week later they moved into the house and things were never the same again, nor were they meant to be. Despite his jokes about work Donald had become a well-concealed predator, a skilled manipulator, something he had learned as a political activist, and was earning a degree in accounting at night school at the University of Detroit. During the longish evenings alone Clare began reading again and hadn't stopped since. Over the long haul she couldn't have endured Donald without her books, but now the idea of the books without Donald seemed rather nice. Two years after Laurel, who had been nicknamed "Papoose," Donald Jr. was born, and when Donald arrived late at the hospital with three dozen roses he announced, in his first tailored suit, that he had been elected a member of the Detroit Athletic Club. Clare put down the book she was reading, a novel called *The Deer Park* by Norman Mailer, in which there were no deer to be found but lots of intriguing bad behavior. She remembered looking closely at Donald, a long pause where she waited patiently for him to mention the birth of his son.

Clare dozed for a half hour, waking fearfully with a deep chest pain, then smiled because she had rolled over and clenched a fist against her heart, mistaking it for an attack. The fire was down to embers and she decided to use the largest of the sticks in hope that it would last until she slept long and deeply, if ever. She strained above the hiss and sputter of the fire to hear something just on the edge of the audible. There it was again. And again. A dog barking far to the south, she imagined in some barnyard at the outer edge of the arc thrown by a porch light, the dog's body stiffening as it barked at the night as Sammy's body had every single night just before bedtime. It was an unimaginably comforting sound and tears of joy formed in her throat. How wonderful it would have been to have the dog with her, not for protection, as Sammy's bravura was mostly fake, but for companionship. Sammy had been afraid of cats and snakes, but her thunderous bark warned away possible intruders and door-to-door salesmen and the irksome approach of Jehovah's Witnesses. For unclear reasons she liked the Federal Express man but loathed the one for UPS. The black furnace repairman once threw her into a fearsome rage which caused Clare to offer an embarrassed apology after she had closed Sammy up in the garage. The black man, who was about her age, looked at her strangely, then offered his hand. It turned out they had been in a civil rights march together well over twenty years before, and the man's little son who had played with Laurel in Hart Plaza now taught high school science in Ypsilanti. When the repairman left it wasn't the happiest occasion because the intervening years acquired the sharpest of focuses. The man had mentioned seeing her name in the *Detroit News* where she had been referred to rather nastily as a "well-heeled liberal environmentalist."

At dinner when she brought up the repairman Donald had become vague and nearly morose for a minute. It had been difficult for him lately as one of his minor saving graces was an abiding concern for probity in government, and the successive scandals in Pentagon procurement, HUD, and the enormity of the savings-and-loan mess disturbed him deeply. She tended to go easy on him on the rare occasions when he became vulnerable, but two summers before, near Bay View in Petoskey, they had come upon a ragged Chippewa selling Korean-made moccasins. Clare had bought several pairs, quipping that the Chippewa apparently didn't own any oil wells, a reference to a Reagan gaff. They usually avoided political discussions, settling for canceling each other's vote at the polls.

Laurel, however, was merciless and could redden Donald's face by saying that she wanted to go to Costa Rica and speak Latin just like Dan Quayle. Laurel was never particularly interested in novels or poetry, and her single misquote was from Yeats, the sense being that while the best lacked all conviction, the worst were full of passionate intensity. That appeared to sum up Laurel's feelings toward the political world. Donald Jr. tended merely to be a more cynical version of his father. Clare herself had come to the point that all the highest hopes of her twenties had dissembled to the degree that she was relegated to writing checks to distant organizations and trying to save the occasional pond, creek or sorry woodlot in Michigan. The heady idealism of the Labor State had died with Walter Reuther, and the prospects for social services and the environment had become dismal in the face of lobbyists' opportunism.

Fortunately, the thought of politics made her sleepy, though sodden might be a better word, she thought. She heard the dog's bark a little more clearly and there was an eerie moment when she thought it might be her own ghost dog, but the image of it barking out its loneliness under the porch light was dominant. The stars and the moon didn't seem quite high enough, and she remembered Donald's chagrin when they added a master bedroom with a sixteen-foot ceiling. Clare couldn't stay in newish hotels where the windows didn't open. She often regretted her mother's gift of a house so soon after they were married. Money tended to derange people when it arrived so abruptly, and the house wasn't, ultimately, fair to Donald. The ceilings were high in Europe but less equitable societies made her nervous after a few weeks. When this was over she intended to live in an apartment or in a smallish house on the far edge of a town. It would be near a woods and farm country. She would find a job in a library or bookstore where she could make herself useful, a sense she had lost since Donald Jr. had gone off to college. The woman who ran the local office for the charity in Costa Rica had said she was an overworked volunteer and that sounded good to Clare. The woman had advised against visiting the child and she was right. The family had been fearful that something might be taken from them, that they were being judged, but they had warmed to Zilpha and the atmosphere had become relaxed in the one-room stucco cottage near Punta Arenas.

Clare traced a finger across the dew gathering on her face. She had learned enough Spanish to translate the thank you notes from the child who was now in her early teens. The parents had been painfully shy but the second child, a boy of seven, was perfectly round and had thought everything about Zilpha was funny. Clare's mother definitely had been a problem drinker and Clare thought again of the nightmares caused by rich, overgenerous alcoholics. The new, homely word "yuppie" had been devised for the grandchildren of the Depression and she wondered how gracefully they would age. Another ugly word was "schmucks." Last Christmas when Donald Jr. came home from Chicago with a rather pretty but vacant girl, he told Clare her "main problem" was that she expected too much from people when they were really only schmucks.

Sleep was too far away for the clumsiest of prayers. She got up, put another stick on the fire and looked at her bed in the brief yellow flare-up. It was the nest of a not very skilled animal, a temporary measure like a deer bed in high grass. She turned and the wider row she had come down a lifetime ago was now aligned with the moon, a darkling path between silvered leaves which a breeze was lightly rustling. It was a path from a children's book of the twenties in the golden age of illustration, lovely, foreboding, irresistible. She decided to walk herself to sleep as she did so often with her dog at home. Donald had bought her a small pistol which she never took along because the presence of a pistol would have changed the nature of the walk. And Sammy, though still frightened by cats, thought she was a grizzly bear after dark. Besides, she was in fine trim, and asked Donald why they'd remained in so otiose a neighborhood if it wasn't the safest in the Detroit area. She could tell he didn't know what "otiose" meant but pretended he did as he watched Pisor, his favorite late-news baritone. *Oh, fuck Donald,* she reminded herself. *I am here because he isn't.*

She set off at a relaxed but steady pace, fixed on the moon as if she were trying to walk to a place directly under it. After a few hundred yards she quickened her gait and felt that delightful sense that her joints had become oiled, and the night air was sweet and drinkable. Dr. Roth liked to say that the overexamined life was not worth living, and that the quasi-upper-class life had become the shabbiest of self-improvement videos. Goddamn but her mind was so exhausted with trying to hold the world together, tired of being the living glue for herself, as if she let go, great pieces of her life would shatter and fall off in mockery of the apocalypse. Or it would simply deflate, letting off its sour air like a punctured rubber ball. She was delighted when she thought she saw the moon move a bit as it must. Time moved the moon. You should be lucky enough to be there when the tree falls in the desert. Dr. Roth, who was fascinated with the history of religions, gave her what he called a "nice Jewish present," *The Unvarnished Gospels*, a new translation by Gaus. The language was so stark and commonplace as to be almost unreadable.

The world is likely commonplace, she thought. There was the amusing memory of the second term of her sophomore year when East Lansing was frozen in dirty ice. She had met a boy in the periodicals room who was reading her favorite literary journal, *Botteghe Oscure*, edited in Rome by Marguerite Caetani. Clare's secret ambition was to be Marguerite Caetani's secretary and meet the French poet René Char, whose long poem "To a Tensed Serenity" was in the latest issue. The boy reading the journal was shabby, condescending, an avowed "beatnik" who smelled strongly of potato chips.

She found him exciting though he looked down his pale, mottled nose at her pleated skirt and gray cashmere cardigan. The boy let her sit near him at Kewpee's, a cafeteria favored by the intellectual and artistic types, the latter having the advantage of smelling like paint rather than something else.

She and the boy would sit as close as possible to a table of seniors dominated by a strange-looking young man who, on alternate days, wore army surplus or the kind of suit and Chesterfield coat worn in her hometown. He was more vigorous and arrogant than her suicidal instructor and she and the boy listened raptly as the young man droned on about Rimbaud, Verlaine, Laforgue, Péguy, Alain-Fournier, Camus, Kierkegaard, Yesenin and the "obvious" structure of Joyce's *Finnegans Wake*. He had taken to glancing at her legs now and then and once loudly told a story about fucking a fat, drunken waitress who wore an ankle bracelet which spelled "Herbert." One day the man looked over at her and asked her if she had read Dostoevsky, especially the new translation of his *Notebooks* wherein there was an entry about a girl who, one cold St. Petersburg afternoon, drank a bottle of wine and committed suicide out of boredom. She answered that she hadn't read Dostoevsky but Turgenev's *Sportsman's Sketches* was one of her favorites (it was actually her father's favorite). "That's good," he said, "but read *Fathers and Sons*. I'm actually Bazarov. Get off your pretty ass and read all of Dostoevsky or you'll become a punching bag for some Grosse Pointe fraternity boy." Then the man stood up and announced to his cronies that it was time to get drunk and play pool. On the way out the man paused by her chair and pronounced loudly that she was "edible" which confused her somewhat.

After she said goodbye to the boy she cut a class and went immediately to the campus bookstore and bought all of the

Dostoevsky in the Modern Library editions, the Constance Garnett translations. She read *The Idiot, The Gambler, Notes from Underground, The Possessed, Crime and Punishment* and *The Brothers Karamazov.* Her eyes were hot red balls in her head but her life was changed. The great Russian had devoured another piece of her each time she wept over a hero or heroine, a grand conception, the marriage of heaven and hell that was his peculiar genius, and spat her out in bones and gristle. But after she and the beatnik boy had returned on three successive empty days they finally heard the young man had suffered a nervous breakdown and had run off to New York City, leaving a wife and child in married housing. Clare stayed in her room for a week until a dorm counselor escorted her to the campus psychiatric clinic where a sluggish doctor advised her to construct some effective shields against her emotional life, a project at which she proved most successful.

Her skin was moist and her breathing harder as the darkness of the path ahead yielded to a lighter shade of gray. There was a hissing, clicking sound which could have been a flying saucer had she not recognized the sound of irrigation sprinklers from the golf course near their home. The cornfield gave way to another huge field she guessed must be soybeans, the sprinklers tossing water into the moonlight as far as she could see to the east. Off to the north were the soundless lights of trucks and cars on Route 80, with the illusion at that distance that they were traveling slowly, creeping toward Chicago or back west toward Omaha. There was a two-track lane between the soybeans and corn and she walked south for a while, hoping to see the light of a farmhouse. She wanted to hear the dog bark and there was nothing, but she suspected everyone must be asleep by now. She followed a thumping in the ground to a tall thicket of grass and weeds growing up around the main outlet and valve for the irrigation system. She slid in a big puddle but maintained her balance, the water pleasantly icy on her hot feet. Where the main pipe curved up and out of the ground there was a wheel to turn the water off and on, and a large connecting pipe to the field, out of which came a steady gout of water from a bad fitting. Clare cupped her hands, pausing to let their warmth cut the water's icy edge to avoid the onset of a headache. The water was clean and marvelous after the tea-colored sludge from the creek and she stooped there drinking until she felt a little bilious. She slipped off her blouse, skirt, panties and bra, bathing herself slowly with her hands. She did not feel remotely sorry for herself which there had been a trace of earlier. Dr. Roth had a theory that self-pity was the most injurious emotion to mental and physical health. In the small desert town near the pain clinic a trinket store sold T-shirts that read, "The Pain People," which they all bought with irony and humor.

Clare let the breeze dry her off. People used to say "buck naked" and that's what she was, with more than a twinge of desire for Dr. Roth at the moment his image shifted out of the dark in connection with Dostoevsky. She felt quite free to think about making love to him because she knew it would never happen. It would break the etiquette of their affection for each other. For an uncharacteristic few seconds she thought that any farmer would do, or even the trucker who ate the four-pound hamburger, but certainly not Donald, who would not be caught dead out here unless he was bent on buying the farm. She was nearly dry and thinking about nothing in particular except how smooth and strong her body was for her age, when Dr. Roth arrived again. She had told him about the

Dostoevsky incident at the bar of the Townsend Hotel and was miffed when he began laughing.

"Life is so unforgiving when you're nineteen," he said.

"And that makes my sad tale funny?"

"If it's not funny by now you might have to shoot yourself. That's what I mean by unforgiving. Actually, if you shoot anyone it should be the psychiatrist. All he did was try to lower the ceilings."

"I suppose he was tired of the anguish of hundreds of nineteen-year-olds."

"Then he should have gotten the fuck out of the business. You have to remain vulnerable to treat the vulnerable."

"I'm not so sure he could have said anything valuable."

"Of course he could. He might have said that neurotic intellectuals can be as dangerous as cheese-brained fraternity boys. He could have said if you really wanted the guy you could have closed the deal before you read all the books, but it probably wouldn't have been a good idea."

"But I didn't know I could have closed the deal."

"That's ladylike bullshit. You knew that on a particular level. I think it's intriguing that you wanted to fuck someone for their mind. I sure could have used that at nineteen." Dr. Roth nearly blushed at this, the first mention of sex between them, albeit abstract.

"I would have been twenty-six at the time, already an old lady for a nineteen-year-old." She was going to let him fry for a moment.

"That's not the way it works. I'd feel more comfortable talking about religion."

"I remember when I wrote about Apollinaire that he said Jesus held the world's high-altitude record. Is that religious enough?"

"It's definitely safer. We always like to think we're on the verge of danger when we're nearly immobile, don't we?"

"I suppose so. It's nice to hear that you think of yourself as no more adventurous than me."

"Now it's my turn to suppose so." He had become strained and distraught. "That's what is finally unforgiving. All of this mythological freedom we grow up on which we usually get to express standing around in a field wearing a baseball mitt. Or sailing a quarter-million-dollar sailboat down the Detroit River hoping the water won't corrode a hole in the bottom."

On the long walk back to her nest Clare remembered that Apollinaire left his wife by merely getting on a train and disappearing, but the idea of her own escape was too obvious to attribute to the poet. The beauty and dread of time was that nothing was forgiven. Not a single minute. The years she had spent in consideration of this act were not only lost, irretrievable, but the recognition of the loss was so naïve as to leave her breathless. And she lacked the convenient excuse of children to care for, or the most central excuse of all, poverty. The bondage for most women was not enough money to live on, especially if there were children. And for men there was the perpetual bondage of work and debt, to which was added so frequently a level of spending far beyond their means. In Clare and Donald's class it meant something quite different. Donald had explained several personal bankruptcies after Black Monday. A number of their club members had been making five hundred thousand a year but regularly spent seven hundred. This fact dumfounded Clare whose extravagances were limited to a good bottle of wine a day and rare books. On vacations she liked deluxe hotels but flew tourist class, which had always irritated Donald. She liked to send the difference to a charity so that it wasn't a matter of being an unpretentious skinflint.

Her brother Ted always seemed a more elegant version of Donald and tended to avoid seeing her except around the holidays when it was pro forma. He had been to Hazelden in Minnesota three times to dry out, and the last trip was to the Betty Ford which still didn't do the trick. What finally worked was a panel of doctors' absolute guarantee that he'd die within a year if he continued drinking. His three failed marriages and obsession with racing sailboats in the Great Lakes and the Caribbean had diminished his trusts by two-thirds, until he was forced to live quite modestly. Clare had loaned him a great deal of money over the years and this made Donald quarrelsome. Her brother liked to make her feel guilty by repeating that she had inherited all the good genes from their father, while he was stuck with the unstable propensities of their mother. Unfortunately, Dr. Roth had said, that was a possibility. The bottom line, Clare thought, was that her brother had been a bully since he was an infant, and had tended to bully himself into the middle of any misery he could find. To an unimaginable degree he had ruined his life and caused a great deal of pain to his wives and children. He was a living poster child for the evil potential of inherited wealth.

Clare was absurdly happy when she reached her nest, as if returning home from a tiring day. She tended to the remaining embers of the fire, bringing them to life with dry grass and sticks. There was a lightness in her body brought about by the fact that she did not give a flat fuck if she ever saw her brother or Donald again. It was as simple as that. She repeated the phrase "flat fuck" with the avowed intent to take up swearing as a pressure valve. The phrase was used by April, a rotund woman Clare and Zilpha met up near Pellston the October before on an outing. It was at a small county park on a lake, the autumn colors so stridently lovely as to approach banality, with Sammy swimming through the red and yellow leaves on the lake. When Sammy finished swimming she came up to Clare and waited patiently for Clare to pick the wet maple leaves off her back, then rolled vigorously in the dust and ashes of a campfire site. Zilpha had started a fire in the small Weber grill they traveled with, using the dry split oak that was kept neatly tied in a bundle. From home Clare had brought the salad, the dressing, and a pheasant Donald had shot at a hunting preserve near Holly. The pheasant had looked a bit lean so she had split it in half before daylight that morning, puréed butter, fresh thyme and sage and forced the mixture gently up under the skin while Donald was already barking on the phone in the breakfast nook.

April was driving down the gravel road when she blew a tire with a shotgun sound not fifty yards from them, and Sammy rushed into the woods, remembering the few times she had been used as a bird dog in her youth. April got out of the car with her five-year-old daughter, a chubby miniature of her mother.

"I can't believe this fucking shitass car," April hollered with a volume that brought Sammy running back from the woods.

Zilpha and Clare went to her aid. There was a bald spare tire but no jack among the hundreds of returnable beer cans in the trunk. Zilpha got the jack from the Toyota and swiftly changed the tire which amazed April. Zilpha's husband was a car buff, and before their marriage had ruptured into boredom they had restored a number of old cars together.

"Lady, you could get a job in a flat-fucking garage," April said. She continued to talk, bearing down on the day's problems, with every sentence peppered with phrases polite folks think of as filth. Zilpha and Clare couldn't help but begin to laugh and April said she was sorry but she always talked that way. Meanwhile the child was off throwing a stick into the lake for the dog, her voice pealing out, "Bring it back, you son-of-a-bitch." Clare asked April if she'd like a drink or something to eat. April said she had just had lunch but "I could use a fucking drink to turn the day around."

They sat at the picnic table drinking white wine with Clare getting up now and then to tend the broiling pheasant, watching the child wrestle with the wet dog. April was a local and worked as a barmaid up the road. Her ex-husband was a welder in Detroit but was in jail on assault. She had had his checks garnisheed but he wasn't getting paid in jail so times were hard. Zilpha took down the information, saying that her husband might be able to look into it. Then April said, "Where do you gals work?" and there was an embarrassed silence.

"We're sort of housewives," Clare said, and April said she had tried that once but it "bored the shit out of me." She liked working in the bar because you could shoot the shit with the customers, and if you got a little horny you could always find someone. Clare had set out a small wheel of Camembert and cut a wedge for the daughter who was eyeing it. The child smelled the cheese, announced loudly that it smelled like poop and ran off again with Sammy. When April left she thanked them profusely, took one more swig from the bottle of wine and said, "You fucking ladies got it all." When she was gone their laughter was mixed with a little melancholy. The pheasant was delicious and Sammy got a chunk of raw shin bone of beef that had been packed for her in a cellophane sack.

That had been their next to last outing before Zilpha's diagnosis had come, right after Thanksgiving. In early December they went off to a spa near Tecate in northern Sonora, just a few hours south of San Diego. The trip had its moments but the diagnosis was too fresh in mind to try to ignore. After the first day of group exercise they gave up the program in favor of hiking in the mountains, most of the time well off the marked trails.

They had been at the spa together a decade earlier, and since then it had vastly upgraded its facilities, and the clientele had become a bit more hard and glitzy. One evening in the dining hall Zilpha said, "We're all the same here," and it was true. Other than a dozen men there were nearly ninety women, between the ages of forty and sixty, but a concentration around fifty. More than age, the women seemed to be fighting a malaise of fatigue and dissociation, of free-floating anxiety so deeply ingrained as to be invisible to the bearer. The regimen of a vegetarian diet and relentless exercise in a lovely setting far from home, the source of the gray-area angst, worked quite well, and within two days spirits were lifted. It was a break, not a cure, a shifting into a pleasant neutral where the body's exhaustion supplanted the brain's dreary machinations. Unfortunately, given the death sentence of Zilpha, the function of the place was too clearly scribed, so they took refuge in the mountains, packing along water bottles, hard-boiled eggs and oranges, descending in the late afternoon to start a fire in the fireplace and drink a glass of wine before dinner. Clare had been thrilled to discover that their small villa had once been used on a regular basis by Aldous Huxley, one of her earliest reading enthusiasms. Zilpha was a steady reader herself but disliked Huxley's brittle intelligence which reminded her of her husband. At dinner every evening Zilpha would look out over the assembled ladies and whisper, "Don't you wish April was here to sweeten them up?"

One afternoon they were sitting on a boulder halfway up Mount Cuchama when a Pacific front swept in over a distant ridge and within a few minutes they were looking down at the roiling tops of clouds with far less security than is felt in an airplane. They were excited and girlish at the experience, noting the occasional hawk or raven that would pop up through the clouds, circle around, then dive back down into the moving fleece. "These clouds aren't comforting enough for the afterlife," Zilpha said, just before they heard a rattle of stone and a ragged, desperate Mexican man appeared before them. He gestured at his mouth in hunger and they handed down a remaining orange and hard-boiled egg from their perch on the boulder. The man pocketed the food, smiled, bowed and scampered up the steep mountain at an alarming rate, with physical verve that Clare pointed out none of the fitness instructors could have managed. Zilpha became depressed that the man was headed for America and might be disappointed, then she began coughing so they headed down the mountain.

Clare sat before her fire and decided that at last she was ready for sleep. She felt a trace of something new and feared she might be like a patient emerging from an asylum, using a cornstalk as a scepter, and saying, "As of today I'm giving up control of the entire world and all of its inhabitants." A half-dozen fireflies had gathered in the darkness around her green cave, and the tiny beams seemed to trace the convolutions of her thought. Life outside the asylum was not necessarily more pleasant. It could be, but it didn't have to be. She tried to recall what her beloved Camus said about "terrible freedom," that once you decided not to commit suicide, whether physically or figuratively, you assumed the responsibility of freedom. The thought blurred with a firefly's movement past her nose. She curled up fetally, rejected the position and stretched out strenuously on her back until there were bone crackles.

When she woke up a few days before this trip she noted that her feet were getting old, and laughed. She met Dr. Roth downtown for lunch because it was his volunteer day. He looked grim in the foyer of the Caucus Club and she feared a bad morning at the hospital, but it turned out an auto dealer had called to tell him his wife was intent on buying the same car she had bought the day before. The restaurant seemed suddenly inappropriate so they walked down the street and bought two coney islands apiece. Clare admitted she had never eaten one in her life but found the frankfurters covered with onions, mustard and chili quite delicious.

"You just saved a hundred bucks," he said, examining a splotch of mustard on his necktie. Clare had always insisted on the check.

"Too bad they don't sell these out our way."

They ducked into a bar, had a quick beer and removed the mustard from his tie. When they left and began walking again it was by common consent they decided not to be witty.

"What would you think if I left Donald?"

"I'd think you were sane" — his reply was quick — "but that's as much as I'll say. When did this come up?"

"About seven years ago. Why won't you say any more?"

"Because I've seen dozens of divorces in my practice and the act is so utterly intimate that outside advice only confuses the issue. Also, anything I'd say would be an abridgment of your freedom."

"I understand that. I've actually reduced it to an abstract principle." She hesitated, feeling foolish.

"Let's have it. Don't leave me hanging. This will be a first."

"I want to evoke life and he wants to dominate it. Is that too simple?"

"No, I don't think so. I'll have to spend an evening with that one. When are you going to do it?"

"I have no idea."

"Where are you going?"

"I don't know."

"Well I don't believe you don't know. In the ten years we've known each other you've mentioned a number of places you'd like to live. Let's see, there was Flagstaff, Minneapolis, Durango in Colorado, Pendleton in Oregon, and Duluth. And the obvious Paris."

"You have a remarkable memory for my nonsense."

"I've never been to any of them, but when you'd mention a place I'd look it up in the atlas and think it over." He was nervous with this admission and looked at his watch. It was then that she understood that at one time, at least, he had cared for her. They walked on in silence for a few minutes, her heart swelling in her throat. When they reached her car he hugged her and rushed off.

Clare was sinking into the ground, into a point well past sleep, or so she thought, with her body sweet, warm, deadened, giving itself up to the bed of leaves and grass, the green odor transmitting a sense she belonged to the earth as much as any other living thing. *I don't need to change. I'm just this.* Her brain had grown larger, its outer reaches vertiginous, grand, so that she could move within it as if taking an evening walk. She understood that she had been abandoned there by her mother and father, Donald, her children, Sammy and Zilpha, and that only being abandoned by Sammy and her children was natural. Zilpha was torn off the earth, taken away. Donald had disfigured himself beyond recognition and bore no resemblance to the man she in innocence had once been proud to love. Her mother smelled of allspice, martinis. Her ears smelled of gin. *Be careful because they'll always try to put their thing in you, dear. No matter what they say, that's what they're trying to do.* Her father had said, *Clare, look at your mother and don't drink anything stronger than wine,* and she hadn't except an occasional brandy. But when she slept in her birthday tent out by the grape trellis with the English setter, Tess, the dog had growled when her mother covered her in a mink coat, then she heard her mother vomit in the yard. Her legs were so thin and she died a year after him, unable to stand on thin legs still smelling of gin after death, beside him in the cemetery Clare could not bear to visit. Now she would, to say goodbye. As a child puzzled by age she'd say, Why is Dad older? Why does he say, *Take the best bite first?* We went for a drive that took all day from the cottage to a man's farm near Gaylord to get Tess bred. We dropped her off and he didn't want me to see it so we went to town for lunch. Mother was in the hospital so I got to eat French fried potatoes, then we went to see the Hartwick Pines, the biggest trees left, then we went to the wilderness where there were only huge old stumps. He said all but a few white pines five feet thick were cut down. *They're like the buffalo,* but I didn't understand. At Christmas he gave me a silver dog whistle with three small diamonds set in it because I could make the setters mind. Sit, stay, come, heel, slow. I never got to go hunting. My brother hated it. Girls don't hunt, he said. My brother hit the dogs with a stick and got spanked. He would always hit me but Mother said I did the bruises myself to make my brother look naughty. The clock said three and I didn't hear Sammy's breath and I knew she was gone. It was May and the lilacs had just come out. I wore my nightgown and put on my hiking boots. I carried her down the hall and Donald looked out of his bedroom door and I said, *Go back to bed Donald this is my dog.* Out at the end of the garden I began digging and it was more than an hour before the hole was deep enough. I got down in the hole chest deep and could see that dumb bastard Donald staring at me out the kitchen window, then he went away. I lifted Sammy in after I kissed her goodbye and covered her with the dirt, and sat down out of breath. At Zilpha's grave they covered the dirt with a rug of fake grass the color of grass in Easter baskets.

Something brushed against her leg and she bolted upright from the waist in alarm with hundreds of yellow dots whirling about her and above the rabbit that paused beside the dim coals of the fire. The moon made shadows of the rabbit's twitching ears. She scrambled out of the green cave and stood, gulping air in fright, the rabbit shooting back into the thicket. She prayed for her heart to stop thumping and looked up at the moon, and there were fireflies above her. As her heartbeat slowed she still did not want to look down at her body or touch herself because she thought she might be seven again. The fireflies were thicker in some places above the thicket, blinking off and on, whirling toward each other so if you blurred your eyes there were tracers, yellow lines of light everywhere. She thought, *Laurel should see this, Laurel would love this,* and then she was no longer seven.

Clare rebuilt the small fire to break the unearthly mood but the fireflies weren't disturbed. She walked up the row fifty feet, turned and looked back, hoping that she wouldn't see herself standing there. The countless thousands of fireflies stayed just outside and within and above the thicket. Quite suddenly she felt blessed without thinking whether or not she deserved it. She went back to her nest, lay down and wept for a few minutes, then watched a firefly hovering barely a foot above her head. She tried out *Now I lay me down to sleep* despite its failure to reassure. *All souls will be taken, including the souls of fireflies.*

She closed her eyes and felt herself floating in memory from her beginning, as if on a river but more quickly along the surface than what had happened to her. Now she saw when it was she had slept on the ground without covers up at the cottage when she was seven, with Tess curled up in her arms, smelling like a skunk Tess had bothered. In March that year, 1947, there was a serious bout of pneumonia and the doctors had given her too much of the new wonder drug, penicillin. At first she was better, though she hated the hospital and asked her parents daily if she could go home and they kept forgetting to bring along her small ceramic dog. All her joints began to redden and swell and her fever rose precipitously. The doctors diagnosed rheumatoid arthritis, a terrible disease, and then she lapsed into a coma for five days. All that she could remember from the coma was that her grandfather had brought into her hospital room his huge Belgian draft horse mare with the rooster perched on its back. When her grandfather left with the horse and rooster, her grandmother came in leading a black bear with a red leash. Her grandmother said nothing but the bear had sat down beside her and talked in a soothing language, and before the bear said goodbye she put Clare's ceramic dog on the nightstand so it was there when she woke up with a big needle putting juice in her arm. No one was there when she woke up though she thought she still smelled the bear in the room. A specialist from the university said she was allergic to penicillin and the drug had poisoned her system. Her parents were happy she didn't have rheumatoid arthritis (they kept saying it) but Clare felt things were never quite the same again. In her child's mind she felt that they had abandoned her because she had frightened them with her illness, an almost imperceptible withholding of affection that became directed to her little brother, or so she believed. When she got out of the hospital it was nearly time to move up to the summer place, but when they got there she was told she was too ill to go fishing with her father. He kept saying, *Maybe next month*. One evening her parents went to a party down the lake, the babysitter was awful just sitting out on the porch with a boyfriend, and her little brother had purposefully broken the tail off her ceramic dog by hitting it against the fireplace. She stayed up late to show the broken dog to her parents, but they came home a little drunk and spanked her for staying up late. She crawled out the window with Tess and slept under the bushes near the garage where the three-legged cat had visited them. Tess liked cats and tried to lick their fur. Early in the morning she was discovered when Tess started barking at a motorboat, and she was spanked for sleeping outside. She never did get to go fishing that summer though she happily threw her brother's favorite teddy bear off the dock and stood there a long time until it drowned. Then her mother had to go to the hospital down near Ann Arbor, Mercy Wood, because she drank too much, though her dad said she was just sick. The good trip was to take Tess to Gaylord to find her a "husband." That's what he said though there was no church, just a farm with English setters. Then came the lunch, the big trees and the buffalo stumps.

When Clare awoke again the fireflies were gone. She rummaged in the bag until she found her watch, lit a match and saw it was four A.M., with dawn less than two hours away. She felt drowsy and unafraid so didn't bother to rekindle the fire. It was pleasant to know she had no idea what she was going to do other than wear a beret in Paris on at least a single walk, she hoped on a rainy August afternoon. Barring small children most women in her neighborhood in broken marriages ran afoul of sheer idleness. Clare knew she was bright enough to make herself useful somewhere, especially when she wouldn't be running the house, which she tended at the moment to look upon as a preposterous imposition put on her by her mother. Her father tended to be naturally morose, taciturn, but the times her mother began drinking again after a supposed cure were hard on him. Once Clare came upon him crying in the den after her mother had fallen down the stairs. She hadn't really injured herself but the family doctor thought it an opportunity for a quick cure. His eyes had also become moist when Clare was dressed up for her first formal dance at fourteen. He had just arrived home from a business trip to New York and stood in the hall with his ponderous briefcase, and as she was leaving, he turned and nodded to her boyfriend standing on the porch, kissed her and said, *This can't be, this is too sudden,* and off she went. The last time was when, despite the pressures of business, he drove her up to East Lansing to enter college. Going to Michigan State was Clare's first act of total defiance against her mother to whom the college was unmentionable. Her mother had insisted on her own alma mater, Smith, and Clare had said, *You're not much of a recommendation, the only thing I've seen you read is Vogue,* and her mother had slapped her for the last time. Clare's favorite teacher had gone to MSU and had set up a program with old professor friends so that after basics Clare would have clear sailing in comparative literature. She envisioned a career that allowed her to read world literature, think about it, and anything beyond that was an irritation. Her father was fairly strict about her spending but gave her free rein with books. Sadly, Clare thought, the only time he truly defended her against her mother was in the choice of a college. But he had become quite upset when he dropped her off at her dorm, and they had talked with an intimacy previously unknown to them about her mother. He nearly begged her to come home as often as possible, if only for his sake. It was an unnerving moment for her, this first time her father was not quite her father but an intimate. Why had he waited until she was eighteen to try to become close, a time when it was no longer achievable, though it might have been later, had he lived? *Oh Father don't worry I'm doing fine,* and then she slept a pure, deep, dreamless sleep.

At first light there were more birds than she had ever heard at one time. It was as if she were *within* the birds, and wrens fluttered skillfully through the branches of the thicket. She heard whippoorwills, mourning doves, the resurgence of the red-winged blackbirds from the marsh beyond the creek. She ran a finger through the dew on her face which was slick as fine oil, and her movement disturbed something beside her. She turned and her heart stopped as a very long, thick, black snake eased himself off into the deeper reaches of the thicket. *Holy Jesus I have slept with a snake.* She laughed as her heart restarted. She gathered up her bag, took a sip of the boiled creek water, which had settled somewhat during the night, and scrambled out into the dawn. If someone would just bring coffee she might stay a few hours more. She began to walk down the row, then turned around, having forgot the cranberry juice can. When she picked it up there was a clear view of her nest, and it reminded her in the first light of a swamp near their cabin where her father said a bear slept. She made a little goodbye bow to the green cave, examined her filthy clothes and set off down the row toward the east where a burnished orange sun was rising. She thought that in the future any place she lived would have to have a clear view of the east.

Two weeks later in a not altogether pleasant room in a small hotel a block off Rue St.-Jacques Clare's view was a scant dozen feet in whatever direction, but the ceiling was high. The room was as close as she could get to the *pension* she had stayed in for three weeks thirty years before, and twenty times as expensive. She had had her walk in an August shower in her beret, without an umbrella, until she was quite wet, and then a coffee and calvados at Café de Flore, where she had overheard an American couple her age asking a waiter where Camus had sat. There are other pilgrims, she thought, without a trace of self-mockery. She read Guillevic and Sarraute in her room, reread Alain-Fournier's *The Wanderer* and planned a train trip into the countryside. In the café where she took her lunch every day she knew she was referred to as "the schoolteacher." This pleased her though it wasn't meant to.

On long walks in the overwarm city she had occasion to think of the cool breezes that came in the evening off Lake Michigan. If she had the whole thing to do over she would have done it differently, but then no one has anything to do over. Down near the end of the corn row a pickup truck passed and she hid as an old man turned off the irrigation for the soybean field which was tinged orange and glistened in the morning sun. She followed the path of the pickup to the back of a barn where there was a field of pigs with small, low-slung sheds in rows, and a smell that would take some time to get used to. She went through a gate into a barnyard where the old man had the hood up on his pickup and was tinkering. A collie mongrel rushed at her, barking, but Clare said a quiet hello and the dog wagged its tail. The old man looked at her without alarm and put his hands in his denim jacket.

"What can I do for you?"

"I've been misplaced. I'd like a cup of coffee."

"If it's coffee you want, we got coffee. You must be the woman we heard about all evening on the radio. You're supposed to be in a red car."

"I spent the night in your field." Her voice began to quiver.
"You had to get loose. The radio said he was beating on
you."

The old man led her toward the porch where a very large
old woman was standing with her arms crossed. "She looks
just like Grandma, doesn't she, Ed?" she said. At the screen
door with a tuft of cotton on it to keep away flies the old man
nodded in assent. Ed disappeared into the house and came
back with an antique gold-leaf mirror with a photo portrait of
a woman framed on the back of it. The woman wore a stiff-
necked black dress and had an amazing resemblance to Clare
who was momentarily disoriented.

"That picture was took in 1890," said the old woman.

"I suppose I should make some phone calls," Clare said.

Laurel arrived in two hours from Des Moines in a police car
with a state trooper who talked farm prices and drank coffee
with Ed while Laurel and Clare sat on a porch swing. Laurel
had come down from Sioux Falls and spent the night in vigil
with Donald in Des Moines. "I never thought you would do
it," Laurel kept saying.

"How's Donald?"

"He's unhappy but he'll survive. He told the police you had
a nervous breakdown, but I had them call Dr. Roth. You have
to tell the trooper that he didn't abuse you within Iowa state
lines."

"The poor thing," Clare said, and began to cry.

Clare spent a scant hour talking with Donald in a room at a
Best Western motel in Des Moines. There was more than a
trace of the vulnerability in him that she once had cherished.
He wanted to put off any decision "in depth" until Clare "came
to her senses," which is precisely what she thought he'd say.

She sat next to her suitcase on the bed near the open window, as always. She couldn't help but notice the day's *Wall Street Journal* and a note pad covered with numbers on the nightstand. He was the same Donald, only paler, and she waited fearfully for some tremor to come, but it didn't. There were a few surprises.

"I can't say I didn't see this coming, but I hoped we'd carry on."

"I don't have anything left to carry on." It was so utterly painful to say it.

"Is it Dr. Roth?" He looked away when he asked this, as if fearing a blow.

"No. Don't be absurd. You were always more than enough."

"What about the house? What about everything, for God's sake?"

"I hope you'll still look after everything. I don't care about the house. I want my books, but the house was Mother's idea." She found that she was three feet from her body again, but craving the immediacy of the thicket. What did fireflies do in the daytime? Perhaps Laurel would know.

"I had a good talk with Laurel last night. Per usual she told me what was wrong with me. When she was little she even told me how to shave. She said you were tired of the life you were living and wanted to do something else. Is it as simple as that?"

Clare looked up and saw that he had begun to cry, but it was Donald crying, not her father. She nodded yes, it was as simple as that. She got up and hugged him, and saw herself hugging him in the wall mirror, with a wave of claustrophobia sweeping through her body.

"We'll talk it over in October," she said, because that was what Laurel told her to say.

Laurel was dozing in the car and awoke with a start when her father put Clare's suitcase in the back seat. Laurel got out and began to cry which was so untypical that both Clare and Donald were nonplused, though it seemed Donald might have felt some subdued pleasure. They consoled Laurel, and it occurred to a couple driving up to the entrance that they were seeing a happy, if tearful, reunion.

In Paris at a newsstand Clare bought a *Rand McNally Road Atlas* of America. Due to the strength of the franc many prosperous French were visiting the States. In her room she spent a warm, humid afternoon looking at the locations that interested her, letting the maps bring back Zilpha, and Sammy sitting expectantly in the back seat waiting for a lunch break or a rest-stop stroll. Clare felt a little lost but then she always had, and supposed easily that it was the condition of life. Lying back on the bed, under the whir of the fan on the nightstand, she decided that she felt less lost than before her night in the thicket, and when the afternoon cooled she would write letters to Dr. Roth and Laurel. If it rained, she would wear her beret to dinner.